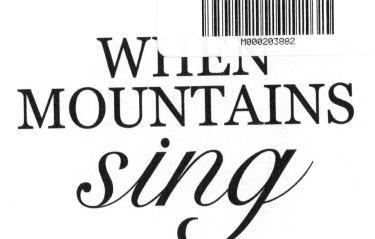

WHEN MOUNTAINS sing

My Father's House series, Book 1
The Mosaic Collection

Stacy Monson

His Image Publications
Plymouth, Minnesota

Welcome to
THE MOSAIC COLLECTION

We are sisters, a beautiful mosaic united by the love of God through the blood of Christ.

Beginning August 2019, **The Mosaic Collection** will release one book each month for the next twelve months, exploring our theme, *Family by His Design,* and sharing stories that feature diverse, God-designed families. All are contemporary stories ranging from mystery and women's fiction to comedic and literary fiction. We hope you'll join our Mosaic family as we explore together what truly defines a family.

If you're like us, loneliness and suffering have touched your life in ways you never imagined; but Dear One, while you may feel alone in your suffering - whatever it is - you are never alone!

Subscribe to *Grace & Glory,* the official newsletter of The Mosaic Collection, to receive monthly encouragement from Mosaic authors, as well as timely updates about events, new releases, and giveaways.

Learn more about The Mosaic Collection at
www.mosaiccollectionbooks.com

Join our Reader Community, too!
www.facebook.com/groups/TheMosaicCollection

Books in
THE MOSAIC COLLECTION

When Mountains Sing by Stacy Monson
Unbound by Eleanor Bertin
The Red Journal by Deb Elkink
A Beautiful Mess by Brenda S. Anderson
Hope is Born: A Mosaic Christmas Anthology

Coming soon: novels by Lorna Seilstad, Janice L. Dick,
Angela D. Meyer, Sara Davison, Johnnie Alexander,
Regina Rudd Merrick, and Hannah R. Conway

Praise for
When Mountains Sing

In *When Mountains Sing*, Stacy Monson beautifully tells the story of Mikayla Gordon's journey to find the truth about who she is. This emotionally raw story is filled with relatable characters, including Mikayla's beloved adventurous father, her adorable guard dog, Lula, and many gracious people who bring hope to her hurting heart. Set in the majestic Rocky Mountains, Monson captures the beauty of God's creation and the peace found only in Him. I highly recommend joining Mikayla on her quest for truth by reading *When Mountains Sing*.

— TIFFANY KUBLY

Mikayla's courage and bravery in the face of so many unknowns inspire me to cherish more deeply the family God has given me. Monson writes with excellence and tenderness as she weaves Biblical principles into the hearts of her characters, and I am all the better for it. With characters so complex and dialogue so convincing I was often surprised to find myself still on my own couch (I far prefer the Rockies!). Another exceptional story!

— CAMRY CRIST

To those who have lost their way, who struggle to know who they are, and to those who find themselves in life's wilderness – know that the God of the universe created you with His own DNA. He will light the way for you, tell you who you are, and lead you out of the wilderness. And when He does, the rivers will clap and the mountains will sing for joy!

Let the sea resound, and everything in it,
the world, and all who live in it.
Let the rivers clap their hands,
let the mountains sing together for joy;
let them sing before the Lord
for He comes to judge the earth.
He will judge the world in righteousness
and all the peoples with equity.
Psalm 98:7-9

- 1 -

The clash of cologne, sweat, and ego assaulted her senses as it did every weekday morning. Even blindfolded, Mikayla Gordon would know she'd entered the office. Testosterone reigned at *Outdoor Experience* magazine. She dropped her backpack on her desk chair and stood a moment catching her breath. The rainy walk from the bus stop had left her strangely winded.

"Big weekend, Gordon?" Leif looked at her over the cubicle divider.

She shrugged. "A little kayaking on Lake Superior." He didn't need to know the twenty-plus miles had rendered her arms nearly useless yesterday. Keeping her hands on the steering wheel during last evening's two-hour drive back down to the Twin Cities had felt like one long isometric exercise. "You?"

"Hot date with a waitress." He wiggled bushy brows and flashed an ego-drenched smile. "Did our own kind of kayaking, if you catch my drift."

His drift was always the same, as was his desire to get a

reaction out of her. His weekend exploits were never something she wanted to contemplate, nor did they ever seem to be outdoors. It was a wonder he could write anything worthwhile about adventures he never took.

What was worth contemplating, although not with him, was tucked in her backpack—a completed proposal she hoped would get her out of this confined space next to Leif. She nodded absently, no longer listening, and retrieved her laptop from her pack. Her lack of response drew a huff.

"You need to get a life, Gordon."

A smile touched her mouth. If that meant jumping from bed to bed with whoever was handy, no thanks. "Got one. Thanks, Leif."

With a snort, he wandered off to share details of his weekend with one of the guys who would no doubt appreciate it more than she had. She hid a relieved sigh and settled at her desk to review the proposal. The idea had percolated for months until she finally sat down to put it on paper. The more she'd written, the more excitement bubbled up.

She ached with the desire to welcome women into the male-dominated world of the outdoors. Women like her were out there. She'd encountered four of them this past weekend up in Duluth. Now to convince her boss this proposal was the right way to find and encourage them, the right time to teach, support, and empower them to find their inner strength. Not an in-your-face, girl-power strength, but true strength of character and capability. And the fun they'd have in the process? Nature was meant to be experienced, not viewed through a window.

She cradled the travel mug between her hands and smiled sadly at the family photo on her desk. Loathe to admit it, she was lonely for female companionship. Even with two sisters she loved, she still wandered in the wilderness that was her life. She adored spending time with Dad outdoors as she had for all of her thirty years, but she craved friendship with women who understood her.

Lindy, her twin, glowed in the photograph. Opposites in nearly every way, from their coloring and stature to their careers, they were best friends. Lin had defended her through their school years when girls ignored her because of her love of the outdoors and guys both welcomed and shunned her as their equal in anything sports-related.

Mikayla sipped her steaming coffee. From elementary school on, Lindy had always had a line of starry-eyed boys trailing her, while Mikayla had been out blazing a trail in the woods. Alone. With Lindy's fall wedding only five months away, she'd be required, as the maid of honor, to do all those frilly things Lindy loved—and she'd do it with a smile hiding her grimace, for Lin.

She studied Maggie, the eldest. So focused on becoming a doctor, the idea of dating had been an almost foreign concept. At least she could sympathize with Mikayla's loneliness working in a male-dominated career. But she'd forged her own path and now worked in New England under a renowned pediatric surgeon in the very position she'd set her sights on years earlier.

A deep breath slid out. Lindy was the pretty one guys wanted to date while Maggie was the smart one they were afraid to date. And she was the one it didn't occur to them to date, the one they hung out with and talked about girlfriend problems with. She wasn't sure they even thought of her as an actual girl.

The phone alarm pulled Mikayla's attention to the meeting with Ted in ten minutes. If she'd done a thorough job, this proposal would set her on her own path to success. Ted would see the hungry market they were missing in the distribution of the male-focused magazine.

She printed another copy of the proposal and sat quietly, breathing evenly over the tremor in her chest. Then she nodded and wound through the cubicles to Ted's office. Leif and Justin, another writer, were settled in chairs at the editor's desk, laughing uproariously while Ted smiled. As she approached, their laughter settled into chuckles and meaningful glances. Ted waved her in, his smile widening in what looked like relief.

"Gentlemen," he said, "I have a nine o'clock meeting with Ms. Gordon."

As the men stood, Leif muttered a comment that drew another laugh from Justin, then brushed past close enough for Mikayla to get a lungful of cologne. Breathing out as long as she could, she offered the young men a professional smile and took Justin's chair. Facing her boss, she attempted a neutral expression.

The older man winked. "I know. I can't take a deep breath when he's in here."

"Maybe you could suggest he tone it down?"

"I did. I think this is his idea of toned down." He leaned

back and clasped his hands behind his balding head. "So how was your weekend in Duluth?"

"Great!" She loved these chats with Ted. He was friendly and professional, and seemed to understand what she dealt with in an office of nearly all men; his assistant Betty was the only other woman at the magazine. She described the weekend of glorious weather and smooth paddling along the endless Lake Superior shoreline, the curious wildlife that had ventured a peek at her, and the beauty of nature's silence.

He nodded, asked questions, and smiled. "Get some good photos?"

A flush of pride swept through her before she squashed it. "A few." More like four dozen. "One of a doe and two fawns is probably my favorite. Although there's a sunrise that turned out pretty good too. I'll bring them in this week."

"Good. We're lucky to have someone with your caliber of both writing and photography skills."

His genuine interest and encouragement reminded her of Dad. She was the lucky one, having two amazing men in her corner.

"So." He rubbed his hands together. "You said you have a proposal for me?"

She handed him a copy, reminding herself not to rush the presentation as she often did when an idea excited her. She might be the last writer hired, but after eighteen months she was done being passed over for the best assignments. She'd taken on every boring and repetitive topic and written award-winning articles for the magazine. Now was her chance to shine.

When she'd finished outlining the proposal, Ted relaxed back in his chair with a smile. "Mikayla, I can always count on you."

Warmth filled her cheeks. "To talk too much?"

He chuckled. "Not only are your ideas excellent, you come in prepared with more detail and supporting evidence than I probably would have asked for."

"Overkill?"

"Not even remotely." He removed his glasses and cleaned them, a thoughtful frown on his whiskered face. "I think this is a tremendous idea, but I'm not going to sugarcoat it—the board of directors will be a hard sell. This is a new way of thinking that'll be difficult for a few of the old guard."

She nodded, the excitement cooling. That wasn't news. "Anything I can do to help grease the skids?"

He looked out the window for a long silent moment, sliding his glasses back on. "The next board meeting is in two weeks. Let's make sure we cover every angle before presenting the idea." He raised an eyebrow at her. "You game for writing more sample articles and including your fantastic photographs?"

She straightened. "As many as you want. And I'll make sure I've covered every topic. And then some."

"Good. But there's one thing I want you to think about over the coming weeks."

She leaned forward.

"While I think this is a great recurring segment idea, it might also warrant its own focus. A separate entity, not just an article."

She pressed a hand over the flutter in her chest. A separate mag? Just for women?

Ted laughed. "Look at that. Mikayla Gordon speechless."

"Well, I... Wow. That would be a dream come true." A dream she'd never dared put in words.

He held up a hand. "Don't get too excited. It would be down the road if it happens at all, but it's a direction I'd like to see us consider. It could be part of, or completely separate from, the online version. We need numbers, Mikayla. Let's show them how this will boost circulation and increase readership, not drain already dwindling resources. Up for it?"

She grasped the chair handles to keep from leaping to her feet. "Yes! I'll do whatever it takes. Thank you."

"Don't thank me. It's your brainchild." He stood and put his hand out, grinning. "Let's make it work."

She gave a firm shake. "Yes, sir!"

The smile in her quaking heart spreading across her face, she left his office clutching the proposal to her chest. A rather dreary Monday morning had burst into color, leaving her breathless with excitement, nearly dancing back to her desk.

"Must've been a good meeting with the boss," Leif commented as she passed.

"It certainly was." She slid the proposal into her computer bag, unwilling to share even a whiff of her idea.

He stood and looked at her over the cubicle wall that reached his chest and her chin. "Getting a promotion?"

"Nope." She didn't want to be the boss. Never had. But to have her own project... She blinked as his smug face swam out of focus. "I'll leave the, uh...the management stuff to the people with the right skills." Her brain was oddly fuzzy.

He grinned as if she'd paid him a compliment, his chest puffing. "Good plan."

"Well, lots...lots of work to do." She grasped the back of her office chair and blinked again. The excitement of the meeting was obviously going to her head. "So if...you'll..."

She tightened her fingers on the chair as her legs buckled and the office went dark.

"What the—?" Leif's voice was the last thing she heard.

- 2 -

"Mikayla? Can you hear me?" The unfamiliar male voice came from far away, prodding, annoying.

She couldn't muster the strength to respond. She was tired. So tired.

"Mickie, wake up." A female voice. "Come on. I know you're in there."

Lindy. Whenever they'd played hide and seek, she'd said that when she thought she'd discovered Mikayla's hiding place. Most often she was wrong. This time she was right. Sort of. She wasn't hiding, just sleeping. Or trying to. *Go away, Lin.*

Large hands engulfed hers. She'd know that grip with her eyes closed. Like now. Hands that had taught her to tie her shoes, bait a hook, and build a fire. "Wake up, sleepyhead. We've got a fishing date tomorrow, and I've got a secret lure. I plan to trounce you this time."

The corner of her mouth twitched. Not that her father was a sore loser, but she'd bested him the last two outings. Why were so many people in her bedroom?

She forced her eyelids open then shut them against the light. "A new lure doesn't scare me," she rasped.

Relieved laughter, male and female.

"Of course not." Dad chuckled. "But it made you open your eyes."

"Can't a girl sleep in once in a while?"

His fingers tightened. "I think five hours is enough, don't you?"

What? She squinted up at him. Bags under his bloodshot eyes, messy hair. He looked terrible and she told him so.

He grinned, running a hand through his dark curls. "You don't look so hot yourself, kid."

"I'm not a morning person."

Lindy appeared at his shoulder, her sleek dark ponytail a contrast to their dad's mess. "Hey, if you wanted some time off, Ted said you only needed to ask." While her twin spoke with a smile, the crease between her perfectly tweezed brows went deep.

"I don't want time off."

"Then fainting at work is a great way to get the attention of an office full of men."

Mikayla closed her eyes. "I don't faint."

"Until this morning."

This morning she was in Duluth, sharing coffee beside a campfire with a group of women she'd encountered...no, wait. She'd had the usual Monday morning exchange with Leif, then met with Ted. She frowned at her sister. "What day is it?"

Dad stepped back as Lindy settled on the edge of the bed, tears in her brown eyes. "It's Monday, you goose. You went to work this morning. Ted said you'd had a meeting that seemed to go well, and then you went back to your desk and passed out. Apparently, you gave the guy next to you a heart attack." Her grin wobbled. "But it turned out it was *you* having the heart problem."

"That's ridiculous." She looked toward the doctor standing to the side. "My heart's fine."

He moved to her bedside. "Hi, Mikayla. I'm Dr. Helgeson. It seems you do have a small issue with your heart. It's called an atrial septal defect. In other words, a hole in your heart. Yours is the most common, called an ostium secundum, located between the upper chambers. That's good news."

"Good news?"

"We can use a non-surgical procedure for the repair."

She stared at him blankly.

"You won't need open heart surgery," he added. "That's very good."

Mikayla glanced around the room. "Where's Mom?" Her heart, which the doctor had just said was defective, fluttered like the wings of a bird she'd startled on her hike.

"She went to get coffee," Lindy said. "She'll be right back."

Mikayla struggled to sit up, and Lindy used the remote to raise the head of the bed. Mikayla's vision blurred a moment then cleared as she looked at the doctor who smiled. If she were about to die, hopefully he'd look a bit more alarmed. "How do you know I have a hole?"

"We ran tests while you were having your beauty sleep to figure out why you collapsed."

That was creepy. She glanced at her father and sister, then

back to the doc. "Why wouldn't we have known this a long time ago?"

"Many people go years and years before it's discovered. Some aren't discovered until there's an autopsy."

"Sorry I didn't give you the fun of finding it that way."

He chuckled. "I'm quite happy about that."

So he was serious about a hole in her heart. The one that beat faster when she ventured into nature, wrestled a northern into the net, and hiked with Dad. "But I can't live with a hole..."

"I'd say you've done quite well for three decades," the doctor assured her. "The repair is relatively simple, as heart procedures go. Something that's done regularly. Your surgeon is one of the best in the country, so I can guarantee you'll be in great hands."

The door opened and Mom entered, carrying two coffee cups. Meeting Mikayla's gaze, she broke into a smile. "You're awake!" She thrust the cups at Dad and hurried to the other side of the bed. "You gave us such a scare. How do you feel?"

Other than humiliated? "Fine." Fainting at work. Great. She'd never live this down. She looked from one beloved face to the next. The only one missing was Maggie, who would understand this medical stuff better than anyone else. "And now that we know the procedure is no big deal, you can all stop looking at me like I'm about to keel over. You're free to return to your regularly scheduled life."

Laughter met her comment, but no one moved.

"Since we have the doctor here," Lindy said, "I'd like to know more about this...condition. How could no one know she had it? Why would it show up now? Do Maggie and I have it too?"

"An atrial septal defect can be a genetic issue or, occasionally, a fluke. We'll need to look into your family's medical history to determine which. I would recommend every family member have an echocardiogram to determine if they might also be at risk. It would be important to know this for the next generation. While the hole in Mikayla's heart is quite small, some genetic issues can be far more extensive in a developing fetus. That said, I wouldn't worry..."

His voice faded as her heart-with-a-hole clenched. Genetic. Her future went dark. Who would marry someone with a defective heart, a problem that could be inflicted on more generations? What about Lindy and her fiancé Beau? She pressed her fingers over the beat she'd taken for granted. The gentle thump continued as it had for thirty years and one month.

"Mikayla?"

She started and looked at the doctor.

"Are you feeling light-headed? Any discomfort?"

She shook her head. If she spoke her fears aloud, it would make this all too real. He gave her a gentle smile and looked at her family. "I think our patient could use some time to rest. There's been a lot of commotion and information that can overwhelm someone who's only been awake twenty minutes.

"I'd like her to rest for the remainder of the evening." He opened the door and stood expectantly. "My doctor's orders are for everyone to go home and get some sleep while Mikayla do es the same. She can go home tomorrow."

"I'm staying," Lindy stated, her fingers tight around Mikayla's.

"I'm fine, Lin. He's right, I need to sleep."

When Lindy's mouth opened to voice the protest darkening her eyes, Mikayla squeezed her hand. "Really. Go. You're always telling me I need more sleep so let me sleep."

"You'll call if you need anything? Or just want to talk?"

"I will. Promise."

Her frown faded and she leaned in for a hug, promising to bring Mikayla's favorite latte in the morning. She rested her forehead against Mikayla's as they had as kids and whispered, "Got your back."

"Got yours too." The simple, familiar exchange knotted her throat.

Their father took her place. "This is a little over the top just to get out of fishing with me, kid," he said. The scratch in his voice outweighed his light words.

"No way would I weasel out of another chance to beat you, new lure or not. I'll see you on the lake." How she adored this man who'd taught her everything she knew.

"That's my girl." He grinned and kissed the top of her head. "Love you, honey."

"Love you more, Dad."

Her mother squeezed Mikayla's hand, tears in her blue eyes. "You've always been the one scaring me with one adventure or another," she scolded lightly. "It's time to stop doing that."

"Sorry." Mikayla nodded. She'd been enough trouble for all three of them. "I promise not to do it again. If I can help it.

Maybe."

Her parents' laughter, though forced, warmed her. When they'd all finally, reluctantly, left, the doctor returned to her bedside. "Are there questions you wanted to ask without the audience?"

She pulled in a slow breath, scrounging for courage. "It's just...when you said genetics and history and children, I realized we're not fooling around here. We're talking about my whole life. Marriage, kids—"

Lifting a hand to stop her, he pulled a chair next to the bed and sat. "Mikayla, before you rearrange your future based on some vague possibilities, let's take this one day at a time. We'll get the procedure done in the next week or so, then we can focus on your family history and get the answers we need.

"There are no guarantees in life," he added. "We could rule out every genetic possibility for every disease we know of, and something else could go wrong. Making major life decisions based on what *might* happen is no way to live."

She bit her lip and nodded. *Deep breath. Falling apart won't help.* "You're right. So how do we fix this?"

"It's minimally invasive," he said, "which means you can go home within twenty-four hours and have a quick recovery. This type of procedure is done in a heart catheterization laboratory with a highly trained staff. You'll be in very good hands."

He stood and smiled. "Now, rest for a bit and then it'll be time for the dinner cart. It's amazing how much better we feel once we've had something to eat." He paused at the door and winked. "Especially a helping or two of this hospital's world renown chocolate pudding."

A smile flickered across her mouth then faded. As the door closed, she curled on her side. There wasn't much that truly scared her, but this... She pressed a fist over her heart-with-a-hole. There was so much life still to live, so many places to explore, adventures to have. She'd just have to hope the doc was right and this would all be over soon.

No way would she miss Lindy's wedding. Her twin would kill her.

- 3 -

From the couch in the townhome she shared with Lindy, Mikayla folded her arms and frowned at her mother. "If I've been just fine for thirty years, I think I'll be fine until next week's procedure. I need to go to work!"

Unruffled by Mikayla's irritation, her mother fluffed a pillow and gestured for Mikayla to lean forward, then stuffed it behind her. "There. Now you can order everyone around from your throne. One more day off work won't ruin your career. And it's doctor's orders."

"Mom, I work with men. Fainting in front of them was about the worst thing I could do. I need to get back there." She could imagine what Leif would say when she returned. Or how the guys would treat her. She'd always hated weakness, and fainting was about as weak as it got.

"You're not a man," her mother pointed out with infuriating patience. "You don't have to act like them."

"I don't have to act like an eighteenth-century woman, either."

Her mother settled into the recliner opposite the couch

and cradled the cup of tea she'd set aside to fluff pillows. "Even men know this isn't the eighteenth century."

Mikayla dropped her head back with a strangled, "Argh!"

"I didn't know people actually said that." Mom pulled a decorating magazine onto her lap and leafed through it. "You've never allowed me to baby you. Indulge me for a bit. I promise I'll go when your sister gets home from work."

Mikayla glanced at her phone. Three more hours. She reached for her laptop and nestled against the pillow to focus on the proposal. She had articles to write, photos to sort through. So much was riding on this—her reputation, her future with the magazine. And now how she was viewed by her coworkers.

If the board approved it, she could push harder for more women to be hired on. And she'd suggest the magazine sponsor wilderness trips for women that she would lead. Her heart shimmied. That would be a dream come true.

She was more than a pretty face, sadly true because Lindy had gotten all of the beauty. A pretty face would probably be detrimental to this profession anyway. She just needed a creative way for them to see past her being female. This proposal was it.

She'd need to go through their family medical history to see where the heart issue came from. She loved uncovering details and finding answers, so she'd no doubt enjoy that process. Even with the procedure looming, there was a lot to look forward to. Questions to be answered. And a future to be mapped out.

Mom stayed true to her word and left when Lindy got home. After Chinese take-out, they relaxed in the living room. Lindy leaned back in the recliner and stretched out long legs, flipping through the magazine their mother had looked at earlier. "Day One down," she said.

"Not funny. I feel like a toddler in need of constant supervision."

"If the shoe fits." Lindy shrugged, flipping her ponytail off her shoulder.

Mikayla pulled a pillow from behind her and flung it at her smirking sister. "One of these days it will be you laid up, and I won't bat an eye when you beg me to get Mom out of your hair."

"I don't get sick."

Mikayla frowned. That was true. While Lindy had rarely been sick through their childhood, Mikayla had caught every little thing going around, and now had this issue. "Huh. So why do I? We've lived the same life. We came out of the womb together, for Pete's sake."

"I'm tougher than you?"

Mikayla burst into laughter. Lin loved fashion and bling and stilettos. Mikayla loved her work boots, which Lindy refused to allow in the townhouse, and lived in jeans and a T-shirt. Lindy had her mechanic on speed dial for her beloved Audi while Mikayla happily dug under the hood of her old jeep though she knew nothing about engines.

"Okay, yeah." She wiped her eyes, still giggling. "That's got to be it."

Bouncing a pedicured foot, Lindy continued through the

magazine, a corner of her mouth twitching. "Laughter is good medicine, you know."

"Well, a few more statements like that and the hole in my heart will mend itself."

They sat in comfortable silence as Mikayla mulled over Lindy's simple declaration. Lindy had been the healthiest right from the beginning, a germaphobe who couldn't stand dirt under her gel nails.

"Remember that time you threw up over the side of the boat," Mikayla said, "after I put the slug on the hook?"

Face twisting, Lindy shuddered. "That was the grossest thing I'd ever seen. And when you pretended to swallow it..."

Mikayla giggled. "I have to admit, that was a good one!"

"That was disgusting." Lindy tossed the magazine on the coffee table and shifted to look at Mikayla, brown eyes glinting. "Remember when you lost the bet about my getting caught sneaking out and had to wear nail polish for a week?"

"On my fingers *and* my toes." Mikayla rolled her eyes. "It lasted all of about thirty-six hours."

"But you admitted it looked pretty. Until you started chopping wood and wrecked it."

They traded memories until tears ran and their stomachs ached. When Lindy went into the kitchen to refill their coffee, Mikayla relaxed against the pillows with a sigh. Even after her wedding, Lin would always be her best friend and sister in crime. They were blessed.

The evening passed quietly as they worked on their computers, sharing occasional observations and news.

"Oh!" Lindy straightened in her chair at the dining room

table. "Here are the results from my cardiac test yesterday."

Mikayla threw off the blanket and crossed the room, dropping down beside her.

"I'm afraid to open it."

An arm around her shoulders, Mikayla squeezed reassuringly. "If you've got the same issue, we'll do the procedure together."

Lindy's finger hovered over the "Open" button, then she closed her eyes and tapped it. Side-by-side, they scanned the report. Finally, she sagged back in the chair. "I don't have it."

Relief and confusion tangling inside her chest, Mikayla smiled. "Yay!"

"But...why you and not me? Why not Dad or Mom?"

"They got their results already?"

Lindy nodded. "Their hearts are fine. Maggie scheduled hers for next week, but the surgeon she works with thinks she's fine. But if the doc thinks it's genetic, one of us should have it. This doesn't make sense."

She forced a shrug. "Luck of the draw, I guess. I'm not sure Mom could handle both of us having this problem."

Lindy swiveled on the chair and grasped Mikayla's hands. "Well, you're not going through this on your own. I won't let you."

Mikayla managed another smile. "Thanks, Lin. No way could I do it alone."

"Now that's a first. Mikayla Gordon admitting out loud that she needs help."

Mikayla shoved her playfully and returned to the couch. "I'm not afraid to admit it when I actually need to. I just don't need to very often."

"That's for sure. You'd rather be covered in grease or dirt trying to figure something out than hire the professionals."

"Why pay someone if I can do it myself?"

Lindy turned her attention back to her laptop, shaking her head. "You're impossible."

"But you love me anyway."

Long after Lindy went to bed, Mikayla sat at her computer. How could she have a serious genetic condition that no one else in the family had? In search after search, the information seemed contradictory at best, unsettling at worst. The journalist in her chafed at the inconsistencies.

She closed the laptop and climbed into bed where she stared at the shadows on the ceiling. She'd always felt like the odd girl out. Now this. With a huff, she rolled to her side and closed her eyes. There had to be an explanation, so she'd continue her search for answers, starting with Mom.

- 4 -

Mikayla strode through the office doors Wednesday morning, chin lifted. The little fainting episode was just that, an episode. Once the procedure was done, she'd be back to normal. She smiled to herself. Better than normal—a force to be reckoned with.

She stopped short at her cubicle. A pillow and folded blanket sat neatly on her chair with...what was the little medicine bottle? Ahh. Smelling salts. It would be funny in another setting.

"We tried to get everything you might need," Leif drawled, elbows propped on the cubicle wall.

"I'd say you did just fine," she replied with a smile. "Nice touch with the smelling salts. You'd better hope you never have an issue here, Leif. I'm an expert at payback."

He chuckled. "Says you. Too bad we'll never find out since I don't faint."

"Good thing mine was a fluke."

"They figure out why you did?"

She shrugged. No way would she mention the hole. "I

23

hadn't had breakfast"—that much was true—"so I think that was part of it. A little dehydrated. And I kayaked about twenty miles last weekend. But I've gotten work done at home and had a big breakfast today, so no worries." She connected her laptop and pulled out the proposal folder. "Lots to do today."

"I can take a hint. You just holler if you need anything, little lady."

Jaw clenched, she held in the grimace until he dropped into his chair, then squeezed her eyes closed and counted silently to ten. There was no question she could out paddle, hike, and fish the big dolt any day. She pulled in a slow breath and opened her eyes. She wasn't going to waste time or energy letting him under her skin. She had a career to build. The folder in her hands was her ride upward.

Hours later her head ached, her stomach growled, and her eyes had lost focus. She glanced at the clock and straightened. Only one column written all morning? She massaged her temples. The words hadn't flowed like she expected. Ideas played hide and seek with concerns about the procedure. For Pete's sake, she'd only be in overnight, with one day at home to recover and a week staying low-key.

Pushing away from the desk, she stood and stretched. Her heart-with-a-hole fluttered, making her pause. How often had it done that over the years and she'd simply ignored it? Or when it raced longer than seemed necessary after a strenuous hike? She'd always pushed through pain, discomfort, even fear to finish what she started. She could certainly do that now.

The ring of her desk phone made her jump. She answered with a chipper, "Yes, boss?"

"Hope you don't have lunch plans because I ordered in for the two of us."

"Ted, I'm perfectly fine," she said, holding back a sigh. Now even her boss saw her differently. She sank back into her chair. "You don't have to treat me like china."

He chuckled. "I've never used Mikayla Gordon and fine china in the same sentence. I ordered in so we could work through lunch going over the proposal."

"Oh." *Over-react much?* "Well, that sounds great. What time?"

"Twelve-thirty, if that works for you."

"I'll join you then. Thanks, Ted." Dropping her head back, she stared up at the ceiling tiles. *Get a grip, Gordon, or you'll become the hysterical female you don't want to be.*

She glanced at the clock again—forty-five minutes to at least outline the columns she planned to write. Words might not be flowing in coherent order, but she could think in bullet points.

"Tell me about your parents and grandparents," Mikayla prodded from where she sat at the kitchen island after work.

Her mother finished peeling an apple. "Not much to tell, as you know. My parents are both alive, living their very privileged life in Michigan without a single health complaint."

Mikayla stole a slice of apple and popped it in her mouth. "I still don't get why they don't care if they see us. I know you've said how busy they are, and how snooty, but still...

They have three granddaughters they barely know."

"Welcome to my childhood." A deep sigh as sad eyes lifted to Mikayla. "I finally had to accept that I didn't measure up when I chose not to live the high-society life. It was a major disappointment for them when I married your father."

"What? But he's amazing!"

A warm smile bloomed as she started peeling another apple. "Yes, he is. But he didn't come from money. He and I only cared about having enough to provide a good life for our family. That was an embarrassment to them. They wanted to boast about us to their friends. Instead, they've pretended we're distant relatives."

Mikayla could count the number of times she'd seen her grandparents. Only twice at their palatial home in Michigan. The rest of the time they'd made the trip to Minnesota with a boatload of gifts, stayed at an expensive hotel, then scurried out of town.

"You're so different from them," she mused.

"Thank you."

Mikayla directed the conversation back to her quest. "So Aunt Beth never had any health issues?" They'd seen her mother's sister even less, since she lived somewhere in Canada.

"None that I ever knew of."

"How about your grandparents? And their siblings?"

Mom added the apple slices to the growing pile in the bowl, then wiped her hands and leaned against the counter. "Honey, I don't know everyone's complete history, but I can tell you there's longevity on both sides of the family, mine and your father's. Your issue is simply a fluke, and we should be grateful it can be repaired so easily."

"That doesn't cut it, Mom. Something doesn't add up. I'm glad it can be repaired without surgery, but I'm thinking about my children."

Her mother raised an eyebrow. "Is there something you want to tell me?"

"What? No!" Mikayla rolled her eyes. "Hardly. But I'm assuming there'll be kids in my future someday, and I'd like to know if there are issues to be aware of."

"Are you finally dating someone? Is that what's behind all the questions?"

Finally? "I'm pretty focused on my career right now. There's no time for dating."

"You have to make the time, honey." She mixed the apples and spices. "I can't believe there aren't any nice guys at the magazine."

And here we go. Her mother wouldn't be happy until Mikayla was married off to a successful businessman like Lindy's fiancé Beau and had given up her outdoor "hobbies." Never mind that nobody gave Maggie grief about not dating.

She stuck another apple slice in her mouth to slow the defensive retort that always shot to the surface.

"I should have let you make these pies," her mother mused. She rolled out a lump of pastry dough. "You need to know how to cook and bake in a kitchen, not just cook burgers at a campsite."

What was so wrong with burgers at a campsite? "So I can have a fulfilling life as a housewife?"

"I can't imagine you being a housewife." She dismissed

the idea with a wave of her hand as if it were too outrageous to consider, then placed the perfect pastry in the pie plate.

Ouch. Not that she could see herself contentedly keeping house, but she still longed for someone to share life with. "Then what *do* you envision for my life? You hate that I like being outdoors, but you can't see me as a wife and mother either. Maybe a spinster living alone in the woods who should know how to cook for herself because no one else will?"

Her mother glanced at her before filling the pie plate with apples. The kitchen warmed with sweetness and cinnamon. "Mikayla, I'm sure your life will turn out exactly the way you've planned, which is good. But I'd like you to at least have the basic skills to feed a husband and children. Not only over an open fire but in an actual house."

Why weren't her dreams as good as Maggie's and Lindy's? "What if I don't want that life? Isn't it enough that Lindy does? She's marrying a great guy who makes a boatload of money. They'll live in a beautiful home and raise perfect kids. That should satisfy your need to have raised the perfect daughter." Lips pressed firmly together, she pulled in a slow breath through her nose. Why did she let herself get sucked into this conversation every time?

After a brief silence, her mother said, "Honey, I don't want perfect daughters. I want happy daughters."

Mikayla met her mother's clouded gaze and released the breath she'd held. Unlike Lindy and Maggie, she'd given her parents plenty of scares with her choices. She'd broken a leg, both arms, and three toes, had a concussion, gotten stitches countless times, and lost track of time while hiking on her own which resulted in more than one grounding.

"I'm sorry I'm not more like Lindy or Maggie. I'm just... me."

Closing the oven door, her mother came around the island and wrapped her arms around her. Mikayla sat stiffly under the unusual embrace.

"I love you the way you are, sweetheart." She went to the sink and rinsed off the utensils. "I just don't know enough about the things you enjoy to have an actual conversation about them. And that makes me feel like I've failed you somehow."

Mikayla blinked. A surprising admission from her always-put-together mother. "Mom, it's not you. I was born one lure short of a full tackle box." One of Dad's favorite sayings. "But I'm happy doing what I love even if it doesn't look like Lindy or Maggie's successful lives."

Looking back over her shoulder, Mom held her gaze then nodded. "I know you are. And not being able to bake a pie isn't the end of the world." She turned back to filling the dishwasher. "I just want you to be happy."

Mikayla's shoulders lowered and she studied her short fingernails. Apparently being able to bake an apple pie was a sign of happiness as well as a domestic achievement. As usual, she fell far short in that department. But she could filet a fish better than Dad and start a fire with a couple rocks and a stick. Not exactly domestic but good skills to have.

Except in her mother's eyes.

Dad knew even less than Mom. As Mikayla sat with him in companionable silence in the middle of the lake Friday morning, casting and reeling, she drew a deep, appreciative breath. Pine, lake water, summer mist. There was nothing better than the peaceful beauty of fishing at dawn.

The cheerful melody of birds darting from tree to tree and the call of a loon filled her heart. Over Dad's shoulder she watched a trout leap out of the water as if in joyful abandon. Nature celebrated each new day, and she wanted nothing more than to soak it in.

This moment was why the proposal needed to go through—for women to know this peace was available to them regardless of income, skill level, or age. Women who hadn't heard nature's invitation to be still and connect with a world far from cell phones and laptops, rush hour traffic, and full calendars.

"Feeling okay?" Dad's question startled her.

"Sure. Just appreciating the perfection of such a morning." Sunlight sparkled through the trees as it lifted off the horizon and lit the royal blue sky.

"Yeah, it's pretty great."

They shared a smile and then Mikayla's pole jerked her attention back to the water. Bingo! She played and reeled, letting the fish tire on the line. Pulling it in, she grinned as her dad swept the northern into the net.

"It's a beauty, kid. Great job!"

"Thanks. What do you think, maybe eighteen inches?" She held it aloft for the usual photo op, then glanced sideways at him as she slid the fish on the stringer. "Time for you to get serious, don't you think, Pops? I'd hate to win so easily. *Again.*"

He chuckled and tapped the visor of her baseball cap. "Don't worry about me. I'm just letting you enjoy a false sense of security. This contest is all mine."

"Well, you'd better catch something or there won't be a contest." A pair of ducks skidded across the still water, quacking quietly. "Dad, you're sure you can't think of anything in your family's history?"

"Sorry, kid. I've tried but nothing comes to mind. Nobody died early or had heart issues. My uncle had Alzheimer's, and my grandma had cancer. Lots of broken limbs and things since they all spent a lot of time outdoors, but no heart thing like what you have."

She sighed. She hated loose ends. There had to be a definitive answer somewhere. Flicking the rod back and then forward, she watched the leech sail toward the sun, then drop with a tiny kerplunk.

She'd have to go back through decades of death records to look at every family member's cause of death. Perhaps there were newborns who hadn't live much past birth because of a deformity in the heart. Or perhaps it really was a fluke and there was nothing to worry about. That would be something to celebrate, after she ruled out a family tie. It was a mystery she'd solve one way or another. With the procedure scheduled for next Friday, she had time to keep digging.

Moments later the issue was forgotten as Dad reeled in a smallmouth bass that wasn't giving up without a fight. The contest was on!

- 5 -

Mikayla laughed at Beau's comment, watching her sister trade smiles with the young man she adored. The mid-September wedding was just months away, which seemed like forever but also like tomorrow.

She envied their relationship—how Beau seemed to accept Lindy and her quirks, with only an occasional lift to his reddish eyebrows. He doted on her, supported her, and applauded her work. He was perfect for her. But once they married, Lindy would move into Beau's house and everything would change. As it should.

Mikayla took a leisurely drink from her water bottle to hide a sigh. They were grown-ups, for Pete's sake. It was time for things to change, for them to move apart and start their own families. They'd lived together since graduating from college. It wasn't like they'd stop being besties.

"Right, Mikayla?"

Beau's question yanked her from her musings. "Sorry, what?"

"Despite preferring to spend her waking hours at a mall

with all the germs of society," he said, "your sister is sickeningly healthy."

"Interesting choice of words. Yes, she's always been as healthy as a horse."

"Nice comparison," Lindy grumbled from where she snuggled against Beau. "Why can't it be healthy as a princess or something?"

"Then we'd have to compare everyone to you, princess," he said.

Mikayla rolled her eyes and laughed.

He winked at her. "Maybe you two aren't even sisters. That'd explain why she's been so healthy and you've had issues. You're adopted," he teased. "Actually, Lin would be the one who was adopted since you look like your mom with the blonde hair and blue eyes."

Lindy elbowed his stomach. "That's not remotely funny."

He shrugged and drained his glass. "If you weren't twins, it would be something to look into."

Mikayla forced a smile past the breath caught in her throat. It was too ridiculous to consider. They were opposites, for sure, but there were newborn pictures of them together in the same crib, Maggie hanging over the side dangling a toy. Birthday party pictures from their first to last month's thirtieth.

Lindy directed the conversation to Beau's new job, while Mikayla's mind played the simple statement over and over. While she looked like Mom, Lin had Dad's coloring. Maggie looked more like Aunt Beth, but she shared a lot of the same mannerisms and quirks as the rest of them.

After watching a movie together, Mikayla pleaded a headache and turned in. With several nights of disrupted sleep behind her, and Beau's suggestion rattling around in her tired brain, the headache was real. And so were the questions. Hopefully she'd sleep tonight out of sheer exhaustion and be able to laugh about his idea in the morning.

Sitting in the rocker at two a.m. yet again, she opened her laptop and searched for DNA information. Curiosity urging her on, she filled out an online form requesting information, then set the computer aside and returned to bed. The peacefulness that settled over her warmed her faster than the blanket. The results would put the silly idea to rest once and for all. After next week's procedure, she would finally be able to focus on her future.

In the morning she read through the reply, requested the DNA testing packet and left for the office. As tired as she was, she completed several more sample columns, words flowing fast and clear. Ted's enthusiastic appreciation of her work spurred her to tweak ideas and words, fine tune photos, and add more ideas to the mag within a mag idea.

When Mom and Dad arrived for dinner that evening, their guest's familiar voice brought Mikayla squealing from the kitchen. "Mags?!"

Maggie tossed her coat on the couch and caught Mikayla in a hug. "Surprise!"

Mikayla squeezed hard, then released her older sister. "How in the world did you get time off? And why? But thanks!"

Dad chuckled as he passed them. "Leave it to Mikayla to cover all the bases in one breath." He gave Lindy a peck on the cheek, then rubbed his hands together. "Someone said there's wine tonight and with the company's audit underway, I'll need at least one glass."

Arm-in-arm, Mikayla led Maggie toward the kitchen, peppering her with questions. Maggie's crazy schedule often left her barely coherent when they tried to connect. That she took time away from her job to be here made Mikayla's heart-with-a-hole swell to bursting. Life didn't get better than having her family under one roof. Unless it was getting them all around a bonfire under a star-filled sky.

After Lindy's exquisite fettuccine, Caesar salad, and homemade garlic bread, followed by homemade strawberry cheesecake, they remained around the table long after the plates had been cleared, laughing over family memories and bad jokes. Mikayla propped her chin on her hand and studied each face. They shared a lifetime of major events and daily skirmishes. It was ridiculous to think one of them was adopted.

Lindy leaned her head against Dad's shoulder as they laughed over something. They shared the same dark coloring though Lin's hair was straight and smooth while Dad's was a curly mess. Mom and Maggie chatted at the end of the table, heads angled toward each other. Their profiles were similar, their smiles identical though Maggie was the only strawberry blonde in the family.

Mikayla sighed quietly. And then there was her. She looked like Mom with thick blonde hair and blue eyes, but her personality was Dad's into her marrow. She might be on the smaller side like Mom, but she had his strength and athleticism.

"Hey, Mikayla." Lindy's voice broke into her thoughts. "Listen to Dad's new one."

His endless repertoire of jokes kept them groaning even as they egged him on. Mom interrupted often with news of the local volunteer work they were doing to balance his goofiness. When she shared that "Aunt" Cindy had broken her leg in a fall from her horse, Mikayla and her sisters bombarded her with questions about their mother's childhood friend whom they considered family.

Maggie's stories of the breakthroughs her team had made recently for the children she worked with brought tears to Mikayla's eyes. After Lindy shared news that she'd been assigned a highly anticipated fashion line to promote and market, Mikayla revealed details of her proposal.

Each announcement was met with excitement, and Mikayla reveled in a powerful sense of thanksgiving. Maggie hadn't been home for nearly a year, which in one way magnified the seriousness of what Mikayla faced, yet reminded her that distance hadn't diminished their bond. Mom and Dad held hands as they laughed with their daughters. And Lindy...

Her sister glanced sideways at her and winked. As always, they knew each other's thoughts and moods without sharing a word. Life was good. And it would be even better after the procedure.

Minutes after Lindy left for work in the morning, the DNA testing packet arrived, and Mikayla breathed a sigh of relief. She had no clue how she'd have explained it. After dinner last night, she'd strenuously insisted she clear the table and do the dishes later, wanting to keep everyone's silverware and glasses in order. The DNA site had said glassware and eating utensils were excellent sources for collecting samples.

Grateful Lindy detested doing dishes and hadn't moved anything on the counter, Mikayla carefully collected her own sample and samples from her parents. Just before sealing the packet, she added samples from Lindy and Maggie as well. While the very idea that she was having her family's DNA tested was beyond ridiculous, it was the only way to silence Beau's voice that continued to whisper from a dark corner of her mind. She readied the package for mailing, then pulled out the pre-op information packet and read through the myriad of pages again.

"Let's get this over with and move on," she said firmly. With so much to look forward to, she was almost excited about the procedure. Almost.

- 6 -

Mikayla opened her eyes and focused on Dad's glowing face, her hand in his. "Hey."

"Hey, yourself. It's over, kid, and everything went great."

She smiled drowsily. "Ready to go home now."

"Tomorrow morning. The surgeon will be here soon to share the gory details."

"She said you were a model patient," Mom added from the other side of the bed.

Mikayla rolled her eyes. "Because I was unconscious."

"Good thing." Dad chuckled. "Otherwise you'd have scrutinized how she made her surgical knots."

"Mitchell!" Mom exclaimed.

Her mind clearing, Mikayla exchanged a grin with her dad. "Someone taught me there's a right way and a wrong way to do things."

"So you *do* listen to me."

"Once in a while. Don't let it go to your head."

"Oh, you two," her mother scolded.

How many times had she said that over the years? Mikayla

closed her eyes with a contented sigh. If Dad was teasing her and Mom was protesting, all was right with the world.

The surgeon entered the cubicle with a broad smile. "Well done, Miss Gordon. You're the most cooperative patient I've had this morning."

A corner of her mouth lifted. "Since I was first on the list, I won't get too excited."

"Still, you've set the bar high for the others. Now, as for your procedure, all went well. You should feel very little discomfort and be ready for a full schedule in about a week. The hole was slightly larger than we'd thought, so I'm surprised you didn't experience more symptoms."

"There were times I was more tired than usual," she said, "but nothing that made me think it was more than lack of sleep. Never passed out and fell out of the fishing boat, or off a cliff."

The surgeon laughed and pressed a gentle hand to her shoulder. "I'll check in on you once you're in your room. Get some rest now. Tomorrow we'll send you home with a fully functioning, strong heart."

As she was moved to a private room, Mikayla touched her fingertips over the beat of her mended heart. Now she could get back to real life. Like launching the proposal Ted would take to the board. And not letting Dad off the hook with the excuse of *her* health. She'd never backed down from a challenge yet, and she wasn't about to let him either. She'd learned it from him.

The email popped up in her inbox Tuesday evening. Funny how she'd nearly forgotten about it since Friday's procedure. While she'd swept any questions from her mind, the waiting and wondering had lurked at the edges.

Before she could open the email, the front door opened and she slammed the laptop shut as Lindy entered laden with bags, Beau straggling behind with more.

"Wedding shopping is hard work!" her sister declared, motioning for Beau to set his collection on the coffee table.

"Hard on the wallet as well," he grumbled.

"Hey. You offered to buy the last three."

"So we could get out of there. I'm hoping you'll return them like you return everything else."

Their playful banter, usually entertaining, now grated as Mikayla folded her hands on the laptop. If she admitted that Beau's harmless teasing had affected her enough to follow that rabbit trail, he'd never let her live it down.

"You okay, Mickie?" Lindy asked, using that silly child-hood nickname.

She nodded quickly. "Yup. I was just thinking I need some of Mario's cold brew lemonade so I'm going to walk over there." She gathered her laptop and a few random papers, glancing sideways at her sister. "You guys sticking around here tonight?"

Beau wrapped his arms around Lindy from behind. "I scored Twins tickets. Baseball under the lights."

"What could be more romantic." Lindy rolled her eyes, then looked up at him with a grin. "But I'll go for the nachos and a chance to get on the Kiss Cam."

"That's my girl."

"Okay, well, you two have fun. I'll keep my fingers crossed for a cameo on the Cam." Mikayla waved as she went out the door. "Taa taa."

The three-block walk to the coffee shop passed in slow motion. She waited at red lights, then weaved around couples pushing baby strollers and people meandering with their dogs. Once she had the lemonade in hand, she sped toward "her" table in the back corner, the perfect spot for people watching or hunkering down to get work done.

She clicked on the email from DNA Testing Ltd., and read through what seemed to be standard verbiage about the report findings, how to get questions answered, and who to contact for any follow-up.

There looked to be individualized reports for her comparison to each parent and to each sister. She opened the first of the attachments. A table comparing her DNA, Subject A, in the first two columns to Subject B, her mother's, in the other two columns revealed row upon row of numbers that nearly all matched. She skimmed the page to the bottom where it stated an index number in the millions and released the breath she'd unknowingly held. "Probability of Maternity >99.9%."

Take that, Beau! She grinned and opened the next attachment, the comparison between her and Dad. The grin dissolved as she skimmed the rows of numbers. Unlike the comparison with Mom, nothing matched between their columns. Row after row with different numbers.

Her gaze leaped to the bottom of the chart. The index number was a zero. She read through the numbers slower. No matches. Did they have different blood types? Was it a natural difference between male and female?

Her newly mended heart pounded against her ribs as she moved on to the comparison with Lindy. She blinked several times. Her number was also a zero. Her comparison with Maggie had some matches, though not as many as with Mom. At least her report had a number, but not in the millions like Mom's.

The final attachment was a recap. Subject A was Mikayla. B was Mom, C—Dad, D—Lindy, and E—Maggie.

Subject A and Subject B = Match
Subject A and Subject C = No Match
Subject A and Subject D = No Match
Subject A and Subject E = Possible Familial Match

Her mother was a match, but not her father? Nor Lindy. But Maggie was a possibility? What did that even mean?

She dropped back against the chair, staring across the crowded coffee shop. The usual hum of conversation and laughter was muted, as if someone had put their hands over her ears. She shook her head, but the muffling remained.

Dad had never treated her as anything other than his own child. And she and Lindy had always been together. Hadn't they? She frowned, racing through childhood memories. Was there a time when they weren't? No. Every childhood photo had the two of them. From tiny infants. Inseparable. She had to be missing something.

The score at the bottom of her mother's report, "Combined Maternity Index," was in the millions, but Dad's "Combined Paternity Index" was zero. Zero. The man she idolized, spent hour upon hour tromping through woods with or sitting quietly together in a fishing boat *wasn't* her father?

Under the Index was a Test Conclusion section. Her mother's report concluded with "is not excluded as the biological mother." Was that a double negative? It seemed to say she *was* her biological mother.

She rubbed her eyes and looked at the Test Conclusion on her father's report. "Is excluded as the biological father." As in definitively? There was no chance he was her biological father?

That just wasn't possible. She was far more like him than Mom. Same warped sense of humor and love of the outdoors. Same skills and mannerisms. She and Mom were from different planets. The same hair color didn't make a relationship, a bond.

Something had skewed the testing. She'd done it wrong, submitted the wrong items. She closed the laptop firmly. She'd call them first thing in the morning and resubmit everything. And she'd tell them what she thought of sending out reports like this to unsuspecting people, using science-speak that was not only confusing but could be life-altering if not read correctly.

Returning home, she breathed a sigh that Lindy and Beau were gone. She didn't trust herself not to blurt out the skewed test results and scold Beau for even suggesting such a thing. She nibbled at a piece of toast, then threw the other slice away. Drank half a cup of coffee before dumping out the whole pot, and folded towels that had sat in the dryer for days. And she swatted away thoughts that poked at her, questioning where she belonged and who she was.

Settled under her covers after blindly watching the news, she curled into a ball as the questions crystallized. *But if it's true...then who am I? Who's my real dad? Who am I to Lindy?* Who knew the truth? And why hadn't they told her?

"Good morning, DNA Testing Limited. This is Barbara. How can I help you?"

Mikayla took a deep breath and plunged in. "Hi Barbara. I received my reports yesterday, and I'd like to request more testing."

"I see. Let me connect you to one of our counselors. Hold please."

As she waited, Mikayla pressed a hand over her raging heartbeat. This whole misunderstanding would be resolved soon.

"Good morning!" a cheerful female voice said. "This is Wendy."

"I just received some test results that I'm sure aren't accurate. I'd like to request more testing."

"All right. First, let me pull up your records. Do you have your client number?"

As the woman reviewed her reports, Mikayla said, "Could you explain the results in simple terms? I'm pretty confused by the wording."

Wendy apologized. "We hear that a lot. The reports are based on scientific findings so unfortunately the results are worded that way. Let's see... It appears that your comparison with your mother resulted in a match that's as close to 100% as testing can get."

"That's what I thought it said."

"And the comparison with your father..." She paused. "That report shows that you don't share any DNA with that sample."

Her world skidded to a stop, and she swallowed with difficulty. "Meaning?"

"That the person from whom you got that sample is not a blood relation to you." Wendy's earlier cheerfulness quieted.

"That's not possible." Her trembling fingers convulsed around the phone. "I share far more characteristics with my dad than my mom. I must have done something wrong with the sample. Maybe I should send in a new one? A better one."

"Actually every sample you sent was very clear."

"But..." No words formed a coherent sentence.

"Since you're here in Minneapolis, would you like to come into the office to continue this in person?" Wendy asked gently.

So they could gawk at a thirty-year-old illegitimate daughter who no doubt resembled a deer caught in the headlights of an approaching semi? "No. I, uh...this is fine."

"All right. Then let's take a look at the other reports. Perhaps that news will be better."

Not if she'd read those correctly.

Wendy compared both Lindy's and Maggie's DNA with Mom's and Dad's. Lindy had zero matches with either parent. And again, Maggie seemed to have some, but only with Mom.

By the time they hung up, an endless twenty minutes later, Mikayla knew one thing for certain. Life as she'd known it—as any of them had known it—would never be the same. And everything she'd assumed as basic fact was simply a facade.

She called in sick to the office, then changed out of her work clothes and headed to her favorite wooded trail. The wobble in her legs made it difficult to navigate the dirt path so she focused her frayed energy into making it to the top of the hill where she sank to the ground.

Staring over the lake below, she struggled to corral her emotions, to isolate even one she could put a name to. Flashes of her childhood poked through the fog—playing hide and seek with Lin, getting math help from Maggie. Hours spent with Dad chopping wood, tying lures, hiking, camping.

Her eyes narrowed on the flight of a distant plane. Time spent alone with her mother seemed fleeting. Catching a quizzical frown on her face, or a flicker of surprise had always made Mikayla wonder what her mother saw in her. Now she knew. She saw *him*. Some man she'd cheated on Dad with.

The clarity of that realization brought her emotions into jarring focus. *How dare she do that!* A blast of anger sent her to her feet. Pacing the quiet spot, questions shot through her mind like fireworks, exploding into confusion. Who could possibly be better than Dad? Why would her mom risk everything for someone else? Obviously she hadn't considered possible repercussions, like the lives that would be destroyed by her indiscretion.

"Has she always known I wasn't his?" she demanded of a squirrel that dashed past. She followed it and continued. "Is that why she treated me differently? Do I look like him?"

She stopped. *Does Dad know?*

Tears shot up her throat. Could he have known and still treated her the way he did? What would the truth do to their relationship? She dropped down at the base of a tree and buried her face in her hands. What would she do if he started treating her differently? If their time together changed, or even ended?

The fury morphed into fear so paralyzing she couldn't breathe. The DNA results had shattered everything that mattered—her relationship with her beloved dad, the connection with Lindy, her family structure. Nothing would ever be the same. The life she knew—*thought* she knew—was gone.

She needed answers. Putting a hand to the tree, she pushed to her feet and stood quietly, pulling courage from deep inside. *Show no weakness. Rely only on yourself.* Her new mantra going forward. Much as she wasn't sure she wanted the answers, she had to know the truth. Where had Lindy come from? Was Maggie illegitimate too? Who knew what about this mess?

Ignoring the stab in her newly mended heart, she set her shoulders and headed down the trail. One person knew everything, so that's where she'd start. But even with answers, the cracks in her heart wouldn't be so easily mended.

- 7 -

Mikayla stood on the front step, the tremble in her legs forcing her against the railing as she drew a slow breath. She put a hand against her chest, hoping the crazed flutter wouldn't re-open the hole. She didn't want this conversation. Didn't want the results folded up in her purse. Anguish burned under her ribs, and she jammed her finger on the bell.

The front door opened, and her mother's face lit with a smile as she pushed the outside door open. "Hi, honey. You didn't have to ring the bell, you know that. Come in."

Mikayla went to the couch where she sank down before her legs gave out.

"This is a nice surprise," Mom said, closing the door and joining her. "I never get to see you during the— Mikayla?" She paused mid-step. "What's wrong? Is it your heart?"

And my life. And my future.

Her mother perched next to her and reached for her hand. Mikayla pulled back and moved to the chair. She'd rehearsed this conversation on the drive over, but now there were no words. Fear locked her jaw.

"Mikayla, you're scaring me. What's wrong?"

Mikayla looked at the familiar face, childhood memories colliding in confusion. This couldn't be true. She pulled the paper from her purse and held it out.

Her mother took it cautiously. "What's this?"

Mikayla blinked and nodded toward it.

After a long moment, Mom unfolded it and read, the blood draining from her face. She put shaking fingers to her lips and closed her eyes. "I see."

I see? Mikayla waited for a denial, a protest. Silence. She blinked hard, refusing the tears that burned. The strangle-hold on her throat didn't allow room for breath let alone words.

"Mikayla, I..."

Mikayla had never seen so many emotions cross her unflappable mother's face. "It's true?"

When her mother folded her arms across her stomach, Mikayla willed her to deny it, claim it was a misunderstanding or that the DNA results were wrong. Something. Anything.

"Apparently."

The last thread of hope unraveled. "Apparently? What does that mean?"

"There's so much to the story, I don't know where to start."

Anger flared. "How about at the point where you decided to cheat on Dad."

"I didn't! I would never have made that decision."

Her breath caught. "You were raped?"

"No! Not that. It was just a...a mistake. A terrible mistake after too much wine."

49

The whispered words shot into Mikayla's heart with a force that knocked her back in the chair. She wasn't even the product of a loving relationship. She was a mistake. "So that makes it okay? Like I should feel better knowing you didn't even care about him?"

Her mother flinched. "That's not true."

"Is Lindy the result of a different one-night stand?"

"No!"

"But she's not my twin."

"No." The word came on a sigh. "You were born within days of each other, and we got her when she was just two weeks old. It seemed best to simply raise you as twins."

"Best for who?" Mikayla stood and paced. "Were you ever going to tell us?"

"Yes." She lifted her hands, then dropped them into her lap. "We had planned to, but we didn't know how after all this time."

"Great plan. If you ignored it long enough, you'd eventually buy in to your own fairy tale." The sarcasm pinched her heart. She'd never spoken to anyone like this, but no one had ever hurt her this deeply. No. Shredded her whole being and tossed the pieces into a cold wind. Who was she? Lin was adopted, but *she* was illegitimate.

"At least Dad has never treated me as anything but his own." There was a sliver of consolation in that.

"He thinks you are."

The world froze. "What?"

They were kindred spirits. She could tie a sailor's knot faster than him now, chop almost as much wood, catch more fish. He'd never known she wasn't his?

"*I* didn't know until right now."

Mikayla turned slowly, swaying. "What does that mean?"

"We'd only been married a few years, but we were having a tough time, and we'd taken some time apart. I returned home after...after the..."

Wait—what? "*You* didn't know he wasn't my father until right now? How could you not?" She dropped onto the couch, staring at the stranger before her. "Who are you?"

"Sweetheart, I know this is a lot to take in all at once." She reached a hand toward her. "This isn't how I imagined the conversation would go."

Mikayla recoiled, watching her mother's face crumple. "Because you were never going to tell me. And you've never told Lindy?"

"No."

"Then I'll tell her. She has a right to know our mother isn't the saint we all thought she was. And that I'm not even her sister, let alone..." She pinched the bridge of her nose to keep the stinging tears back, the nausea from surfacing.

"Of course you're sisters, Mikayla. Blood isn't the only thing that makes a family."

"Honesty seems pretty essential, but we obviously don't have any of that."

"We're a family by choice."

"Whose? Certainly not mine. Or Lindy's. What about Maggie? Did she get a choice?"

Her mother lowered her head. "We adopted her as a newborn as well."

Wow. Mikayla fell back against the couch, rubbing her temples. This got more bizarre with each revelation. "I'll guess she doesn't know either."

"No," came the whispered response. "We were so thrilled when each of you came into our lives, we never made a plan about how to explain it once you grew up."

"So why does some of my DNA match Maggie?"

"It's complicated, honey. Each of you has such a different story."

"There's nothing complicated about the truth," Mikayla snapped, then her head came up. "Unless none of it was legal?"

"Of course it was. Maggie and Lindy are our children in every way."

Mikayla flinched. "And then there's me. Legal but illegitimate."

"Mikayla, I have no excuse for not telling you except trying to save face," her mother admitted quietly. "But it's not as bad as it sounds."

"You're going to put a positive spin on having an affair?"

Silence followed by a deep sigh. "I'm not proud of what I did"—she held Mikayla's gaze—"but I wouldn't change it for anything because it gave me you."

The declaration hung between them—humility edged with defiance.

"I want to meet him." She would tell him exactly what she thought of a man who did something like this and then sauntered off into the sunset.

"I hope you can," her mother said, "but you'll have to track him down first."

"Is he some kind of fugitive?" If she had to be the black sheep, she might as well be as black as possible.

"Don't be silly."

The fondness that colored her mother's smile made her heartbeat stumble.

"When I knew him, thirty years ago, he was funny, and sweet, and determined not to put roots down anywhere." She took Mikayla's hand. "A free spirit, just like you. You have his love for the outdoors, his joy for living. And you look a bit like him."

She yanked her hand away. She was Mitch Gordon's daughter, not some bum who couldn't be bothered with a child. Maybe she didn't look like Mitch, but they'd been connected at the soul her whole life. "So how do I find this paragon of virtue?"

Her mother leaned back. "I wish I knew. Back then he lived and breathed the outdoors. In the winter he worked the ski slopes out west. In the summer he took odd jobs, which is where I met him. At Aunt Cindy's resort in Michigan. Now," she lifted her hands, "he could be anywhere."

"What's his name? I'll find him online." She needed facts, not a romanticized version of what her mother wished were true.

There was a heavy pause before her mother answered. "I only knew his first name. Kenny. Aunt Cindy will have his employment record."

Mikayla couldn't breathe in or out. Her mouth opened and closed without a sound. Her mother hadn't even known the full name of the guy she slept with?

"This is nuts." Jumping to her feet, she headed for the door. She couldn't handle one more surprise. "I can't do this. I have to get out of here. Away from you."

"Mikayla, please." She reached out again. "Once you know the whole story—"

"I'll what? Think it's all okay and forgive you for cheating on Dad?"

She flung the door open, then glared back at her weeping mother. "Your choices and your lies have ruined my life, and they'll destroy our whole family." The disjointed pounding in her chest made it difficult to draw a breath. "I can't believe *you're* the only one I'm actually related to. Just...stay away from me."

In the car, she pulled blindly away from the curb, sucking in gasping breaths, tears flooding her cheeks. Two blocks down she turned at a side street, lurched to a stop, and rested her forehead against her hands on the steering wheel. She tightened her grasp as if she could hold onto her life that was crumbling into a heap. And she sobbed.

- 8 -

The days that followed were a hazy mess of questions and wildly fluctuating emotions. Not telling Lindy made her complicit in her mother's lies, but what could she say that wouldn't ruin Lin's life as well? She stayed away from the townhouse until she could slip in and go right to bed. Work, she explained when Lindy asked. And that was true. The only place she felt somewhat normal was at the office.

By Monday it was impossible to concentrate. She and Ted had reviewed the proposal and the presentation she'd created for the board of directors meeting, tweaking it, tightening the wording and rechecking the financials. She'd asked to present alongside him but reluctantly accepted his explanation that since none of the board members knew her, it would be better coming from just him. While it was her baby, her ideas and vision, she was relegated to off-stage, unable to present and defend her proposal. That grated.

She sat at her desk Monday, unable to focus on anything other than Ted in the board meeting. When her phone buzzed after lunch, she snatched up the receiver. "Hi, Betty."

"Hi, hon. I wanted you to know I put a two o'clock on your calendar with Ted."

"Okay. Did you get a sense how it went?" *Was he in a good mood? Did he give any indication at all?*

"I didn't, but he only stepped out of the meeting for a minute."

Heart in her throat, Mikayla thanked her for the heads-up and checked her calendar. Proposal discussion, two p.m. She leaned back in the chair and forced the sudden jumble of nerves away. There was no way to predict their response, despite Ted's enthusiasm for the project, so it would be better to prepare for the worst. She smiled to herself. Easier said than done.

In the ensuing ninety minutes she finished two more columns, putting her six weeks ahead of schedule. That would allow her more time to focus on the project, to get everything lined up and ready to go. If they gave it a green light, she'd show them their faith in her hadn't been misplaced.

By ten past two she realized it was she who had misplaced her faith.

"They asked a number of good questions," Ted said as they met in his office. "But there were a few, as we'd suspected, who couldn't understand why we'd want to consider this."

Listening to Ted deliver the rejection as gently as he could, Mikayla sat rigid and silent, knuckles white as she tightened her clasped hands. Her past had been obliterated, and now her future was blurry at best.

Not a reflection on her work, they'd said. "Nor on your being female," Ted insisted.

A nice man but delusional if he believed that.

"One of their arguments was that current readership wouldn't accept it, and since no one is clamoring for it, there's no reason to take the financial risk."

"Of course they're not clamoring for it because they don't know it's even an option for them!" Nerves screaming for movement, she stood and paced behind her chair. "We could be on the cutting edge of this becoming big business, Ted. I've met our new readership out on the trail—hiking, camping, rock climbing. I'd think the board would want to be on the front lines, leaders of change, innovators."

"The money men in the group only see loss right now," he said. "They can't see it being profitable because they can't think outside the box. To put extra salary into creating it, even as an online product, just didn't fly for them." He sighed heavily. "I'm sorry, Mikayla. The presentation you created was excellent, but I didn't do a good enough job selling it."

Then she would. She leaned her hands on the back of her chair. "Let me meet with them. You and I could do a follow-up presentation together." Hope fluttered at the edges of her dying proposal.

"Well, that's worth a try, although the next board meeting won't happen until sometime in September. I'll get us back on the agenda."

September? A lifetime from now. With the search for Kenny, and Lindy's wedding preparations, would she have the time and energy to rework the presentation? Did it even matter? The wings of the last bit of hope lay still.

"Take the afternoon to process this, Mikayla," he said.

"I'm not giving up on the idea. It's just going to take time to change the culture. We'll do it one small step at a time, okay? We'll have a new presentation ready for their next meeting with more statistics, even better financials." He folded his hands on his desk, his salt and pepper eyebrows tented. "We aren't giving up."

His encouragement fell short, shattering into jagged shards at her feet. She nodded, forcing a smile. Then she walked on stiff legs past Betty's worried expression and Justin's tiny basketball hoop with crumpled paper balls littering the floor, and Leif's cubicle, thankful he'd taken the day off. Deep voices, guffaws and chuckles filled the space until she wanted to press her hands over her ears.

She stood at the opening to her small cubicle, seeing it clearly for the first time. Seeing her life clearly. She didn't fit here; never had. She wasn't making a difference; she was just taking up space. A tiny bit of space as a token female.

She didn't fit with her family either. Maggie and Lindy were a choice their parents made together, but she hadn't been planned or chosen. She was a mistake. It hadn't been her choice to be conceived in a night of drunken passion by people who barely knew each other. She was a product of other people's choices.

The buzz of her cell phone startled her, and she yanked it from her pocket. Another text from her mother. As she'd done the last three days, Mikayla hit delete without reading it. There. That was her choice. Never speaking to her mother again would be her choice.

Ted had said getting them onboard would take time. So

she could spend the summer working even harder on the presentation and hope they saw it differently. Or she could move on and find a better fit in a place with a vision like hers. Those were her choices. As was finding the man who'd drunkenly made her mother pregnant and telling him exactly what she thought of him. It was time to live her life the way she wanted.

Within minutes she'd stuffed her few personal belongings into a plastic bag, then printed off a brief letter of resignation and handed it to a wide-eyed Ted with her thanks for his support. No, she wasn't angry. The board's decision made it clear it was time for her to move on, pursue other options that would better suit her career plans. Yes, she'd be happy to get a letter of recommendation from him.

She told him where he could find the columns she'd written which would keep that slot filled until he found her replacement. Then she gave Betty a hug and a promise to keep in touch. On the way out, she stepped into Leif's cubicle. After considering the greatest impact, she slid the keyboard shelf out and set the rubber snake he'd left under her desk two months ago on the keyboard. She slid the shelf back in and left his cubicle with a smile playing at the corners of her mouth.

Without speaking to any other colleagues, she left the building. They wouldn't care that she left. If Leif were there, he'd send her off with an "About time." Standing outside squinting against the afternoon sun, she waited for an emotion. Any emotion. Instead her spine stiffened, her chin lifted. From now on, every step she took, every decision made would be intentional.

Show no weakness. Rely on yourself. The mantra she'd

told herself after getting the DNA results would now be her life's mantra. In this new life, her first decision was to find her biological father and get her medical history. After that, she'd figure it out. On her own.

- 9 -

Planted at her laptop, Mikayla fired off searches with what little information her mother had provided. Countless Kennys surfaced with each search—Kennys who skied but were too young or too old. Kennys who didn't ski and were too young or too old.

Releasing an irritated breath, she pushed away from the desk and closed her eyes, massaging her temples. Simply typing his name brought a sour taste to her mouth. She refilled her coffee cup and stood at the sliding door, her resolve slipping like raindrops down the glass. Mom said he was an outdoorsy guy who lived to ski. There'd have to be some record of him working at a ski resort somewhere. Like at Aunt Cindy's resort.

Mom had suggested that but in her fury it had barely registered. Why was she wasting time on the computer when she could just call Cindy and Jim? Better yet, she could drive up there for a visit. That would hopefully lead to another resort or at least a direction to look.

A sigh fogged the glass. If she didn't have this heart issue, she'd just forget he even existed. She had a dad. She certainly didn't need another one, especially one without a moral compass. Would her childhood have been different if Dad—Mitch—had known the truth about her? Would his attention have gone to Lindy or Maggie instead?

A corner of her mouth lifted. Maggie with her nose always in a book. Lindy teetering around in Mom's heels from the time she could walk. Hard to imagine either of them dressed in waders standing in freezing cold water with a fishing pole. Or learning to set up a tent in driving rain.

A broken laugh erupted, and she shook her head. Nope. But she'd loved following him anywhere, shivering in a deer stand, reeling in a bass as he cheered, camping under the stars. Anything just to be with him.

She frowned. Maybe they were wrong. She was like Dad in every way. Well, except for her blue eyes. And the tangle of wavy blonde hair. But that came from her mother. She was Mitch's daughter in every other way.

Modern medicine wasn't always right. She straightened in the chair and glared at the folder holding the DNA results. They could have mixed her sample up with someone else's. Her spine wilted. But how many people sent in that many samples for testing? And her mother's story only solidified things—important things like she'd had an affair, Dad wasn't her dad, nor were Lindy and Maggie her actual sisters.

She set the cup down with a bang and retrieved her jacket. She'd find this Kenny character and come to her own conclusion. But one thing was fact. She'd never call him "dad."

At her parents' house she let herself in, relieved Dad's car wasn't in the driveway. "Mom!"

A brief silence then, "Mikayla? Oh, honey. I'm so glad you're back." Her mother appeared from the kitchen wiping her hands on a dishtowel, relief in her smile. "We have so—"

"I need more information on that man. More than a first name. You've got to have a photo or a letter with his address or something."

Mom stopped short and blinked. "I don't. It's not like we kept in touch after..."

Disgust surged. "You slept with someone and didn't even know his name!"

Pink filled her mother's pale face. "If you'd let me explain a little more, you'd understand."

"What's to explain? You slept with the guy. I showed up. He waltzed off into the sunset while I grew up in a family where I never belonged. The rest is just excuses."

"Of course you belonged! All three of you belong. To us and to each other."

"You *chose* Lindy and Maggie," Mikayla shot back, the words sharp against her tongue, "but you were stuck with me. A reminder of something you never wanted anyone to know about."

Tears spilled down her mother's cheeks. "Honey, I have never for one second been ashamed of you. I love you!"

Who was this woman weeping before her? Who said she wasn't ashamed yet had raised Mikayla at a distance while refusing to acknowledge what she'd done? "I've never been like Lindy or Maggie which has always made you crazy. I'm probably more like *him* than you'd ever want to admit. You didn't know what to do with your unexpected prize, so you pretended I was the awkward twin of the adopted daughter you *did* know what to do with."

The angst of the words spilling from her mouth knotted her lungs until she couldn't breathe. She needed distance from this mess. From her mother. "I'm going to Aunt Cindy's. Hopefully *she'll* be honest with me. Then I'm going to find him and make sure he knows what kind of man he really is."

Her mother approached a few steps and Mikayla backed toward the door.

"You don't have to drive all the way up there. I'll call Cindy right now and get more information. Sweetheart, please talk to your father before you do anything."

"He's not—" She closed her eyes as another piece of her heart shriveled. "What would I say to him? 'Gee, Dad. Thanks for everything, but I'm not really your daughter so now I'm going off to find the sperm donor.'" She shook her head sharply. "I'm not doing your dirty work for you. And there's no way I want to see his expression when you get around to telling him the truth about me.

"Your lies have destroyed every truth I ever thought I knew. I don't know who you are, and I sure don't know who I am. Don't you dare tell Dad about me until I'm gone. And don't call me or text or anything else. I'll let you know if I get to the point where we can talk again."

She strode to the car, ignoring her mother's tearful plea behind her, and pulled away from the curb with a spray of gravel. She'd leave first thing in the morning. Without seeing Dad one last time. It would kill her, literally, to see the disappointment in his eyes, the disgust he would no doubt feel toward her and her mother. She'd have to cut the cord herself; she couldn't watch him do it. A searing pain broke her heart in two.

She'd figure out how to get the answers she needed on her own. And maybe one day, when she could stomach seeing her mother again, she'd come back. For Lin and Maggie and Dad.

- 10 -

"What do you mean, you're going on a trip?" Lindy paused, needle and thread in mid-air, to frown at Mikayla. "We're planning my wedding!"

Mikayla tucked more socks into the corner of the suitcase. "I'm hardly helping."

"Of course you are." Dropping her hands to her lap, Lindy studied her. "I can't do it without my other half. I won't."

Wincing at the words, Mikayla returned to the closet and pulled out several shirts. She used to think that way. Now they were halves that didn't make a whole. Leaving felt like she was cutting off her right arm. Maybe a leg as well. "You're getting married. Your other half is Beau."

Lindy sighed noisily. "Did the anesthesia do something to your brain?"

Mikayla focused on folding a pair of jeans. "I know it sounds like it, but I've got to get some stuff figured out. This whole stupid heart thing has thrown me off." She looked down at the folded jeans in her hands and added softly, "I need to dig into the family history so I know I'm not defective."

"My gosh, Mikayla, you're not defective! You had a hole in your heart that was fixed. Why isn't that enough?"

"Because—" The truth crouched just beneath the surface, waiting to burst forth and spew her pain into Lindy's life. It would be a relief to share it with someone. But she couldn't, not before the wedding. "Because I do."

"I hate to make it about me, but what about my wedding? How long will you be gone?"

"Only as long as it takes to track down the information. I would never miss your wedding, sillyhead."

Lindy gave a half-hearted giggle at the childhood nickname.

"And you know if it were up to me, you'd be getting married in a meadow somewhere, so it's best if I stay out of it. That's what your frou-frou girlfriends are for."

Lindy snorted, a usually funny habit they shared. "My girlfriends are not frou-frou. But they do have better fashion sense than you."

"Everyone has better fashion sense than me. That's not exactly a compliment to them."

Lindy sat silently watching her pack. "Since you quit your job, how are you going to pay for this?"

"I have savings. And I can write freelance articles on the road." She dropped onto the edge of the bed and closed her eyes. "Why can't anyone understand I need answers? I just..." Her voice broke. "I need to know."

Lindy's arms came around her in a fierce hug. "Don't cry, Mickie. I get it. I do. It's just so unexpected. And the timing is terrible."

She turned into Lin's embrace and soaked in the love. She rarely gave in to fear but leaving her best friend was terrifying. *Show no weakness.* She leaned back and wiped her face. "I know it seems sudden, but it's all I've thought about. Mom and Dad don't have the answers I need, so I'm going to do some digging for all of us. Then I'll be back."

"Before the wedding parties begin, right? Showers and stuff that you hate?"

"Of course! Wouldn't miss it." She hated parties where they sat around with their ankles crossed, eating tiny sandwiches and making small talk. And Lin knew it.

"At least for the wedding. Promise?" Doubt clouded Lindy's eyes. "I won't get married without you there."

How could she promise anything right now? But she would for Lindy. "I absolutely promise to be here for the wedding."

Lindy grasped her hands. "I hate that you're leaving without telling me everything. We've never kept secrets."

"I'm—" She'd almost said she wasn't. But this secret would upend Lindy's life as it had her own, and that wasn't fair before the wedding. "I need answers. It may require digging and you hate getting dirty so I can't drag you along."

Lindy gave a short laugh. "Are you digging up dead people?"

"Sorta feels that way. More like digging through old records and stuff."

Lindy leaned forward and rested her forehead against Mikayla's. "You'll call if you need anything? Money or help or food? And send me updates? I don't like you being out there alone."

If she'd been able to pick a twin, it would have been Lindy. She bumped her forehead lightly against Lindy's and offered a wobbling grin. "I'm the one who goes camping on my own, remember? You're the one who hates being alone."

"Oh, right." They shared a giggle, then Lindy reached into the closet and pulled out a sweatshirt. "I want some photos of you in this."

Mikayla rolled her eyes. The hideous green sweatshirt with a multi-colored geometric design across the front had been a gag gift a few years ago. Now they snuck it back and forth into each other's closet. She stuffed it into a corner of the suitcase. "Fine. When I'm someplace I know no one can see me."

Lindy helped her pack the jeep, rolling her eyes at the fishing pole, tent, and camping gear already loaded, sniffing when Mikayla slid her suitcase and duffel bag into the backseat.

"I know you have to do this, but it feels like you might never come home," she sighed as they went back inside arm-in-arm.

"Of course I will. Everything I know is here." *What I thought I knew.* She turned and grasped her sister's hands. "My best friend is here. And there's a wedding I wouldn't miss for anything. I'll be back before you know it."

Lindy's brown eyes, so like Dad's, studied her. "Got your back."

"Got yours too."

Long after Lindy had gone to bed, Mikayla sat on the couch in the dark living room looking out the window. She'd always been a decision maker. Loose ends made her crazy.

With her world now upside down, she had no clue how she'd fix it. She'd just have to find the truth somewhere along this journey and be back in time for the wedding of the century.

- 11 -

The rolling beauty of the wooded Wisconsin hills, the vibrant green of acres of farmland dotted with cows failed to hold Mikayla's attention. Despite repeated attempts to pull her thoughts to the scenery, the road blurred and she blinked furiously. She'd left without seeing Dad. He'd have known in an instant she was hiding something.

Dad was...Dad. Strong, encouraging. Steadfast. She nodded. That's what he'd always been in her life. Her rock. She brushed at the tear that burned down her cheek. No matter how the truth changed things going forward, she'd hold onto all that she'd learned from him, their times together, the safety she'd known with him.

The truth had severed her relationship with her mother with the ferocity of a lightning bolt. She'd never trust her again, never believe her. Anger raged hot under her ribs. How could she keep such a secret knowing the longer it went, the more damage it would do?

"If she'd just owned up to it," she said, smacking the steering wheel. "If she'd thought of someone other than herself,

our family wouldn't be a big lie. Maybe Dad would have—"
Pain creased her heart. Maybe Dad would have gotten used to
her not being his biologically. Or not.

What would her life look like if he hadn't shared his love of
the outdoors with her? Had never taken her camping, shared
peaceful early mornings on the lake, hiked with her in heat
and snow and pouring rain? Who would she be without that?
What did a future without that even look like?

She shuddered, then blinked against the bright lights
sparkling in her mirror. A siren drew closer, and she signaled automatically and pulled onto the shoulder. The lights
remained in her mirror, pulling closer until she realized the
state trooper had stopped behind her.

With hiccupping breaths and a wildly thumping heart,
she wiped at her face and rolled down the window. The tall,
stern looking man in reflective sunglasses stopped just short
of her door.

He bent slightly to look at her. "Good morning."

She managed a trembling smile. "Hello."

"Do you know how fast you were driving?"

The speed limit? Way over? Or maybe under. "Right
around the limit? I thought I had the cruise on."

"Eight miles over, ma'am. And I noticed you were driving
a bit erratically. Were you on your cell phone?"

"No. It's...I think it's in my purse. Do you want to see it?
I can get it—"

"I don't need to see it. Have you been drinking?"

"I don't drink." Heat rose in her cheeks. "I was...crying."

He removed his sunglasses and studied her. "About

what?"

She managed a shaky laugh. "If you have all day, I could explain it."

"How about the Cliff Notes version?"

"I had heart surgery about a week ago, and then found out that my father isn't actually my father. And right after that my boss told me the proposal I'd pretty much staked my career on was rejected by the board of directors." Anger flared. "A bunch of guys who don't think women know how to fish or hunt or camp. So I quit."

The corners of his eyes crinkled. "You showed them."

She sighed, shaking her head. "I sure did. Now I'm unemployed, illegitimate, and have no clue what I'm supposed to do with my life. Oh, and I turned thirty last month. And my twin, who's not really my twin, is getting married in September to a really great guy who makes tons of money, while I haven't been on a date in two years."

"Where are you headed now?"

"My aunt's resort near Iron Mountain. In the UP. I guess that's...that's where I was..." She swallowed a lump of humiliation and lifted her chin. "I'm looking for my biological father to find out if my heart condition is genetic or not. I know he's not there, but it's a start."

She rubbed her temple. "I'm sorry. You must hear sob stories like this all the time. I'm not crazy, I promise."

"May I see your driver's license please?"

"Oh. Of course." She handed it out the window. *Nothing like starting this stupid trip with a big fat ticket.*

"Sit tight. I'll be right back."

She dropped her head back against the rest as he returned to his squad car. What a mess her life had become in a mere four weeks. And now she'd joined the ranks of women who cried in front of law enforcement. She thumped her head back a few times. *Get. A. Grip. Even if Dad never speaks to you again, you can at least honor him by not falling apart after a few bumps in the road.* Along with a speeding ticket.

"Stand strong, kid." Dad's deep voice, always edged with laughter, resonated in her heart. "Don't let a few waves knock you out of the boat. Get your feet under you and ride it out." The longing to lean into the words, lean into him ached deep inside.

"This is a warning, Miss Gordon."

She startled at the voice at her window.

"If you're stopped again," he continued, "it will be a hefty ticket, and neither of us wants to add that to everything you're dealing with."

Tears burned at the kindness in his voice. She nodded, accepting the yellow paper and her license.

"Good luck, Miss Gordon. I hope life gets straightened out soon."

"Thank you," she croaked.

He touched the brim of his hat and returned to the car. She set the paper on the dashboard as a reminder, put her license away, then carefully signaled and pulled back onto the highway.

A reprieve. Drawing a steadying breath, she set the cruise control and continued toward the UP.

Parked in one of the few open spots, Mikayla climbed out and stretched her arms overhead. As usual, the place was brimming with activity. How she'd loved visiting Aunt Cindy and Uncle Jim's resort. They were her parents' closest friends, so while she had an actual blood aunt somewhere in Canada, Cindy and Jim seemed more like family.

She turned slowly to drink in the familiar sight—the two-story resort nestled among rolling hills, a riot of floral color spilling from window boxes, the full-length front porch as welcoming now as it had been decades ago. Swings at either end beckoned her to "set a while," as Cindy often said. "No use hurrying through life when all we have is what's here in front of us."

With the past upended and the future uncertain, the invitation had never meant more. She would get the information she needed, and then maybe she'd set a while before heading out. Ride horses, hike, soak in the peacefulness. Find the courage to follow this through.

Mom had been here. That man had been here. She narrowed her gaze. Where had they met? Had they gone riding together? Hiked the trails? Or simply slept together and then moved on with their lives?

"There you are!" From the front porch, Cindy and Jim's daughter Sara waved.

So Sara knew she was coming. No doubt Mom called. Who else had she told? Mikayla approached the building slowly. Long and lean, Sara bounded off the porch like a gangly foal and flung her arms around Mikayla, who returned the hug. She, Lindy, and Sara were inseparable when the families got together. How in the world would she explain her messy life?

"I've been counting the minutes since Mom mentioned you were coming."

Heat crawled up her neck. What had Aunt Cindy told Sara?

Hooking an arm through Mikayla's, Sara steered them into the building. "I'm so glad you're here. It's been way too long."

As they crossed the wood plank floor of the foyer, Sara asked one of the front desk girls to bring in some coffee, then they went into the office.

"After six hours in the car, you probably don't want to, but sit anyway," she ordered Mikayla, closing the door and waving a hand at the leather couch. "I'm dying to get caught up."

Mikayla paused before the framed family photos on the wall. "Wow, look how tall James has gotten. Is he taller than your dad?"

"By two inches now."

"Funny. He'll always be twelve in my head." She turned back. "Mom told us Aunt Cindy broke her leg. It sounded serious."

Sara nodded, frowning. "Got her foot caught in the stirrup when Whiskey hit a hole. Broke both her fibula and tibia. Got a nasty bump on the head as well."

"That's awful!"

"It was. It happened on...boy, everything's running together lately. Two weeks ago tomorrow. She'll move to rehab on Monday and probably be there at least eight weeks. In a cast for another couple of months after that."

Mikayla settled on the couch. "Wow. I'm so sorry."

"Thanks." Sara offered a lopsided smile, dropping down beside her. "Nobody's sorrier than she is. She's never been a sit-still kind of person, so this is making her, and thus all of us, crazy. Her fingers work just fine on the phone and computer."

A quick knock at the door, then it opened and the front desk girl entered with two mugs of coffee. A tiny dog zipped in behind her and bounded toward Mikayla with a happy expression. Mikayla bent down to pet the creature, dancing on fragile-looking back legs, eyes bright as she pawed the air with dainty front feet. "Well, hello! Aren't you the cutest thing?"

"That's Lula, Mom's dog." Sara thanked the girl for the coffee and waved off her offer to take Lula back out with her. The door closed with a click, and Sara set Mikayla's mug on the coffee table. "That dog has been an absolute pest since Mom's accident. Lula, stop it!"

Mikayla scooped her up, laughing when the tiny tongue plastered licks across her face. "What is she?"

"I can never remember. A cross between a Chihuahua and a Papillon. That long hair and the color are more Papillon, although she's only got the one black ear instead of two." She rolled her eyes. "And thank goodness they aren't as big as a true Papillon's. She can already hear me across the building."

Mikayla giggled. "She's adorable."

"I used to think so, but I don't have time to give her the attention she wants, which is pretty much 24/7. She can be your buddy while you're here. She's only three so she's still a bit of a puppy. Mom can't get home fast enough for so many reasons, but that dog is definitely at the top of the list."

Holding the nearly weightless dog with one arm, Mikayla sipped the coffee. "What I remember most about your mom when we were young is thinking she must have more than two arms because she always had about ten things going at once—something yummy in the oven while cooking something else on the stove, a phone at her ear, and helping run the front desk all at the same time."

"She's still that way only she's doing it from a hospital bed." Sara sobered and leaned her elbows on her knees. "She told me your mom called."

No doubt to excuse her behavior of thirty years ago. "And said..."

"That you were heading this way looking for information."

"About?" She hadn't planned to divulge more details than necessary.

"About her...indiscretion."

"Huh." Hadn't thought of describing herself that way. It went along with accident, unwanted, unexpected, mistake.

Sara's fingers closed around her forearm. "Mikayla, don't go there. I know what you're thinking. You've never had a good poker face."

Mikayla stood and moved to the window. "So everyone tells me. What was my face saying?"

"That you're a mistake."

Along with Lindy, Sara had always been able to read her. "Well, I am. Not in a crybaby way, but as fact. I hardly think they meant their little rendezvous to end up in a pregnancy."

"Probably not," Sara conceded, "but that doesn't make you, Mikayla Gordon, a mistake. You are exactly who God meant you to be."

God had obviously been busy elsewhere when their tryst happened, or He'd have stopped it. Fodder for another discussion. "Regardless, I need to get some information from your records." When Sara was quiet, she added, "Please."

"Can you stay a couple days or are you heading out right away?"

A deep longing stole her breath. Once she left here, she'd be on her own. "I'll hang around a day or two, if that's okay."

"Right answer." Sara leaned forward and hugged Mikayla warmly. "I'm happy you're here."

"Me too," Mikayla whispered.

- 12 -

After her first restful sleep in weeks, Mikayla perched across the desk from Sara, both willing her to find the information and hoping she didn't. If there was none to be found, her search would already be at an end. That might be okay. But then she'd live the rest of her life with a question mark stamped on her true identity.

Lula trotted daintily into the room and stood at Mikayla's feet with bright eyes and a wagging tail. Unable to resist, Mikayla swept her onto her lap.

"Mom would still be using paper for all of our records if I let her," Sara muttered, frowning at the computer screen. "Unfortunately, I haven't had time to get all of the old info entered. Looks like...hmm." She lifted a crooked frown to Mikayla. "We'll need to dig into the file cabinets. I haven't gone back farther than twenty years."

"Anything I can do to help?"

"Sadly, no. With HIPPA laws the way they are, I shouldn't be sharing any of his information, but..." She shrugged, unhooking a packed keyring from her belt loop. She unlocked the side door and motioned for Mikayla to follow. The smaller room held a copier, four tall file cabinets, and shelves of marketing materials. "I'm swearing you to secrecy as to where you got your information." She threw a mock frown over her shoulder. "I'll disavow ever knowing you. And these files will self-destruct."

Mikayla laughed, then locked her lips and tossed the imaginary key behind her. "Mum's the word." Lula licked her cheek.

Sara fingered through the top two drawers crammed full of manila folders, then pulled a chair closer and started on the third drawer. "Speaking of mums, how are things with yours?"

Bile instantly stung Mikayla's throat. "It will be fine... eventually. Maybe." If she could disavow her mother, she would. There was still no way to process what she'd learned in the past week or decide which was worse—seeing her mother for what she truly was or fearing Dad would never speak to her again.

Sara paused to offer a sad smile. "It's rough when we find out our parents aren't who we thought they were. Or maybe it's just discovering they're like us—people who made some poor decisions along the way."

"This wasn't just a poor decision."

"True." She rested her arms across the open drawer. "But I suspect there's more to the story than you know."

"Did your mother tell you anything?"

"Nope. Just that you were coming for information and why. I don't think she knew more than that."

Mikayla pursed her lips and looked away.

"Why don't you ask her for details? She'd love a visit."

"No way will I leave without seeing her." She needed to do that before hitting the road. If anyone could corroborate, or disprove, Mom's story, it would be Aunt Cindy. "I'll stop by on my way out of town."

Sara turned back to the folders. "Okay, let's find the information. It's gotta be here somewhere."

Mikayla stood at the window soaking in the warm comfort of the small dog in her arms and the sun on her face. She forced her attention to the beauty of the resort, her gaze following the chair lift lines. She'd hiked up there with Dad on nearly every visit.

The fond smile faded and she shivered. While she willingly took on challenges that involved water, hills, even rocks, she'd never mastered a paralyzing fear of heights. Her mother and sisters had tried bribing her to take the lift, but Dad firmly stated it wasn't something she needed to "get over." His acceptance allowed her to wave happily from the ground as her family sailed upward, skis dangling as they waved back.

"Got it!"

The triumphant words pulled her from the memories, and she hurried to Sara's side. "What does it say?"

Sara's dark eyes swept over the information, then she looked up. "His real name is Walter Kenneth Johnson. Looks like he went by Kenny."

Kenny Johnson. The man who'd wrecked her life before it even began. The hand stroking Lula's silky head trembled.

"Mikayla? You okay?"

"Sure. Fine." She pushed her shoulders back. "Does it say why he left?"

"Let's see...voluntary termination. Seasonal hire. Says he was heading back to the ski circuit in Jackson Hole."

"A ski bum." Wouldn't he be disappointed to find out she'd never skied down a hill bigger than what was on a cross-country course.

"Mom's comments are 'excellent employee, solid work ethic, personable. Definite rehire.' But he never came back." She flipped through the few papers. "Oh. Here's a photo." She held it out. "Remember you're sworn to secrecy."

Mikayla reached for it, nausea bringing sweat to her hairline. Lula snuggled under her chin as if in support. The wallet-sized photo revealed a tanned and smiling young man, blond curls, sunglasses perched on his head. Leaning against the corral fencing, he looked strong, healthy, and carefree.

"Cute guy," Sara commented. "I'll make a copy of it." She moved to the copier, allowing Mikayla a moment to scramble for control.

"Remember," Sara said when she turned back, offering a paper folded in half, "you didn't get this from me."

"Get what?" The feeble joke was the best she could manage as she folded the paper again and stuffed it into her back pocket. "Thanks, Sara. I think I'll go for a walk."

Sara gave her a quick hug. "This will all work out, Mikayla. I know it."

One way or another.

Weaving through the guests visiting and milling in the foyer, she set Lula down and filled one of the coffee cups stacked beside the pot at the front desk, then went out into the glaring sunshine. Now that she knew that man's name, she could begin the search in earnest. She should be energized, anxious to hit the road. Without completing this mission, she couldn't go forward with life. Yet...

She hadn't allowed space in her quiet moments to consider how she might react to her findings. What if the medical history she uncovered suggested it would be risky to have children? And once she got the answers she wanted, then what? Going back to the magazine wasn't an option. Reconciling with her mother didn't seem remotely possible. The thought of facing Dad stopped her breath.

A group of guests gathered beside the corral, getting instructions from the trail guide. Another cluster of five appeared ready for a hike with drawstring backpacks and caps from the resort. The sunny morning hummed with conversation and activity. Just the way Aunt Cindy liked it.

Mikayla headed toward a familiar trail that wound into the woods. Lula trotted behind her, darting after squirrels then returning to stay just behind Mikayla. That the tiny dog had her back made her smile, and she drew a deep breath of coffee and pine, dirt and fresh air. Maybe she should sign on here, help Sara while Aunt Cindy was laid up. Sara would no doubt welcome the suggestion; she looked exhausted.

Birds scolded from high branches. No. She'd just be putting off what she had to do. Regardless of what happened afterward, she needed these answers to begin rebuilding her life. The foundation had been shattered. Hiding out in the UP wouldn't restart her life, and it wasn't how Dad had raised her.

"Look up and forward," he'd often said when they were hiking. "Know where you're going, even if it's just two steps ahead."

She lifted her trembling chin. She had no clue where she was going but she'd do it for him.

After supper that evening, she answered Lindy's call, assuring her she was perfectly fine as she ached to tell her everything. Under a black sky sprinkled with stars, she sat with Sara beside the fire sharing childhood memories, then finally crawled into bed with Lula curled at her feet. It was hours before the questions quieted enough for her to sleep.

- 13 -

Aunt Cindy's face lit with a bright smile as Mikayla greeted her from the doorway Monday morning. The familiar face had more wrinkles than two years ago, but her hair was just as dark, and her eyes still twinkled with laughter. She lifted her arms in welcome. "Hello, darling girl! Come in, come in."

Mikayla strode to her bedside, grateful for the warm hug. When she straightened, she put her hands on her hips. "Now what is this all about?"

A heavy sigh. "I know. I can't believe I was so dumb."

"At least you're on the mend." Mikayla pulled a chair close to the bed. "I hope you're behaving and doing what they say."

"Of course. Most of the time." Familiar mischief colored her smiling assurance. "I'm trying anyway."

Mikayla wagged a finger at her. "If you want to get back to work, you'll have to do better than that. Although I'm sure it's made you crazy already being cooped up here."

She nodded. "You know me well. So, tell me what's happening in the world. How's your job at the magazine?"

Mikayla shared an overview of the demise of her job, and

the dream that remained on her heart to share her love of the outdoors. Aunt Cindy had been an early influence when they'd visited, encouraging her to explore the resort with Sara. Mikayla had envied Sara and James growing up free to roam such beautiful countryside.

"Well, just because that magazine doesn't recognize the value your idea has," Aunt Cindy declared, "doesn't mean another one won't. I don't want to hear that you've given up such a wonderful dream."

Pursuing it would have to take a back seat to her search for her elusive bio dad, at least until she ran out of leads.

"I'm sorry you're going through that," she added, "on top of what you learned from your mother."

Mikayla pressed her lips together against a surge of humiliation.

"You know, your mother has been my best friend my whole life. But for all we've been through, I'll admit I was shocked when she called and told me what was happening. She didn't share all the details; only what the DNA results said." She released a long sigh, gazing sadly out the window. "It's completely out of character for her."

Mikayla would have agreed before the DNA results. *Maybe it's more in character than she ever let on.*

Cindy turned back. "I hope you don't mind that I told Sara. I hoped that would make it easier for you than having to explain it when you got here."

Mikayla shrugged. Everyone would know eventually anyway. "That was fine. What do you remember about...him?"

"A hard worker. Nice guy. Nothing stands out."

"And he and Mom..."

"Were friendly, nothing more. That's why I was so surprised by her news." She shook her head slowly, her gaze distant. "The only thing I really remember is how sad she was when she and Maggie got here. She wouldn't talk about what was happening, only that she had a decision to make. Kenny made her laugh. He was one of those perpetually cheerful guys people were drawn to."

"She was drawn to him, all right," Mikayla muttered.

"Honey, I'm sure there wasn't anything like that going on."

"Seriously?"

Pink filled Aunt Cindy's cheeks. "Well, something happened, of course. But whatever it was, it didn't go on the whole summer."

Which was worse—being the product of a one-night stand or a full-fledged affair? She snorted. Like it mattered.

"Sara told me you have his name and a general idea where you're going. I understand you're angry and hurt, Mikayla. I would be too. But keep your expectations low. I love you like my own, and I don't want you hurt any more than you are."

That wasn't possible. "I have zero expectations. I probably won't be able to find him."

"If you do?"

"I'll tell him what I think of him. Then..." She shrugged. "Maybe I'll head back here."

A brisk knock at the door interrupted, and a young woman in blue entered with a smile. "Hello, Cynthia. Time for some PT fun."

Mikayla stood and slid her chair back to the wall. "I'm going to hit the road. You're sure you're okay with Lula going with me?" After a weekend roaming the resort with Lula at her heels, Sara had suggested she take her along as her guard dog. The image made them laugh while the idea of not being totally alone took root.

Aunt Cindy nodded. "I know she's making Sara crazy, and it could be months before I get home, which makes *me* crazy." She lifted her arms and Mikayla bent into the hug. "Be safe, sweetheart."

"I will." Mikayla breathed in her familiar floral fragrance, then straightened and forced a smile. "I'm just going on a little adventure."

Aunt Cindy kept hold of her hands. "I know you can't right now, honey, but give your mom a chance to explain. There's more to this than we know." Her fingers tightened around Mikayla's. "Don't forget how much your parents love you. Both of them."

Jaw clenched, Mikayla blinked the burn from her eyes. "You take care. And do what they tell you so you can get out of here."

She left the hospital with a knot in her throat and an ache in her heart. Lula greeted her with excited yips as she climbed into the jeep. "All right, little girl," she said, letting the sadness slide away. "Let's do this."

She pulled onto the highway and settled into the flow of traffic, glancing at where Lula rode shotgun, looking out the window. The perked ears with long hair fluttering in the breeze, the teeny quivering nose, and black eyes shiny with curiosity made Mikayla smile. The comfort she found with this high-spirited dog was a surprise since they'd never had pets when she was young.

She'd always wanted a dog, but Maggie's allergies had nixed that early on. She'd dreamed of a fearless German shepherd, or a big, solid lab to hunt with. Even a happy golden retriever as a hiking companion. She'd have laughed at the idea of a...whatever Sara had called Lula. Some kind of Chihuahua and Papi-something. Now she was just grateful to have "someone" to talk to during the long miles ahead.

Three hours later she made yet another stop to clean up Lula's mess, then texted Sara while the dog daintily lapped water. *Does Lula get car sick?*

Sara's response came quickly. *Oh no! I mean yes. Shoot. What do I do?*

Forgot to send pills with u. Sorry.

Mikayla pinched the bridge of her nose and breathed deeply. To turn around now would mean a wasted day of travel. She hadn't thought about the consequences of traveling with an animal. Didn't even know they got car sick. Her phone pinged with another message.

Vet will call prescription to wherever is closest. Where are u now?

She checked the map on her phone. *1 hour to Duluth*

K. Will send name of vet to go to. Really sorry!

Mikayla leaned back against the tree trunk with a sigh and ran her hand over Lula. "Poor thing," she said. "I guess now I know to ask questions. I'll just have to figure out *what* questions before we get to the vet. Think you can handle another hour?"

Lula trotted behind her to the jeep, seemingly unfazed by her constant retching of the past few hours. For a moment Mikayla stood debating where to put the dog. The last episode had narrowly missed her lap, so holding her was no longer an option.

She pulled a ragged towel from her camping gear and bunched it into a nest on the passenger-side floor. Lula climbed in, circled three times and curled into a ball, nose tucked under her feathery tail. Mikayla patted her head, then climbed behind the wheel and prayed the miles to Duluth passed without incident.

The animal hospital Sara sent her to provided a quick check on Lula and a prescription. The technician ooh'd and aah'd over the dog, who reveled in the attention with licks and non-stop wagging. Mikayla smiled with a strange sense of maternal pride for a dog that wasn't hers. But she was for this trip, and Mikayla would take the very best care of her she could, knowing nothing about caring for a dog.

When she admitted that to the tech, she received several pamphlets on the health and wellbeing of a dog, a bag of treats, and a tiny brush with instructions on how to care for the fly-away hair. Mikayla mentioned they'd be doing a lot of hiking, so the tech suggested a front carrier as well.

Back on the road, Lula curled in her nest on the floor, Mikayla sat straighter behind the wheel. Armed with a little information and some equipment, she felt better prepared to care for her sweet companion. She could do this.

They covered another one hundred and fifty miles before the sun angled downward. Just past Fargo, Mikayla followed the GPS to a campground not far off the freeway. She'd take advantage of every opportunity to be outside on these beautiful summer evenings.

Once the tent was up and the coffee pot heating over a glowing fire, she wrapped her favorite old blanket around her shoulders and settled into a chair, Lula snuggled in her lap. This was where she was happiest, where she could admire the splash of stars in a black sky and the hoot of an owl and feel part of something far bigger than herself.

Memories danced in the firelight. She and Dad had had wonderful, in-depth talks beside a campfire and spent just as much time enjoying comfortable silence together. She'd been secretly glad her sisters and mother didn't enjoy camping. One trip together had convinced them all that it would not be a family activity.

She lightly stroked Lula. When it was just her and Dad, she could let her guard down, not worry about choosing the right words or if she wore the right clothes. She was confident and comfortable outdoors, far less so inside with crowds of people. Or even a handful of people. She knew who she was out here.

Or she had. Tears blurred the flames into a swirling kaleidoscope. Her life—past, present and future—was a question mark. She had no guarantees about what she'd discover on this journey; perhaps not even the truth. But she'd search until she turned over every rock, followed every lead, and ran out of questions.

She slid down in the chair and closed her eyes, a hand resting on Lula's warm back. At least she wasn't completely alone.

- 14 -

The rising sun chased Mikayla and Lula west across the flat expanse of North Dakota. With the new medication, her companion stood bright-eyed in the passenger seat, eagerly watching the scenery pass. There was nothing to stop them now other than an occasional leg stretch and potty break. Nothing to slow their progress as they hurtled toward the unknown. The plains gave way to green-topped bluffs, breaking up the scenery if not Mikayla's circling thoughts.

The surprise of the bluffs was not unlike the surprise of her mother's revelation. From the familiar plains of her life had come unexpected and immovable rock formations. Where she'd once been able to see miles into her future, she now couldn't see past the next curve of the highway.

Her emotions had done the same, from the steadiness of doing daily life the way she'd done it for years to rising and falling with the uncertainty of what lay ahead. Though she tried to see this as an adventure, a deep longing for the past kept her throat knotted. Lula whined and Mikayla pulled off the highway for a break.

Lula did her business in a daintily efficient process, then happily darted this way and that along the path to explore new scents and unfamiliar items, always stopping to check Mikayla's whereabouts. They wandered a path of Teddy Roosevelt National Park, photographing the breathtaking expanse of river, rocks, and forests, pausing for Mikayla to read the informational signage. Perhaps she should have become an environmental scientist to study areas like this, how best to protect them, how the ecosystems worked together. With a new life to map out, that might be an option.

Back at the main entrance, they settled on a patch of grass and nibbled crackers and cheese. With a deep sigh, Mikayla rested her elbows on her knees. She didn't want to be on this trip, didn't want to be driven by emotions. She just wanted life to go back to the way it was before she found out who she was. And wasn't.

Lula climbed into her lap and licked her chin as if in sympathy, and Mikayla pulled her into a hug, nuzzling her sweet face. "Okay, Lu. Let's get a move-on." She eyed storm clouds darkening the western horizon. "I'd like to get to Billings before the rain hits."

When the Montana state sign appeared, she cheered. Progress. If she had to do this, at least she'd do it as fast as possible. Clouds stacked higher, thicker and darker in the endless sky as she headed into a vast expanse of brown. Lots of brown. Even the bluffs and expanding hills were now brown.

A bang followed by the abrupt tilt of the jeep toward the right made her clutch the steering wheel as she fought to keep the car from veering off the asphalt. She slowed to a stop and sat still, waiting for her pounding heart to slow as well.

Ordering Lula to stay, she climbed out and rounded the front, discovering a gaping wound in the tire. Great. This couldn't have happened at the rest stop? Or near an exit? Or not at all? The highway sign indicated the next exit was five miles ahead.

She lifted her face and hands toward the darkening sky. "Really? Isn't it enough that I'm even out here?"

A distant rumble of thunder was the response.

"Fine. Fine!" she yelled. "I can fix this."

Changing a tire wasn't on the long list of things Dad had taught her, but dogged determination was. She could figure this out. Muttering about her mother's indiscretion leaving her stranded, she stood at the back of the jeep and fiddled with the spare tire carrier until it swung open, then pulled out her phone to search how to change a flat. Not much reception in the middle of nowhere. A long minute later, with thunder rumbling closer, the instructions appeared. A jack? Lug nuts? Did she even have those?

Another search was followed by an irritated snort. Of course. They were underneath everything she'd so neatly packed. She opened the rear hatch of the jeep and yanked things out, stacking them on the side of the road. Lula's big-eyed curiosity as she repeatedly jumped into the back didn't help, and Mikayla shooed her to the front.

"Lula, no!"

Ears drooping, Lula hopped to the front seat and stood trembling on the console. Regret stung, but Mikayla continued emptying the trunk. She paused to look up and down the empty stretch of highway, the weight of being alone putting a hitch in her determination. If she were Lindy, some handsome cowboy in an expensive pickup truck would already have stopped, changed her tire, and invited her to dinner.

She shook her head as she put the last of her gear beside the jeep. She wasn't Lindy, and that had never been how her life unfolded. Lindy had the looks and charm, while she had grit and strength. Frustration stung her eyes as she turned back to the empty trunk. This was Mom's fault. Mom and Kenny. She wouldn't be standing here in the middle of nowhere, raindrops now splatting on the top of the jeep, if they hadn't—

She pulled the carpet aside. There. That looked like a jack. Sniffling, she pulled out the rest of the tools, scanned the empty highway again, and channeled her inner Dad for help. "Stay focused," he'd say. "Frustration and impatience will complicate the simplest of jobs. Don't rush the process."

That might have been about learning to tie knots, but it should work here too. She reread the instructions, then struggled to loosen the lug nuts, needing her full body weight on the first two. Once they were all loose, she turned to the jack. When the car lifted slightly off the ground, she smiled. *Thanks, Dad.*

Wiping sweat from her forehead, she shivered in the rain that soaked her back. She wrestled the spare into place, then lowered the jeep and removed the jack. As she finished tightening the last lug nut, a state trooper pulled up behind her. Great timing.

"Good afternoon. Flat tire?"

"Yes, sir. I've got it taken care of."

"Really?" He seemed to recognize the disbelief in his voice and cleared his throat. "Good for you."

How would Lindy act? Mikayla offered a smile. "I've never done it before, so I hope I've got the lug nuts on tight enough." Acting helpless never sat well with her.

He studied the tire. "How about I double check?"

Lindy would bat her long lashes right about now. Mikayla nodded. "That'd be great, thanks."

As he checked each nut, she put the tools away and hefted the damaged tire on the holder, then quickly repacked everything, shaking as much water off as she could. He joined her and handed over the wrench.

"Nice work." This time there was appreciation in his tone. "Everything was plenty tight. You said you've never done it before?"

She shivered. "Never had the opportunity."

"You did a great job." He pulled a card from his pocket and handed it to her. "Best to get the rim looked at when you get the tire fixed. This is my mechanic in Billings. Give him this card and he'll check everything over for you."

"Thank you." A bright spot in this inconvenient day. "That's where I'm planning to stop tonight so I'll make sure to see him."

He tipped his hat. "I hope the rest of your travels go more smoothly. Drive safely."

"I will. Thanks for stopping."

Back in the car, she turned the heat on and pulled onto the highway. *Take that, Mom and Kenny.*

Mikayla marveled at the smoother ride as she and Lula raced across the miles toward Jackson Hole. The difference two new tires made, provided yesterday at a discount by Trooper Dan's automotive friend, convinced her she'd have to invest in the other two as soon as she got home.

Home.

What would that even look like when this whole adventure was over? Lindy would be married, living with Beau in their new house. Without a job, Mikayla couldn't afford to keep the townhome they'd been renting so she'd have to find a cheap apartment. Hard to do without a job.

She lowered the window and pulled in a breath of warm sunshine. She'd received the DNA results more than two weeks ago and been on her search over a week now. The freedom she'd suddenly been given was terrifying. It might even be exciting if she weren't on this particular mission. She had the unexpected opportunity to reinvent herself, to start fresh wherever she wanted, be who she wanted.

But where would she find a fishing buddy like Dad? Who else could she count on the way she had him? Who would want to spend early mornings sitting quietly in a boat, or afternoons hiking trails and setting up camp?

The loneliness she'd kept at bay swept in through the open window, ruffling Lula's feathery fur where she snuggled into her blanket on the floor. The future was a blank slate, but she was on her own to create a new design. Even Lula would eventually be gone, delivered back to Aunt Cindy.

An eighteen-wheeler roared past on the left, sending a gust through the window. It forged ahead with purpose, set on a destination. She glanced at Lula. Their destination was a question mark. Jackson Hole would undoubtedly be just the starting point. It'd be far too convenient to find Kenny still living there after thirty years. And maybe too soon. She wasn't prepared to encounter him quite yet.

What could she say in the way of an introduction? *Hi, I'm your daughter.* No. Daughter implied relationship, like what she'd had with Dad.

"Nice to meet you," she said aloud, then scoffed. Hardly truthful.

"Hey. You're Kenny Johnson, right? I'm Mikayla Gordon. Your offspring."

She laughed. Made her sound like a tadpole.

"I'm Mikayla Gordon. Daughter of Rachel Gordon. From thirty years ago? You know, the married woman you slept with in Michigan? Or maybe there've been too many for you to keep track of."

Whoa. Harsh. And an uglier possibility than she wanted to consider. She might have half-siblings all over the country. She released a snort. Nope, couldn't go there. Lula looked up, head cocked, and Mikayla offered a wry smile. "Sorry you got stuck with a nut case for a driving companion."

The tiny pooch gave a heavy sigh and stuck her nose under her tail.

Mikayla echoed her sigh. "Sort of how I feel, Lu."

Her phone pinged with an email notification.

"That's a good signal to take a break," she announced. "I need to stretch my legs, and I'd better see what Lin has to say about the trials of picking the right beverage napkins."

At the rest stop, they did their business and spent a few minutes chasing each other around the pet area before Mikayla pulled out her phone. The name on the email stopped her midstride. *Dad?*

She sank onto the nearest picnic table, Lula at her feet, and started to tap on the email, then jerked her finger back. If Mom told him— Chin quivering, she straightened her shoulders and tapped the email, biting hard on her lip.

> Hey kid.

The familiar greeting loosened the grip of fear.

> Im not much of a typer, as you know, so you'll have to put up with mistakes as I try to pound out a message. And no editing comments just cause you write for a living. Id rather call but I want to respect that you need some distance.
>
> So your mom and I have had some long talks since you left. Not pretty. Now I know why you left but I wish you'd have said goodbye. I get why you didn't, but finding out you left from your sister was hard. Hard on your mom too.

She rolled her eyes. Mom created the whole mess.

> Mikayla, I don't say it much but I love you. Nothing can change that. You are every inch my daughter.

Just like your sisters. Stay safe and come home
soon.
love Dad

The words blurred. She managed a simple response of
Thanks before wobbling like a drunk to the car. Once inside,
she dropped her face into her hands and sobbed.

- 15 -

Signs for Jackson Hole sent a tremor up Mikayla's spine. After several days of travel, the real search could begin. Much as she'd tried to absorb it, the beauty of Yellowstone had been mostly lost on her as she pushed through. Seeing bison from the main road had been a thrill, and the early morning fog over the prairie as she'd taken down the tent had stopped her breath, but the pull of Jackson Hole had overridden everything else. The photos she'd taken would have to be enough for now.

She checked the GPS and exited the highway. Thanks to an early start, they'd reached the ski resort campground before noon. Maybe she'd find the answers she needed today, and this whole journey would be over before the sun set. The hum of the busy campground affirmed her decision to call ahead to reserve a spot. Hers was the only one left, tucked back in the corner.

Once she'd set up camp, Mikayla whistled Lula to the car and drove to the main lodge. After her conversation with Sara, she'd had to consider other ways to gain information without going to the HR departments that would turn her away. It seemed doubtful there would be any workers left who'd have worked directly with Kenny, but while his reputation made her cringe, she hoped it was enough to get a few leads. She wouldn't mention her relationship to him in case his reputation was worse than she expected.

She made the turn into the main resort driveway and pulled in a breath. "Wow! It's beautiful, Lu."

Nestled among towering, snow-capped peaks, the chalet beckoned her along the gently curved drive. People filled the vibrant green lawn, playing bean bags, tossing frisbees, and relaxing on white Adirondack furniture as they enjoyed the summer day. The simple joy of the moment broke through the cloud that had shadowed her life for weeks, filling her with a welcome lightness. If she never found Kenny Johnson, she'd at least have had this adventure. And if she did find him...

She pulled into a visitor parking spot. Lula shot out of the car to do her business and then quickly made friends with the nearby children. Mikayla stretched her back, filling her lungs with clean mountain air. How could she even consider going back to a desk job when the outside world beckoned? There were plenty of alternatives. She just had to find one that would pay the rent.

Over the next hour, she and Lula wandered the property, pausing to chat with those charmed by the energetic dog, getting a map of the area, and soaking up sunshine in one of the chairs as she sipped an iced latte. The white peaks against the brilliant blue sky, the scent of the pines that marched up the mountains to the snowline—perhaps she'd just stay here for a week or forever.

The kids serving coffee in the chalet and those standing at the information desk were far too young to know anything about Kenny. She'd have to find people who worked the runs, who probably lived a life like his. And that meant finding a way up the slopes.

From where she relaxed on the terrace, her gaze followed the chairs that swung upward on the lift. Did it ever stop working and leave people stranded? Or worse, break and send them tumbling onto the boulders and trees below? A shiver raced up her spine, and her latte wobbled. She tightened her grasp on the cup, and icy liquid splashed across her lap. With a squeal, she scrambled to her feet, dropping the cup.

"Ma'am?" A resort worker appeared beside her, napkins in hand. "Here, let me help you. I'm so sorry this happened."

Mikayla mopped her legs and shorts, letting the young man dispose of the soaked napkins and retrieve more. "Thanks."

His apologies didn't stop. "I'm so sorry for the inconvenience. We can get those shorts cleaned for you."

"No, really, I'm fine." She waved off more napkins and smiled reassuringly. "It was my own fault. I wasn't paying attention. Really, it's all good. No, no more coffee, thanks. Really, I'm fine. Thanks very much."

He seemed determined to help somehow. "Do you have plans for this afternoon? You'll need fresh clothes."

She shook her head, then paused, glancing at the chair lift. "There is something you could help me with."

His young face lit. "I'm happy to."

"I'd like to do some exploring up"—she swallowed and waved up the mountain—"up there, but I'd rather not use the lift. Is there a path you can suggest?"

"Exploring? On your own?" He frowned at her sandals. "We have several guided hikes scheduled throughout the day. I'd be happy to get you signed up."

"No, thanks. I write for an outdoor magazine, and I'd like to talk with some of the people about what it's like to work on the mountain, and what kind of work they do." She smiled. Brilliant. It would make for an interesting article someday. "The off-season is a whole different world on the mountain."

"You write for a magazine? Which one?"

"*Outdoor Experience.*"

"That's cool." No recognition showed on his face as he nodded. He was too young to be the targeted audience anyway. "What do you write about?"

"Women in the outdoors. Hiking, camping, fishing. I was a trail guide in college, taught survival skills, so hiking in the woods is nothing new for me, but I'm hoping for a fast way up the mountain other than using the lift." *I'd rather walk backwards the whole way up.*

His gaze moved from her to the chalet as if debating his answer, then he turned and pointed toward the chair lift. "Probably the fastest way is to follow the chair lift line. That's the area that's been cleared the most." He looked down at her sandals again. "But it's not an easy climb, so I'd recommend decent hiking shoes."

Mikayla smiled past an eye roll. "That's the first order of

business. Along with dry shorts."

"And remember, the sun sets quickly so you won't want to get stranded up there in the dark."

Or worse, have to ride the chair lift down. "Thanks for the reminder. You've been a lot of help"—she glanced at his nametag—"Bryan."

He beamed. "Anytime."

After a quick change of clothes and shoes, Mikayla settled Lula into the front carrier, thanking the vet tech yet again for suggesting it. She swung her backpack of hiking essentials over one shoulder, her camera over the other, and headed toward the chair lift, energy in her stride. This was the first step toward locating Kenny and letting him know what she thought of him and the mess he'd created. Hopefully today she'd get a solid lead on where to find him.

Lula peeked over the edge of the carrier, ears up. Mikayla patted her rear through the canvas. "Always looking for the next adventure, aren't you, Lu? Thanks for doing this with me."

The dog looked up and licked her chin before returning her focus to their upward trek. The difference from eight hundred or so feet above sea level in Minneapolis to several thousand feet set Mikayla's lungs burning as she climbed. Several water and rest breaks later, it seemed they'd reached the halfway point. Maybe. Hard to tell where the top was now that she was on the slope.

Settled on a boulder, she lifted her face to the sun and sighed. What could be better than being outdoors in refreshingly crisp air, listening to birdsong in tall pines that reached up to a breathtakingly blue sky? Life held such potential when she was out in the open. "This is heaven, Lu," she murmured.

Male voices from above yanked her attention back, and she scrambled off the rock, nearly dumping Lula out of the carrier. In yellow hard hats and reflector vests, the men carried axes, rope, and shovels. Yes!

As she approached, their conversation stopped. "You lost, ma'am?" the taller one asked.

"Not at all." She smiled. "Enjoying the view. But I'm glad I ran into you. Do either of you remember an employee named Kenny Johnson? I think he was also a skier a while back. Not sure where he's working now."

"Kenny," the older man repeated. They looked at each other, then shook their heads. "Nope, doesn't ring a bell."

"Did he ski around here?" the redhead asked.

"I'm pretty sure he did. I'm guessing he's moved on, but I hope to catch up to him somewhere."

"He in trouble or something?"

Not the kind he was probably referring to. "Not that I know of," she said pleasantly. "Tracking him down for a friend of mine."

The older man shrugged. "If he was on the circuit at some point, he'd probably be in the local papers. You could try the library."

Why hadn't that occurred to her? "That's a great idea."

"No address or cell number for him? Email?"

Plenty of info on the thousands of Kenny Johnsons out there. "Not that I've been able to find. I'll check out the library. Thanks for your time."

The men moved on, and she continued the hike upward. Her steps slowed as she reached a plateau, and she settled against a tree to think. Now out of the carrier, Lula dashed from tree to rock to scrubby brush sniffing and exploring, checking back on Mikayla before prancing off again.

Far below, the resort and chalet looked like children's toys, nestled at the base of the chair lift. She pointed her camera to catch the beauty of the view, thankful her fear of heights didn't extend to being on the ground. Feet were meant to be on terra firma, she'd told Dad numerous times when he'd suggested a zip line or parasailing.

Nope. She was game for most adventures, but there was an immovable line in the sand when it came to heights. If her feet couldn't touch solid ground, she didn't partake. When she and Lula finished their snacks, she started down. Checking the library seemed a better use of her time and energy than chasing around a mountain trying to find other people. If it looked like Kenny was still here, she'd do more canvassing. Otherwise she'd follow the leads.

In the Friday morning quiet of the library, Mikayla scoured local papers from previous decades. Kenny Johnson, local ski racer and instructor. Numerous photos showed a cocky, broad smile as he posed with his arms around what were no doubt his fans and groupies. Grudgingly she acknowledged he was sort of cute with his longish blond hair, Ray-Bans, and engaging smile. Obviously her mother had fallen for that look too.

He'd had some success on the local circuit. Photos showed him on podiums, medals around his neck. Speeding down mountain runs. Celebrations. Champagne spraying over a group of partiers. It seemed he'd skied in Jackson Hole for about five seasons.

A title stopped her scrolling. *Local ski hero arrested for drug possession.* Then another—*Brawl between ski teams results in property damage, jail time.* She scanned both articles, then dropped back in the chair. Great. A troublemaking womanizer. Maybe she didn't want to know more about him if the news continued to go south.

"Finding the information you were looking for?" inquired the young librarian who'd gotten her set up.

And then some. "Yes, thanks. I'm wondering—can I print any of these? And the photos?"

"Certainly. There's a five-cent charge per page."

"Okay." She indicated those with the most information and photos about Kenny. "And I have another question. Do you know how I can find out if he's still living here? I write for an outdoor magazine and I'd like to do a story on him." That could be true. She wouldn't want to, but she could.

"Hmm. I'd suggest the general 411.com site which gives the most current info and past living locations."

Tried that. "Okay, thanks."

"You can pay for the copies at the front desk. Anything else I can help with?"

"I'm good. Thanks."

Settled back at the campsite, Lula in her lap, Mikayla searched the articles for clues about where he went after

Jackson Hole. Denver looked like the best option. He'd apparently done some racing there as well.

Running her fingers over Lula's fur, she rested her head back and sighed. Tomorrow she'd check a few other resorts in the area, then head to Denver. She'd started this adventure with one goal—find the man who'd messed up her life. Now it seemed there'd been something hidden. She'd wanted to find a decent guy who would explain what happened in a way that would somehow make it palatable. Make her feel less illegitimate. Instead, her parentage was becoming even more embarrassing.

"Maybe I should give it up before it gets worse, Lu," she mused.

Lula lifted her head, feathery ears perked up as their eyes met.

"You're right. If I don't follow this through, I'll always wonder. Fine." She released a sharp exhale. "We'll do some more exploring and then get back on the road tomorrow. Happy?"

Her riding companion licked her hand and snuggled back in. If only her life was as uncomplicated as this dog's.

- 16 -

As Mikayla packed the car for Denver, her phone pinged. Lindy again? Her heart leaped. Dad. She settled on the edge of the open hatch and read.

> Hey Kid. Yup, its the old man again. I think I could get used to talking without you interrupting. Ha ha. I was fishing this morning. Its not the same alone. I always knew youd get married someday and have a new fishing partner but I thought we had more time. Makes me think about how we take things and people for granted. And how that can make us do stupid stuff and not let people know how much we appreciate them.
>
> Theres so much I want to tell you but Im sure talking about family is hard for you right now. I hope youll let your old man share some things over the next few days in emails that might help. And I hope youre coming home soon.
>
> Missing my fishing buddy. Dad
>
> Oh. Almost forgot. I thought you'd like this photo

of todays catch. Would have been easier to get it in the boat if you'd been there, but I managed.

She opened the attachment and burst into laughter. A swordfish had been photoshopped into Dad's hands where he sat in the fishing boat. No doubt his idea but Beau's handiwork. Such a goofy grin on Dad's beloved face. So ridiculous, so *him* to send her something like that.

She studied the photo—his dark tousled hair, the camo jacket he wore every time so the fish wouldn't see him coming. A flash of pain creased her heart, then burning resentment heated her from within. How could Mom have done that to him? Maybe he wasn't perfect, but he was as close as it got. He'd been the best dad, and a solid husband who'd provided a great life for his family. After sending back a laughing emoji, she forwarded the photo to Lindy and Maggie, knowing they'd get a giggle out of it.

And this Kenny guy. Sleeping with another man's wife! What kind of person did that? Even in the moral chaos of the twenty-first century it was still wrong. Suddenly she couldn't wait to find him. She had plenty to say, and he wouldn't like any of it. Wrestling the anger back into its corner, she tucked the phone into her pocket. She had to stay focused. Letting her emotions run wild wouldn't help. Denver was calling. She slammed the hatch shut and whistled. Lula dashed around the car and flew into the passenger seat, planting dainty paws on the dash, tiny pink tongue hanging out.

Mikayla giggled. "All right, Lu. Let's head out. Denver, here we come."

The uneventful ride passed quickly as they left Wyoming behind and headed toward what she hoped was their final destination. Crossing the plains of eastern Colorado, the distant mountains of Denver grew larger, and her heart beat faster. She checked the GPS, relieved the campground was only twenty minutes farther. She needed a good hike to shake off the building adrenaline.

Standing in the campground office, Lula in her arms, she stared at the manager. "The website didn't say anything about no dogs."

He shrugged, working around her to help two kids with their soda purchase. "I don't work on the website, lady. I just enforce the rules. And it says right there"—he pointed over his shoulder at the posted guidelines—"no pets. That's a poor excuse for a dog, but it's still a pet."

Mikayla's arms tightened. "The size of something doesn't guarantee quality," she replied, glancing at the man's protruding tummy. Her parents had taught her better than that, but a flood of frustration overrode common sense. Insulting the manager wouldn't get her a spot in the campground.

The young man behind her snickered while the man at the counter ignored the comment. "Look, I can't help you. No pets means no pets. Not even if you keep it in the car. We get way too many complaints about barking dogs, and a yipper like that could get me fired. Sorry. Next."

"Do you have a supervisor?"

He brushed unruly bangs from his forehead and resettled his knit cap. "I *am* the supervisor. And the trash collector, and the guy who tells people to shut off their blasting music in the middle of the night."

Teeth clamped, she spun and flung open the screen door. There'd be no headway with him. In the car, she tried to pull up the confirmation email from the camp, then banged her head against the headrest. Of course—no connection. She was halfway up a mountain.

She climbed back out. "C'mon, Lula. I can't drive when I'm this mad." She'd learned that the hard way when she was younger. A lesson that had resulted in losing car privileges for a month. "Let's go for a hike."

Fastening the front pack, she settled her companion into it, filled her water bottle at the spigot by the campground map, and chose a light, short path. She also knew better than to hike into the mountains unprepared.

Once they left the paved sidewalk, the path meandered in and out of the woods, offering glimpses of snow-capped mountains of varying hues in the distance. A gentle breeze set yellow, white, and purple wildflowers dancing along the path. She soaked in the view from a rocky ridge, snapping photos.

She'd have to start journaling so she could remember the details—the variety of colors, fresh aromas, and peaceful sounds. Column ideas piled in her head. Maybe she'd start a blog about the trip, under a pseudonym to protect the innocent. And the guilty, unfortunately.

With the distant laughter of other hikers, the strength of towering trees and the call of a nearby stream, her heart swelled, the earlier frustration forgotten. Her shoulders lowered, muscles unknotted. This was her life, at least for now.

Lula growled as a squirrel raced up a nearby tree, and

Mikayla laughed. "You tell him, Lu. Okay, let's go find a place to stay tonight."

"Can I get you a refill?"

Mikayla looked up from the map on her phone and nodded at the coffee shop barista with the pink-tinged hair. "Yes, please. I'm in desperate need of more caffeine."

The young woman's hand-written nametag was written in curly swirls—*Jill*. "Some mornings are like that," she said, refilling Mikayla's cup. "Our coffee will get you up and running. Have you had anything to eat? We have award-winning, homemade cinnamon rolls."

Mikayla's stomach growled in response to the aroma of fresh-baked pastries. "I was so focused on getting coffee, I didn't eat. A cinnamon roll sounds great."

The girl winked, her eyebrow piercing catching the overhead light. "I'll grab one." A moment later she returned with a four-inch square, sweetly fragrant roll.

"Wow! That's enormous." Mikayla breathed deeply, mouth watering. "And it smells amazing."

"Taste's even better," came the assurance. "The owner's secret recipe. Enjoy!"

"Wait. How much do I owe you?" Ten dollars based on the size of it.

"It's on the house." Jill grinned. "We get to pick one person each day for a free treat and you're mine."

The unexpected kindness stung the back of Mikayla's

eyes. "Really? That's so nice."

"So are you. Oops, there's a customer." Moving toward the register, she waved ring-lined fingers. "Enjoy every bite."

Before digging in, Mikayla took a picture and sent it to her sisters. After the first bite, she had to force herself not to stuff the rest in her mouth. She closed her eyes in delight.

"Was I right?"

Mikayla grinned, licking her fingers. "I can see why they've won awards. If I lived here, I'd gain ten pounds just coming to your shop."

"Where are you from?"

"Minnesota. I'm just passing through looking for someone. Sort of like looking for a needle in a haystack."

Jill dropped into the opposite chair. "Maybe I can help."

"I don't have a lot to go on—just a name and a few facts about him being a skier."

The girl's pencil-thin eyebrows quirked. "That sort of describes everyone here."

Mikayla laughed. "I suppose it does. He was in Jackson Hole for a few years and skied on the circuit, but then he came this direction."

"Recently?"

"That's what makes it so difficult. It was twenty-five years ago. There are so many ski resorts and towns around here, I'm not sure where to start."

Jill's breath set her pinkish bangs fluttering. "You're right. This is a tough one. Have you got photos or anything?"

Mikayla pulled out the copies from the library and slid them across the table. Showing his picture stirred a strange sense of vulnerability, like she was airing her family's dirty laundry. Which she was.

After studying them a moment, Jill lifted her gaze. "Cute guy." She cocked her head, eyes narrowing. "You look like him. This a relative?"

She shrugged. "I think so. That's why I'm trying to find him. Any guesses where I should start looking first? He's nowhere online."

"Hmm. A man off the grid. Have you tried the jails around here?"

Her breath caught. "Uh...no. I hadn't thought of that." Not so far-fetched based on the Jackson Hole articles. *Do I even want to know if that's true?*

"Maybe try that last," Jill said, handing the papers back. "I'd suggest checking out a few resorts close by. Start with Loveland and Arapahoe Basin. Then I'd say head to Winter Park. He'd probably have skied all of those places at least for a while on the circuit. My dad has said lots of the old skiers settled up in Winter Park."

Mikayla bobbed her head. The prison search would be last. "Hopefully somebody at one of them will remember him. Thanks."

"I'm sure they'll have other ideas if you don't find him there. And when you head home, be sure to stop by here if you come through Denver. I'll be wondering if you found him." She leaned forward. "Can I pray for you before you go?"

Nobody had ever asked that before. And she'd never have guessed a tatted barrista with pink hair would be the first to offer. "Oh. I... Sure."

Closing her eyes, Jill offered a simple prayer for safety and answers. Then she reached over and squeezed Mikayla's forearm lightly before getting to her feet. She slid the chair in and offered an encouraging smile. "I'll be praying that God keeps you on the right path, so you find the guy soon."

"Thank you." The words forced their way past the lump in her throat.

Jill returned to the register, and Mikayla ambled out to the jeep and climbed in, absently petting Lula as the prayer tumbled around in her head. Did God really care if she found Kenny? And if He did, then couldn't He have prevented the event in the first place? Maybe then she'd have been born as Mitch's daughter, not an imposter of thirty years.

"Don't go there," she said firmly. It was good for Jill if she believed God would help, but Mikayla knew better. She'd find Kenny on her own, and not waste energy being angry at God. It was enough to be angry with her mother.

Every employee she encountered at the Loveland resort seemed younger than her, so it wasn't a surprise no one remembered Kenny. After a quick hike with Lula dancing along beside her, she drove to Arapahoe Basin, where she encountered a young employee on one of the trails who didn't remember Kenny but thought some of the other crew might. He made a call on his radio, then told her an employee named Squinty remembered Kenny and would meet her at the base of the chair lift.

Mikayla stopped short of hugging the unsuspecting young man as she thanked him. Nerves tingling, she kept her steps slow and steady, though she ached to race down the slope. She still had no plan for how she'd approach Kenny, but this conversation might give her an idea.

Reaching the bottom, she perched atop a boulder and snapped photos of Lula exploring the wildflowers and scrub under the chair lift. When her head popped up from behind a patch of black-eyed Susan, Mikayla laughed and took another photo.

"Well, ain't that a tiny dog," came a male voice, and Mikayla turned as Lula bounded forward, barking fiercely where she stood between them. "It *is* a dog, right?"

Mikayla slid off the boulder. "Don't let her hear you say that," she admonished with a smile. "She thinks she's part German shepherd, part mastiff."

He laughed and extended a meaty, calloused hand to Mikayla, towering over her like the pines. His wide grin was missing a tooth. "I'm Bob, better known as Squinty."

"Mikayla. And that"—she gestured toward Lula who had apparently decided he was a friend and now stood with her paws on his leg—"is my ferocious guard dog, Lula."

He reached down and greeted her with a surprisingly gentle touch. "You do jus' fine as a guard dog, Little Lula. Don' let anyone tell you different." Years of being outdoors had darkened his skin and carved squint lines, or perhaps laugh lines, in his face. "So I hear you're askin' about Kenny Johnson. That's a name from the past."

"Did you know him?"

"Skied the circuit with him for years."

She couldn't picture his massive frame, solid as an oak, barreling down the slopes. "Did you work with him too?" Hope danced in her chest.

"Yup. How come you're looking for him?"

She handed him her business card as the magazine line slid off her tongue. Maybe she *would* write about him someday. Or maybe not.

Squinty studied it and nodded. "Okay, then. How 'bout we grab some food from the cafeteria, and I can tell you what I remember."

Mikayla forced down a rush of excitement as she followed his lengthy stride toward the lodge. With Lula tucked in her pack, they waited at an outdoor picnic table while Squinty retrieved lunch. Over hotdogs, chips, and sodas, he shared what life had been like on the ski circuit decades ago.

"These kids nowadays," he said, "they don't know how easy they got it. Back then, a lot of these resorts were still small scale. The racers had to set up the course and do all the race day prep work, as well as get in time to practice, and get our regular work done. Now they jus' show up, ski, collect their money, and move on."

He shook his head of shaggy salt-and-pepper hair and chewed thoughtfully. "It was a good life. We worked hard and played harder. We knew how lucky we were to get to live this way. But"—he turned his squint to her—"it wasn't a good life for having a family. Too much moving around, goin' where the work was in the off-season. We didn't make much money and drank away a lot of it."

Or used it for bail. "So how did you meet Kenny?"

He finished his hotdog. "On the circuit. He was from Montana and showed up at a race in Jackson Hole. Just a kid, cocky son of a gun," he added with a snort, "but he was good. Real good. On the course, we were competitors, but when the race was over, we were friends."

"I know he worked in Jackson Hole for a while." Mikayla crumpled her empty chip bag. "When did he move to Denver?"

"Like I said, we played hard. Sometimes Kenny played a little too hard. After his last stint in jail there, he got fired from his job so he moved here to start fresh."

Inwardly she flinched. "What did he go to jail for?"

"Stupid sh—" He glanced at her and corrected his language. "Stupid stuff. Drinkin' and fightin'. A lot of fightin' because he wasn't good at keeping his mouth shut. Thick-headed kid. Couldn't tell him anything."

"Did he get in trouble once he moved here?"

Chuckling, Squinty nodded. "Kenny was pretty much always in trouble for somethin' or other. The ladies loved him. Actually, most people did. He could charm the socks off a shoe salesman. And though most of the racers thought he was a pain in the...uh...neck, they knew he could kick their butt on and off the slopes."

"Did he ever get married?"

"Kenny? Married?" His laugh echoed up the mountain. "No way. He wasn't afraid of nothin' except commitment. He was the poster boy for livin' the bachelor life. Most of us, once we were done racing, ended up getting married, but not him. Not that I knew of, anyway."

"He's not still living around here?"

The smile on his broad face faded. "He got injured real bad in a race. Goin' stupid fast in a storm just to win. After that he had an attitude and got in lots of trouble. Last I heard, he took off for parts unknown to get away from some guy he'd crossed—mean character who'd told people he was gonna take Kenny out. He meant it too." He rubbed his broad nose, frowning. "Might've been a gambling debt or somethin'. I tried to find Kenny a couple times, but he just vanished."

Mikayla pushed back against a surge of disappointment. Her search couldn't end here. Not without knowing what happened to him. "When was his injury?"

"Boy, that was a while back. Let's see..." He rubbed his forehead slowly. "Prob'ly twenty years now. All these memories make me want to check up on him again." He studied her until she squirmed. "You sorta look like him."

She forced a laugh. "People say all blondes look alike."

"Not the hair. Well, that's sorta like his. But more your eyes. A couple times as we've been talking it's felt like I'm lookin' at him."

"Well, that's certainly interesting." She gathered the remains of their lunch and stuffed them in the trash can. "Squinty, I really appreciate you letting me use up your lunchtime. I've learned a lot."

"Happy for a chance to talk about the ol' days. Kids don't want to hear about 'em now, so I was glad to share. You got any other questions?"

"Not right now. You have my card, so please call if you think of anything else, or someone gives you a clue about where Mr. Johnson ended up." She offered her hand. "Thanks again. It was fun hearing about your racing days."

"You be careful out there." He kept hold of her hand. "A pretty gal like you shouldn't be wanderin' the mountains on her own."

"I'm tougher than I look," she assured him, then whistled for Lula who came running. "And remember, I have my guard dog."

They parted on a laugh. Standing beside her jeep in the parking lot, Mikayla watched the large man amble back toward the slopes. When he paused to look back, she raised a hand. Frustration blurred her gaze as she and Lula climbed into the car. After all this, Kenny Johnson's trail couldn't disappear. There had to be a way to track him down.

He might have gone into hiding, but she had a lot more on the line than some big bully from twenty years ago. She'd find him one way or another.

- 17 -

The winding drive up to Winter Park kept her attention focused on the road, leaving little time to think about her conversation with Squinty. Though she was anxious to continue the search, she took pity on Lula's sweet, miserable face and stopped often to let her out to explore and restore her equilibrium. Pausing at the continental divide, Mikayla took photos, romped with Lula in the patches of snow, and chatted with a Japanese family visiting the U.S. for the first time.

When she pulled into the Winter Park campground, she finally acknowledged the nervous energy that had her stomach in knots. The information Squinty shared affirmed some of her assumptions about Kenny, but also raised more questions. She had to find him so they'd all get answered. She was tired of him taking up space in her brain.

Once camp was set up, she and Lula meandered through the pretty town looking for lunch and Kenny Johnson. Any man who appeared to be her parents' age received extra scrutiny. Several times she pulled out the tattered papers to study his features and compare them to men she passed. Tempted to inquire about him at every store, she held back. If he were indeed hiding out here, it might spook him to hear that someone was looking for him. Blindsiding him, as discovering her parentage had blindsided her, was how she preferred to meet him.

On the pink leash Mikayla had bought from the vet, Lula trotted beside her, ears up, eyes alert for another friend to meet along the sidewalk. Her enthusiasm for life cooled Mikayla's ire. She needed to take a page from her tiny friend's book—see the best in everyone, look forward to the next adventure around the corner or down the street. Expect good things. A little hard to do right now, but she'd work on it. Right after she found coffee.

Tucked down a side street, she discovered *The Wildflower Café and Bakery*, a charming coffee shop with window boxes overflowing with color, and wrought iron bistro tables under bright umbrellas. Mikayla chatted with the owner, Violet, as she waited for a latte and sandwich at the pickup window.

"That's my husband's handiwork," Violet said with a smile. "He's an iron worker, so he agreed to try making bistro tables when I opened the shop."

"He made those? They're wonderful. Does he sell them?"

"He does now." Violet handed her a steaming white mug. "Here you go, hon. I'll bring your sandwich out in just a minute."

True to her word, Violet appeared moments later with a plate heaped with chips and a panini that made Mikayla's mouth water. "Would you like some company while you eat?"

"I'd love some. Mmm, this sandwich is delicious."

While Mikayla devoured her lunch, Violet told her about her beloved adopted home of Winter Park. Her Southern twang was evident as she shared funny stories and information about the town, the people, the weather. Drawn into an effortless conversation, Mikayla soon revealed a few details about her journey.

"So you headed out here all on your lonesome to look for someone you've never met?"

Mikayla nodded.

"That's pretty brave, darlin'."

"More like determined," Mikayla said with a shrug. "I feel like I can't move forward until I get answers. All I have to go on is a name and a few older photos." She stopped her reach for the backpack she'd left at the campsite. The photos were in there. "His name is Kenny Johnson. Does that sound familiar to you?"

"Kenny Johnson." Violet's orange-hued hair lifted in the breeze as she frowned. "Sounds a bit familiar, but I can't think of anyone named Kenny, sorry. I'll think on it some more. Maybe it will come to me."

"Thanks." The photos might jog her memory. She'd have to remember to bring them the next time she came into town. "I found someone who remembered him but that didn't pan out." She released a tiny breath. "I'll just have to keep at it until I have the answers I need."

A sympathetic light glowed in Violet's green eyes. "Good for you. I don't do so well myself with questions hanging over me. My poor husband ends up getting the brunt of it when I'm trying to work something out. Sometimes I think he makes up an appointment just to get away from me and all my questions."

Mikayla laughed.

"Speak of the devil." Violet waved an arm in invitation, bracelets jangling. "Abe, honey, come over here and meet my new friend, Mikayla."

A lanky man in overalls, with a neatly trimmed reddish beard and a shy smile approached from the side of the building.

"Mikayla Gordon, this is the nicest man in Winter Park, Abraham Meehan."

He offered his hand, long, calloused fingers enveloping hers. "Good to meet you," he said in a surprisingly cultured tone. "Any friend of Vi's is part of our family."

"Thanks. It's nice to meet you too. Your wife is such a delight."

Violet hooted with laughter. "Not sure Abe would use that word, but I'll take it."

"How long are you in Winter Park?" he asked.

"Just passing through so probably not long, although I'm tempted to stay a bit and enjoy the scenery and the wonderful people."

"Lookin' for a lost relative," Violet told him, then pushed to her feet. "The regulars are starting to mosey over, so I'd better get inside. Mikayla, darlin', you stay put as long as you like. And make sure you come back to see me before you leave town, you hear?"

"Definitely. Thanks, Violet."

Bracelets jangled again as she dismissed Mikayla's

comment. "I'm just Vi to my friends."

She returned to the coffee shop and Abe smiled at Mikayla. "If you have any questions about our town, be sure to ask. Vi knows everyone and everything." He leaned toward her, hand at his mouth as if sharing a secret. "Even things she shouldn't know."

"Somehow that doesn't surprise me." Since she didn't know Kenny, he must not have settled in the area. He'd probably passed through on his way to hiding somewhere else.

"I'd best get back to my workshop. You have a good day, ma'am."

As he strolled away, Mikayla smiled. Had she ever been called ma'am in her life? It was sweet. As much as she preferred making her own way in the world, she still enjoyed the chivalry of nice men like Abe. And Dad.

"Let's head back to camp, Lu. I'd better catch up on Lin's wedding report." Lindy's emails had stacked up the past few days, which wasn't fair. Mikayla had promised to stay involved in the wedding, so she'd make responding to the bride a priority. And then she'd consider responding to Dad's with at least a full sentence. That he insisted she was still his daughter brought a tearful smile every time she thought of him. Maybe their relationship would be okay.

Mikayla studied the hiking map she picked up at the grocery store the next morning. Five miles up the Lone Pine Lake trail would help her acclimate to the altitude and allow her to mentally prepare for the next step in her search.

Parked in the trailhead lot, she settled Lula in the front pack, then hooked the hydration pack onto her backpack and shrugged it into place. While families and hikers meandered around the trailhead, she glanced at her watch and started up the mountain. She should be able to complete the hike in five or six hours, with breaks sprinkled along the way.

The dirt trail wound through a forest of lanky pines and up rock-hewn stairs, following a stream that dawdled at points and gushed over falls with a refreshing mist at others. Making better time than she'd anticipated, she settled on an expanse of rock worn smooth by decades of hiking boots and mountain weather and listened to the water dashing along below.

She shared bites of her lunch with her sweet traveling companion, laughing at Lula's enthusiastic exploration after each mouthful. She couldn't imagine being on this journey without her. She'd have abandoned the search several times if Lula's bright-eyed expression hadn't offered the encouragement she needed.

Back on the trail, they needed only one brief stop before reaching the top. Breathless, Mikayla stood, hands on her hips as she surveyed the beauty of the hidden lake surrounded by trees and craggy cliffs. Lula darted back and forth, sniffing, listening, peeking cautiously over the edge of the rocks.

"This is well worth the effort, wouldn't you say, Lula?" Mikayla sat at the base of a gnarly old tree and opened her backpack. She filled a cup with water for Lula, then drank deeply from her hydration pack, leaning back with a contented sigh. From overhead came the sweet twitter of birds as they danced from branch to branch, and from below the splash of water that spilled into the lake. The knots in her back had steadily loosened with each step upward, the stress of days in the car littering the path behind.

Lula climbed into her lap and licked her chin. Mikayla smiled, stroking her small frame. "I'd be happy to just stop time and spend a month or six in this very spot. I don't really need to find that guy, do I? My life was just fine before..."

The words trailed. Before knowing she had a hole in her heart. Before DNA. Before everything blew up, and she was left with the shell of her life.

"I da winner! You da loser. Again." The gloating male voice, accompanied by the scuffle of many feet, startled her from her musing. Lula shot off her lap and stood yipping protectively between her and the teen boys that emerged from the woods.

"Hey, look at Bigfoot over there." One pointed at the fierce pixie.

Mikayla laughed and got to her feet, scooping Lula with one arm. "Watch it. Attitude counts for something. At least it does when you're this small."

The boys joined her, laughing and jostling each other to pet Lula, who now wagged her feathery tail, protectiveness forgotten under the attention.

"She's definitely got attitude. What kind of dog is she?"

"A Chion, a mix of Chihuahua and Papillon. Tough, isn't she?"

Three teen girls joined them, squealing with delight. "Oh, she's so sweet! How cute is she? What's her name? Can I hold her?"

The boys raced off to explore the area while the girls crowded around Mikayla. A bubbly brunette with a high ponytail coaxed Lula into her arms and snuggled her close. Mikayla told them what she knew about Lula, able to laugh now at her discovery that Lula got carsick.

"So what do we have here?" The male voice was older, tinged with laughter.

"Look, Daws. Isn't she cute? She's a...a..." The brunette glanced back at Mikayla.

"Chion."

"A cheeon," she enunciated. "She's so adorable. And she has the cutest name. Lula. Want to hold her?"

The young man blinked as Lula was thrust into his hands, then held her up for inspection. She stared back at him, wide-eyed. "Well, you sure are a tiny thing. That's the littlest nose I've ever seen on an actual dog. You can't weigh five pounds soaking wet."

"Five very fierce pounds." Mikayla laughed, accepting the dog when he held her out.

"I believe it." He winked and Mikayla's heart thumped.

"Dawson! Check this out!" The boys waved from the rocks on the far side.

"Nice to meet you, Lula." He stroked Lula's head then lifted a smile to Mikayla. "And Lula's mom. I'd better get back to work to keep them from falling off the mountain."

The girls had wandered away, so Mikayla settled back at the base of the tree and watched Dawson join the boys. He was relaxed and cheerful as they bantered, keeping an eye on the girls who sat chatting and admiring the view of the lake below. Solidly built, a bandana tied over dark curls, his aura of strength was offset by the gentleness she'd seen in how he'd handled Lula.

He called the group together at the far side of the plateau. They sat in a haphazard circle listening to whatever he was saying. He had an easy command of their attention, making them laugh, asking questions and then listening intently. Conversation flowed among the group, then they quieted and bowed their heads.

Ahh. A church group of some kind. Elbows on her knees, Mikayla propped her chin in her hand and turned her attention to the lake. An interesting twist to the trail guide idea. Using nature to talk about faith. Or was he using faith to talk about nature? She knew a lot about nature, but nothing of faith. It hadn't been part of their family except for holidays and an occasional wedding or funeral. And Sunday mornings had their own sacred ritual—fishing with Dad in sun, rain, snow or ice.

Now, with the mess her life had become, it was doubtful faith in a God she couldn't see would change much. Her vision blurred and she blinked against the sting. Maybe if she had something like that to hold onto, she wouldn't feel adrift in this ocean of anger and uncertainty.

The group finished their prayer and started back toward the trail, the girls waving farewell. Mikayla waved back and watched them disappear into the woods. For them faith was probably real. For her it would just be a crutch, a way to get through a tough time. That didn't seem right. Either you believed it or not. She rubbed her eyes and sighed. She'd always relied on herself. And Dad. She couldn't just manufacture faith in something she'd never understood and expect it to give her answers.

She'd focus on accomplishing what she set out to do, the way Dad taught her. There wasn't time for spiritual musings, not now anyway. Maybe someday. She'd keep her mantra at the front of her mind—*show no weakness, rely only on yourself.*

Pushing to her feet, she dusted off her jeans and called Lula from her wanderings. She wouldn't see any wildlife on the way down following the noisy church group and their cute leader. She smiled and started after them. She'd rather look at him anyway with that curly hair and long lashes over smiling brown eyes. If she hurried, she could catch up...

Twenty minutes into the downward climb, she found them gathered at the side the path. The leader was on a walkie-talkie while several girls crouched beside the brunette with the ponytail.

"Hey, guys," Mikayla greeted them as she drew closer. "Something wrong?"

"Hannah tripped and hurt her ankle," came the jumbled response from the group.

Kneeling beside Hannah, Mikayla held back a grimace at the sight of the swollen joint.

Tear-reddened eyes looked up at her. "Is it...b-broken?" Hannah hiccupped.

"Hard to say, honey. Definitely sprained. An x-ray will show what's wrong when we get you down the mountain."

"B-but how?" Tears spilled over. "I can't even s-stand up."

Mikayla laid a gentle hand on her arm. "We'll wrap your ankle so it's stable, and then the others can help you."

"Hey," came Dawson's voice. "Thanks for stopping."

Mikayla glanced up with a nod. "No way would I just go past Lula's favorite new friend. Speaking of which..." She unhooked the front pack. "How about if Hannah watches Lula while we get her ankle wrapped?"

She ignored the lift of his brow as she slid out of the pack, Lula still snug inside, and leaned toward Hannah. "Could I ask you to hold her for a minute, hon?"

Hannah held out shaking arms, and Mikayla slid the straps of the front pack up to her shoulders. "Thanks. This way she won't get lost while we get you ready to head out. Sound good?"

Hannah nodded and buried her nose in Lula's fur. Mikayla stood and followed Dawson a few steps away where he faced her.

"Thanks again for stopping. I've radioed ahead so there'll be an ambulance waiting. Once we get her set, a couple of the guys will help her get down."

"I have a few things in my backpack that might help."

He didn't hide his surprise. "For splinting?"

"Among other things."

"That's great. I've got a few things as well. Can you start getting her leg stabilized?"

"I can."

Before she stepped away, he thrust out a hand. "I'm Dawson, by the way."

"Mikayla."

His smile revealed a dimple at the corner of his mouth as he released her hand. "Thanks, Mikayla."

"Glad to help." She returned to Hannah and knelt beside her, pulling a rolled newspaper, small blanket and cloth strips from her backpack. "Hannah, let's get your ankle wrapped up snug. That will keep it protected and make you more comfortable. Can you lift your leg a bit so I can slide this blanket under it?"

"I don't... It hurts," Hannah whimpered.

"I know, hon. Here, I'll help you. Just up a bit." She deftly slid the blanket under the girl's leg. "There. Perfect."

Dawson joined them, and they worked quickly to complete the wrapping. Hannah's sniffling stopped once the injury was set, and she managed a smile when Lula licked her cheek.

"Why don't you head down with the rest of the group," Mikayla suggested in an aside to Dawson, "and I'll hang back with the boys who are going to help Hannah."

Fists on his hips, he frowned. "I don't like leaving part of the group behind."

"I get that, but there's no point in all of us creeping our way down," she countered. "It'll be way past dark at that rate. Get the other kids down and then, if you need to, head back up to check on us." Not that she needed checking up on, but she understood his reluctance to leave part of his group with a complete stranger. "We'll work our way down slowly."

He unclipped the walkie-talkie from his belt and handed it to her. "You can let me know your progress. Zeke knows how to work it."

Mikayla pressed her lips together against a swift retort. He wouldn't know she did too. "Good. We'll see you at the bottom."

Dawson relayed their plans to the group and prayed over Hannah's injury and for safety for all of them before hurrying off with five of the nine kids. Zeke and another boy had fashioned a surprisingly effective crutch for Hannah and stayed protectively beside her as they started down, a third boy behind them.

In the front pack now fastened securely on Hannah, Lula proved to be a wonderful distraction, licking Hannah's face and snuggling against her neck. After making introductions, Mikayla kept the conversation going as they moved carefully down the rugged path, asking about each of them, their group, and Dawson.

They took turns responding. They were participating in an adventure camp, learning how nature and faith connected, developing leadership skills, and getting to spend lots of time outdoors.

"Daws is amazing," Zeke said. "I want to do what he does when I'm done with school."

"And he's cute," Hannah added with a wan smile.

Mikayla winked at her, then steered the conversation to what they'd learned about leadership.

While Peter walked ahead, Zeke and David alternated giving Hannah a piggyback ride when the path allowed it, helping them make better progress than Mikayla expected. As sunlight faded and the path darkened, she pulled a small headlamp from her backpack, silently thanking Dad for his insistence she always keep it handy. Mugging for the group, she fastened the strap proudly on her head, handed a smaller flashlight to David, and took the lead, leaving the boys' teasing comments behind.

The walkie-talkie crackled to life occasionally, and Zeke provided an update. After situating the group at the trail head, Dawson was on his way back up. The chatter dwindled as they continued their downward climb, and Mikayla shared a few more stories of her journey. When Dawson and a medic appeared with two large flashlights, relief pulsed through her tired limbs. She and the boys stood to the side, watching the brawny medic use a specialized harness to put Hannah firmly on his back.

A cheer went up in the distance as they emerged from the darkness into the blinding lights of a waiting ambulance. The kids, along with what looked to be Hannah's parents, rushed forward to surround her with welcoming chatter and hugs.

After removing the headlamp they all now admitted had been necessary, Mikayla collected Lula and the front pack, gave Hannah a quick hug, then stepped out of the way. As activity buzzed around the teen, she trudged toward her car, aching for a warm bath and a comfy bed. She'd settle for something to eat from a drive-through and her toasty sleeping bag.

"Wait!"

She turned and paused as Dawson jogged toward her.

"I can't thank you enough," he said, offering his hand again. "You were a Godsend, that's for sure."

She shook his hand. "I don't know about that but you're

welcome. It was a pleasure getting to know the kids."

"So how did you know how to do that?"

"I was a trail guide in college, and most recently was a columnist for *Outdoor Experience* magazine. And I've had a lot of outdoor readiness training."

"Really?" He cocked his head as he studied her then grinned. "That's cool. Well, this hike didn't exactly go as planned, so I'm thankful you were there."

"Glad I could help."

"Daws, they're ready." One of the boys waved from across the parking lot.

Dawson waved then turned back with a smile. "Mikayla, right?"

"Right."

"That's pretty. Thanks, Mikayla. Hope to see you around."

She'd be on her way home before that happened. "See ya."

As he jogged toward the waiting kids, she climbed into her jeep and headed toward town and the nearest drive-through. That had been an unexpected twist to a much-needed hike. Dad would be proud. The thought sent loneliness zinging through her, and she pressed the gas pedal a bit harder. His emails had become the encouragement she needed to keep going.

- 18 -

Morning sun warm on her back, Mikayla sipped the iced mocha Violet had brought her with a cheerful greeting. When she'd set out on yesterday's hike, she'd looked forward to clearing her head and reveling in the stunning mountain beauty before continuing her search for Kenny. The encounter with Dawson's youth group had been an unexpected bonus. The satisfaction of splinting Hannah's ankle and helping the group back down the mountain had filled her sleep with dreams of past adventures.

"Well, good morning!"

The male voice startled her, and she looked up into smiling brown eyes framed by thick eyelashes. "Hey. Good morning to you. How's Hannah?"

Dawson dropped into the opposite chair. "No break, which was great news. But she'll be keeping that leg elevated for a few days, so she won't be able to finish camp this week." He leaned his elbows on the colorful ceramic tiles. "Thanks again for your help."

"I was happy to. Any friend of Lula's is a friend of mine."

His answering chuckle sent a flutter of delight across her skin. "I was glad you had that pipsqueak along for protection against bears and mountain lions."

Mikayla straightened with feigned indignation and whistled. The pipsqueak raced out of the shop, and Mikayla pointed at Dawson. "Sic him, Lu!"

Lula leaped into his lap and joyfully licked his face. Mikayla rolled her eyes. "I didn't say lick him, I said sic him."

Dawson laughed as he tried to fend off her lightning quick movements. "Okay, okay. I give!"

Mikayla called, and Lula pranced across the table and into her lap. "Lula! Where are your manners? That wasn't polite. No walking on the table."

"Now I've seen everything. A guard dog that doubles as table décor."

Mikayla shared his laughter. "We're a multi-purpose team."

"Dawson Dunne! I'm amazed to see you out of the woods on a weekday." Violet joined them, hands on her broad hips. She turned to Mikayla. "This young man spends most of his days leading groups up, down, over and around the mountains. We only get to enjoy his presence on weekends when he comes into town for supplies."

Dawson stood and shared a hug with the older woman, then grinned at Mikayla. "This is one of my most favorite people in all of Colorado."

"She's become mine too."

"Good choice." He settled into his chair. "Vi, could I trouble you for a large regular?"

She set a hand on his shoulder. "Of course you can, honey. I heard about your long night at the hospital."

He raised an eyebrow at Mikayla. "No secrets around here."

"You spent the night at the hospital?" she asked as Violet returned to the shop.

He shrugged. "Just until Hannah was sleeping. Made us both feel better."

Mikayla sipped her drink and studied the young man. Who did something like that?

"So." He met her gaze and her cheeks flushed. "I actually came into town to find you."

"Me?"

"You mentioned you'd been a trail guide. And I'm in desperate need of hiring someone. One of my guys fell rock climbing two weeks ago and broke his leg. I've got some overnight trips coming up, and they can't happen without two guides."

"It's just the two of you?"

"I've got eight people working with me, but we're already crazy busy, so none of the other staff are available to fill in for Bucky."

Her eyebrows lifted. "Bucky?"

He chuckled as Violet returned with a large to-go cup. "On the house, hon," she said, then smiled at Mikayla and turned toward new customers.

"I love that woman's heart," he commented, then grinned at Mikayla. "Bucky has been his nickname forever, I guess. It came from—"

"His teeth?"

"The fact that he gets bucked off a horse every time he tries to ride."

She stifled a laugh. "That's terrible!"

"Actually, it's pretty funny. They see him coming and go crazy because they know it will be a wild ride. He's not careless," he added, "just a little...energetic, I guess." He sipped his coffee. "He's been banned from most of the stables around here just because it takes a while for the horses to settle down after he's been there. He'd make a great rodeo clown, but he's afraid of bulls."

Mikayla met his gaze, trying to decide if he was serious, then joined his laughter. "I'm curious but not sure I'd want to meet him."

"He's a character. So back to why I was looking for you. Any chance you're looking for a job? We pay pretty good, as guiding goes, and it would be steady work. You'd probably end up working mostly with me, however, so that might affect your decision."

She could think of worse things. "I'm not sure how long I'll be here."

He relaxed in his chair. "Can I ask what brought you to Winter Park?"

"I'm looking for someone."

"No luck so far?"

"So far no, but I just got into town."

He nodded, seeming unfazed by her evasive answers. "Vi knows everyone, so she's a great place to start. I'd be happy to help, though I know a fraction of what she knows."

"You grew up here?"

"Colorado Springs. I moved up here ten, twelve years ago. Needed a change." His gaze became distant. "Turned out it was exactly where I needed to be. Met some great people, got involved in guiding, and found my calling." His phone buzzed, and he pulled it from his pocket. "Sorry. I need to take this."

She waved him away with a nod, relieved to have a moment to digest his offer. He paced slowly as he talked, nodded, and laughed. He was cute, cheerful, and seemed sweetly genuine. She could use a friend like him. Someone who loved being outdoors as much as she did, who wasn't afraid to work hard. And who seemed to truly care about others. She'd work with him in a heartbeat if she didn't think it would distract her from what she'd come to do.

He returned to the table, slipping his phone into his back pocket, then he pulled a card from his shirt pocket. "I have to get back to camp before the next crew heads out. Here's my card. It'd be great if you decided to work with us, at least for the summer." His hopeful smile sent a tingle down to her toes. "Pray about it and let me know."

Mikayla watched him climb into a dusty black pickup, lifting a hand in response to his wave. She had no clue how to pray. If she did, it would be about finding Kenny so she could stop thinking about him.

The brilliant afternoon sun sat above the mountain peaks when Mikayla parked in the crowded resort parking lot. Anticipation pulled her from the car. Perhaps the energy thrumming through her was from sharing coffee with Dawson, or the easy rapport she'd developed with Vi. Answers seemed so much closer now. Or maybe the thinner air was affecting her thinking.

She settled Lula in her carrier, slung the backpack over her shoulder, and set off for the slope. As she'd experienced at other resorts, locating workers was half the battle. She followed the whine of a distant chainsaw up and around the mountainside until finding three men clearing branches.

Her inquiry about Kenny received a response similar to the other places—name didn't ring a bell, the photo didn't look like anyone they knew. They went back to work, leaving her fighting the need to scream in frustration.

"Ma'am?"

She turned to face one of the men she'd talked to.

"There's an old timer that might know of him," he said. "Old Joe. Lives in Tabernash, just a bit down Highway 40 from here."

"Does he have a last name?"

He chuckled and shook his head. "I'm sure he did at one time, but not that I ever heard. Everyone around just knows him as Old Joe."

"Tabernash. Old Joe. Got it. Thank you so much."

"Hope it helps."

"I hope so too." She waved and hurried down the slope, her feet barely touching the ground as she headed for the jeep. Someone named Old Joe had to know about Kenny. She giggled. And the debonair, womanizing Kenny was now probably known as Old Ken.

The drive to Tabernash moved in slow motion though the dashboard clock read only fifteen minutes. After inquiring about Old Joe at the gas station, she made her way up the mountain to his cabin, surprised they gave out his information so freely. Definitely a city thing that made people suspicious and guarded about sharing information.

At the end of the winding dirt road sat at a tiny log cabin. There couldn't be more than three rooms in such a small space. Or maybe it was just one room if he was the sole occupant. She took stock of the neat, sparse yard. Aside from a sprinkling of yellow and purple wildflowers, and the ever-present pine needles, nothing spoke of a female touch.

A wooden bench beside the front door was perhaps big enough for two. A couple of lawn chairs sat nearby, pieces of nylon webbing fluttering in the gentle breeze. Just past the cabin an outhouse leaned slightly to the side.

While she preferred a simpler life than Lindy, hers wasn't nearly this clutter-free. Maybe instead of looking for an apartment she could afford after Lin's wedding, she should build a little log cabin in the woods. With indoor plumbing.

She climbed out and rapped lightly against a flimsy screen door that looked ready to fall off the rusty hinges. The only sound was a gentle rustling from the wind in the treetops. She rapped harder. Silence answered. Perhaps he was in the backyard.

She walked around the cabin and found cold ashes in a firepit but no sign of life. Back at the jeep, she leaned against it with a sigh. This lead had felt so promising, so—

"Joe's not here."

She straightened and turned toward an elderly man with white hair that curled from under a knit cap. "Hello!" She sounded like an over-zealous cheerleader. "Are you his neighbor?"

"Live right over there." He pointed over his shoulder, though no structure was visible in the woods. "Such a shame."

"What is?"

"Joe havin' a heart attack. Just last week." He shook his head and tsked. "Told him not to try movin' the logs hisself, but he's a stubborn ol' goat."

No. No, no, no. "Is he—"

"Dead?" He waved a gnarled hand and chuckled. "Nah. It would take somethin' more'n a heart attack to take him out."

Her legs wobbled. "Oh, that's good. Do you know where I can find him? Is he coming home soon?"

He spat to the side. "His daughter made him move to her place to get his strength back. Made him darn mad, I'll tell ya. He wants to live life his way. But she played the grandchild card and he went. Loves them grandkids somethin' fierce."

"Does she live around here?"

"Alabama, for gosh sake. Who lives there?"

Old Joe's daughter and grandkids, apparently. Now what?

"You a friend of Joe's?" He squinted at her, rubbing his white-whiskered chin. "You don't look familiar."

"I've written columns for *Outdoor Experience* magazine, and I'm hoping to interview him and a few other skiers from the past to get their perspective on what life was like back then, how the ski circuit has changed."

He continued to study her. "Huh."

She forced herself to hold his gaze, keeping a smile at the corners of her mouth. "I'm glad to hear Joe is recovering. When do you think he'll return home?" *Don't sound so desperate.*

"Said he'd be back in a few weeks. That was right before he left. I'm thinkin' she'll be glad to send 'im back by then."

Mid-July. He was the best lead she had at this point. The only lead. She couldn't leave here without talking to him. She'd just have to stay in the area and keep digging until Joe got back.

"Do you know if he knew a guy named Kenny Johnson?"

"Kenny." His brow dropped as he thought. "Don't know about a Kenny. Joe has lots of friends, though, so maybe."

"Would it be all right if I drop by again in a few weeks to see how Joe's doing?"

"'Course it would. Joe loves company. 'Specially"—he said with a wink—"pretty young women who want to interview him. He loves talkin' skiing and life and such."

She pulled a business card from her pocket. "I'll look forward to that. Here's my phone number, in case he wants to call me. I'm Mikayla, by the way."

A calloused hand engulfed hers, surprising in its strength. "Pete. Good to meet ya. You come on back in a couple a weeks, and Joe'll put the coffee pot on."

Retracing the road to Tabernash, Mikayla looked at Lula and sighed. "Sure feels like doors keep shutting on us. But we're not giving up, right?" Despite the defeat pressing against her lungs, she nodded. "Right."

Kenny Johnson was behind a door somewhere.

- 19 -

After the disappointing visit with Pete, Mikayla struggled to keep her spirits up as she made lunch. Moping wouldn't change anything, however. What had always worked back home was writing something—an article, her thoughts, new ideas. Settled in at the campsite, a travel mug of fresh coffee nearby, she ate her sandwich and then opened her laptop and pounded out her frustration on the keyboard. Words flowed and thoughts tumbled over each other as they raced to the screen.

With Lula snoring quietly at her feet, energy pulsed as Mikayla poured out impressions of the people she'd met, descriptions of the unexpected beauty of where she'd landed, and the hope that pushed her onward. In the angst of the past month, she'd forgotten how writing freed her, untangled emotions, and buoyed her spirits.

Hiker Girl on a Mission. She'd blog about these experiences without using her real name or sharing anything personal about her family. If someone stumbled upon it in cyberspace, hopefully they'd enjoy her photos, her thoughts about the freedom in nature. If not, she'd have chronicled the journey for something to look back on someday.

She sent the blog link to Linnea and Maggie then closed the laptop with a snap, startling Lula to her feet. "Sorry, Lu." She cuddled her sweet traveling companion as she savored the satisfaction of creating something new. Her search might be stalled for now, but writing would keep her busy and bring her sisters along on the journey. She could create columns from the blog to send to some of her magazine contacts. Making money while she waited would be a good thing.

"Why didn't I do this at the start?" she mused. Lula licked her chin. "You're right. They'd have been over-the-top emotional. Not exactly what the mags are looking for."

She breathed deeply. They wanted photos of beautiful scenery alongside stories about interesting people, and detailed wilderness experiences.

"Like our hike the other day. I'm wondering how sweet little Hannah is doing, aren't you?" The teen's tearful smile swam before her, followed by Dawson Dunne's dimples. Focused on getting close to finding Kenny, she'd already forgotten his offer at Vi's shop. At the time, she'd expected to be on her way back to Minnesota within a few days. But now...

In the tent, she dug through her clothes until she found his card. *Dawson Dunne, Executive Director, Outlook Adventure Camp. Where faith and potential connect.* An image of smiling brown eyes, hair curling from under a bandana jumped before her. A warm handshake. Laughter in his voice.

He has to be desperate to want to hire a stranger.

And she was desperate to fill her time while she waited

for Old Joe.

"Come on, Lu. I need to think so let's go for a walk." She locked her laptop in the jeep before they headed out. Twenty minutes later she reached the *Wildflower Café & Bakery*.

"Well, there's my Minnesota darlin'." Vi's voice rang from inside.

Mikayla stepped into the cool shade of the coffee shop and inhaled. Hazelnut, cinnamon, pastries.

"Sit yourself right down, and I'll get you some coffee." Violet refilled the cups of the customers sitting by the window, then returned to Mikayla. "How about a pastry? Homemade."

"You make them?"

"All of them," Vi said, a wide smile on her face. "That's why we opened the café. If I didn't have a place to sell my pastries, I was going to outgrow my house. And not in a good way," she added with a wink, patting her hips.

"Then I'd love one. And a glass of orange juice?"

"Coming right up." Moments later, Vi set a tall glass of foaming juice before her followed by a chocolate croissant. "This should take the frown from your pretty face. Now you just sit there and enjoy."

As Violet bustled about behind the counter, Mikayla wrestled with the crazy urge to work with Dawson. "Vi, what do you know about Dawson Dunne and his camp?"

Vi tossed a smile over her shoulder. "Other than he's probably the cutest man in Winter Park? And did I mention eligible?"

Mikayla rolled her eyes. "He offered me a job."

"You don't say. Well, that's something. He's very particular about who he hires."

Unless he's desperate. "What kind of reputation does his camp have? What's he like to work with?"

"Both have a solid reputation. As far as I know, there've been no complaints or safety violations, no illegal activities, no police reports against the camp or the guides." She leaned a dimpled elbow on the counter. "As for him, he's a doll. He came to the camp with some issues but seemed to thrive there, so Walter hired him on as a staffer the next summer. When Walt died, he left the camp to Dawson. That young man takes running it very seriously."

"But," she added, turning back to the coffee pots she'd started, "if you ask me, he needs more fun in his life. Works day and night for the camp. No time for anything else."

"So he's a micromanager?" Red flag there.

"Dawson?" Her burst of laughter made Mikayla smile. "Hardly, honey. He's got a gift for hiring and training the best staff around. That's why they've got waiting lists for kids to come both to work with him and to attend the camp."

Mikayla studied her glass as she swirled the remaining juice. If she took the job, she'd still have to go home the first of September. He probably wanted more of a commitment.

"Honey, if Dawson Dunne wants to hire you, that's high praise. He has a sixth sense about people. Hasn't hired a blooper yet."

Mikayla giggled. "A blooper? I'd hate to be the first."

"You won't be. Talk to him," she encouraged. "Find out about the job, ask him hard questions. Then make your decision. I, for one, would be thrilled you'd be hanging around for the summer. You're a gem, honey."

She moved away to greet a new customer, leaving Mikayla to ponder her words. She pulled Dawson's card out and fingered it thoughtfully. Since she had to wait for Old Joe's return, maybe she could help Dawson in the meantime. Heart fluttering, she retrieved her cell phone and dialed his number before she could change her mind, then left a brief message. There. She'd know if she was supposed to stay or not after meeting with him. If he returned her call.

In the meantime, she'd add another post as Hiker Girl about decisions, options, and figuring out what the future held.

Four hours later, Mikayla drove under the rustic metal sign signaling Outlook Adventure Camp and parked in front of the main lodge. The single-story log and timber building sat in a clearing among tall pines, its green metal roof reflecting the afternoon sun. Atop a rock foundation, a porch stretched across the front with three pairs of Adirondack chairs awaiting campers. An extended roofline offered shaded protection for anyone enjoying the view. She smiled. The porch beckoned her to "set a while" as she had at Aunt Cindy's.

The screen door of the main entrance swung open, and Dawson emerged with two coffee cups. "Hey, Mikayla. Any problems finding us?"

She climbed out and accepted the cup he offered. "None at all. Thanks for this. I've only had one cup today."

"Where are you staying?"

"Idlewild." She sipped and sighed. "Mmm, this is good."

"My secret blend," he said with a wink, then added, "You can have your little friend join us. This is a creature-friendly place."

"If you're sure..." At his nod, she let Lula out of the jeep. "Behave, Miss Lula or it's back in the jeep for you."

She darted off to explore, and Dawson swept an arm toward the lodge. "Come on in. So you're camping at Idlewild while you're here?"

"I camp whenever I get the chance," she said, preceding him into the building, Lula on her heels. "Camping season is pretty short in Minnesota."

In the spacious gathering area, a stone fireplace reached to the rafters, battered leather couches clustered before it. She breathed in the aroma of wood, edged by fragrant lilacs in a nearby vase, and a lingering whiff of past fires in the fireplace. At the left side of the room was a dining area with two long tables before a swinging door she assumed led to the kitchen. To the right side were what looked to be two smaller meeting-type rooms.

She could envision nervous kids checking in at the counter to the left of the front door, laughter and meals shared around the tables, a roaring fire while snow fell outside the tall windows flanking the fireplace. If she started a camp like this for girls and women, maybe her lodge would look like this someday. She'd have to take lots of photos to remember the details.

"Let's sit in my office while we finish our coffee, and I'll tell you about the camp."

She and Lula followed him to the room immediately to the right of the front door. Windows along the front and side walls brought in natural light, making the small room airy and inviting. His oak desk had seen decades of use, as had the black office chair behind it. Above the desk hung a photo of Dawson and another man in silhouette shaking hands, broad smiles on their faces. His dad, perhaps? Shelves along the opposite wall held framed photographs, wood carvings, a small set of antlers, and a variety of books.

He gestured to the chair by his desk, then dropped into his and grinned. "Welcome to Outlook. I was glad to get your voicemail."

"Thanks." She returned his smile. "I'm interested to hear about the camp, how it got started, how you got involved."

"Hope you've got all day," he said with a chuckle. "Nah, I'll give you the half-day version. The camp was established about twenty years ago by Walter Smith. Great guy. I met him the first time I attended camp. I was seventeen at the time."

His smile dimmed and he looked away. "That's a story for another day. Let's just say Walt pointed me in the right direction. I loved everything about the camp. I think I drove him crazy with questions, but he hired me the next summer after I graduated high school. Been here ever since. I think he saw some of himself in me—the part that needed a little firm guidance to get on the right path."

"So you signed on for life?"

"That wasn't the plan, but when Walt got sick a year or so ago, I ended up taking over a lot of his work. When he died, I found out he'd left the camp to me." Pain darkened his face. "That's when I became a lifer. I can't imagine doing anything else. I want to keep his memory alive by continuing the work he started and making this camp a household name."

"I bet he'd like that. How does the camp run? I didn't see cabins when I drove in."

"When Walt started Outlook, he built the first version of this lodge one log at a time. He didn't have money to build a structure for the campers, so those first kids had to rough it. Turned out it was a great experience for them, actually being out there living in nature instead of talking about it."

"But not year 'round." Much as she loved to camp, winter camping was a whole different creature. She shivered.

"Nope. We have day activities through the winter but not overnight. Mountain weather's unpredictable enough during the summer months, so to try it in hundreds of inches of snow? Not worth the risk. And the extra insurance is insane."

Hundreds of inches? What did that even look like? Snow back home was measured in the tens of inches.

"We offer several adventure choices," he continued. "The main program is the seven-day Outlook True Adventure camp for high school and older. We start with two days of prep here, and then take them out for five days of mountain camping. That program requires at least two guides. We have day programs throughout the year where younger kids, elementary and junior high age, come on-site every day. At night they stay down the road at a local church with their own chaperones."

"There's something going on all the time," she noted, to which he grinned.

"We've been blessed. And in case you didn't know, this is a faith-based camp. We have a ton of fun, but we take our faith in Jesus seriously. Our goal is for the kids to leave here with a solid foundation of knowing who God is and who they are as His children. Hopefully we've created a desire in them to learn how to be who God designed them to be, and to want to make a difference in the world."

"That's a lot to cram into a week, along with all the camping, hiking, fishing and other instruction they get." Vi wasn't kidding when she said he lived and breathed this camp.

"It's been a learning process for us," he agreed. "Over the years we've developed a program that blends it all together."

She leaned forward. "How?"

He looked out the window, tapping his fingertips together. "Okay, let's take knot-tying." He laughed when she quirked an eyebrow. "Stay with me. So for a lot of reasons, it's important for them to learn to tie several kinds of knots, right? While we work on it, we get them talking about the big and little things that make them anxious or confused or frustrated. That tie them in knots internally."

"How does that relate to faith?"

"Good question. While we talk about what gets our emotions knotted up during a normal day, we also share what the Bible says about trusting God, bringing our impossible knots to Him to untangle. And how we can learn to avoid the things or people that get us in a knot in the first place."

"Ahh." She nodded, leaning back in her chair. "Sneaky."

"Not sneaky. The foundation of Outlook is plainly stated on our printed materials, on the website, on registration and release forms. We figure out the most natural ways to get them talking about life and then provide hands-on activities and visuals to help them use their faith to deal with issues."

Cute, smart, *and* creative. Impressive.

"Every activity is built on an element of faith. For us, it all goes back to that."

"How would you do that with, say, cooking?"

"God's provisions. Caring for others."

"Fishing?"

"Jesus said His believers would be fishers of men. Fishing is a great way to learn about God's creation while providing 'daily bread,' so to speak, and learning how to share our faith."

"Hiking?"

"Taking care of our bodies. Being healthy while enjoying God's artistry."

"Setting up camp?"

"Teamwork. The importance of working together, helping others, sharing resources and knowledge. It highlights our different gifts."

They looked at each other a moment before laughter erupted.

"You're good," he said, wagging a finger at her. "I can see working with you will keep me on my toes."

"And you have an answer for everything. In a good way."

He shrugged. "I'd better. This is my livelihood. Come on. Let's take a quick tour, and you can quiz me some more."

Behind the lodge a pole barn housed neatly arranged supplies and equipment from a 4-wheeler to snowshoes, tents, fishing poles, camping equipment, and backpacks. Beside the barn sat a brick shower house with changing rooms and toilets. Behind that was a two-story bunkhouse for staff complete with a kitchen and laundry, a main living space, and ten small bedrooms with sinks. Lula's tiny feet ran double-time as she tried to explore and follow Mikayla at the same time.

"While the True Adventure staff are obviously off-site most of their camp," he explained where they stood in the bunkhouse kitchen, "the rest stay here. And most of the camp staff aren't local, so they need housing."

"Do you live onsite?"

"I do. Had an apartment nearby for a while, but there was too much running back and forth, so I moved to the bunkhouse. I'm not in my room all that much anyway, so it's worked great. It helps me get to know the staff better. And I just feel better being on the grounds."

They wandered into sunshine that sparkled through spindly pines, and Lula dashed away. "So camp staff come here from around the state?"

"Around the country, actually. We've set up programs with several colleges as a field placement option for their recreational management students."

It seemed he'd thought of everything. "How in the world do you keep it all straight and lead camps yourself?"

"I have a great staff. You haven't met Brenda yet. She's the true brains around here. She's out with the day campers, but she'll be back soon. She runs the office, my life, and basically this side of the mountain."

The sound of young voices floated through the woods, and Dawson lengthened his stride. "Come on. Let's see if we can catch the end of what they're doing."

Mikayla scurried behind as they headed toward the noise. When they rounded the main lodge, the kids rushed toward him.

"Daws, that was so cool! We saw three eagles. And a fox. And a moose in the distance," they shouted, surrounding him. "And Brenda can climb a tree faster than Rob. She's like a monkey, she's so fast. Ooh, look at this little puppy! She's so cute!"

He laughed as they continued describing their adventures and oohed and aahed over Lula, glancing back at Mikayla where she stood to the side. "I guess it's break time," he said then turned his attention back to the kids.

A young woman joined them in hiking boots, shorts, and a red bandana around her head. With a dirt smudge on her cheek, a long dark braid hanging over one shoulder, and leaves and sticks clinging to her long-sleeved Outlook T-shirt, she looked like the kind of woman Mikayla had longed for as a friend. A yellow lab wearing a matching bandana lumbered into the ruckus, tail wagging as he woofed at Dawson.

At his deep voice, Lula dashed toward Mikayla and stood fiercely barking at the other dog who looked at her in surprise, as if he'd never seen a dog so small.

Mikayla scooped her up. "Lula, hush," she scolded. "That's a friend."

Dawson chuckled, patting the big dog's head. "This is Bruno. He's harmless."

Lula continued a low growl as she stared down at Bruno. Mikayla shushed her again. "He's not going to hurt us."

Fingers to her mouth, the girl's whistle silenced the kids' clamor. "Snack time at the picnic tables *after* you wash up. Five minutes. Go!"

The kids rushed past the lodge to the shower house, the sound of chaos fading as they disappeared. The young woman paused to introduce herself. "I'm Brenda. We sure could use another woman around here," she said. "Let me know if you have any questions."

"Thanks. I will."

The lab woofed again, and Lula barked in reply. Brenda patted his thick frame as he smiled up at her, tongue hanging out the side of his mouth.

"Bruno is one of the camp dogs. Don't let his goofy expression fool you. He's actually trained for mountain search and rescue."

"Wow. Nice to meet you, Bruno." She squatted to put him and Lula at eye level, a short distance apart. As Lula growled menacingly, he sniffed at her, tail wagging. "This is Lula. The two of you will be friends when she gets used to you. She's a big dog in a teeny body."

Lula stretched her neck to sniff at the lab, her tail slowly swinging.

"Good girl, Lu. See? He's not so scary."

Brenda and Bruno followed the kids, and Dawson directed Mikayla back to his office, grabbing two granola bars from a basket on the lobby counter. As they settled, he handed her a cup of water from the jug behind his desk, then leaned back in his chair. "Fire away."

"What's the job description?"

He flipped open a folder and handed her the top sheet. "Here you go."

She set Lula down and skimmed it, impressed with its clarity and thorough description. She wouldn't get rich doing this work, but she'd loved being a trail guide in college, teaching, encouraging, and helping kids. If she hadn't been sidetracked by the allure of working for the magazine, mistakenly thinking she'd have a greater impact on women there, she'd probably have made more headway simply working with smaller groups like this.

"Anything I can clarify?" he asked.

She looked up. "This is very thorough."

"Brenda gets the credit. Her degree is in human resources, so all that stuff is her expertise. I just lucked out that she also loves being outdoors, so we got a two-fer."

"I hope you pay her for that." The words slipped out before she could censor them.

"I do. I'd give her the moon to make sure she's happy here. I couldn't do this without her."

His affectionate smile gave Mikayla pause. Perhaps there was a camp romance going on. But it wasn't her business, and she wouldn't be here that long any—

His laugh made her jump. "Don't ever play poker with these guys," he said. "About a million things just crossed your face."

How often had Lindy said the same thing? She lifted her chin and shrugged. "Perhaps that's just to throw them off."

"Ooh, good ploy," he said with a chuckle. "What else can I answer for you?"

She wanted this job, wanted to spend the coming weeks outdoors amidst a breathtaking landscape. And she wanted to work with Dawson, learn from him. Watching how he worked would be invaluable for starting her own camp someday.

"My twin sister is getting married on September 20th. I'll have to leave here by the fifth at the latest, so if you're looking for someone long-term, I'm not your gal."

"But if I'm okay with that, you'll take the job?"

She hesitated. "There's one other thing. I'm not sure what I think about God. I'm not, like, against it or anything," she added quickly, "but I couldn't teach lessons about faith and God and stuff. I don't really know anything about it, and I don't...I'm not..." At a place where she could explain God to others when she wasn't all that sure He was up there.

"Thanks for the honesty. I'm okay with that, too, if you are." There'd been a flicker of something in his eyes, but his calm demeanor stayed in place. "We don't force our faith on anyone. It's just who we are, what we stand on. How about you teach the skills part, and we'll take care of the faith part. That work for you?"

Their gazes held. Did it? What if one of the kids asked her something she couldn't answer? What if— The doctor's words from a lifetime ago crystallized. "Making decisions based on what *might* happen is no way to live." He was right.

She nodded, and a wide grin broke across Dawson's face, his excitement infectious. He stuck out a hand which she shook automatically. "Welcome to Outlook!"

"Thanks." The unemployed, illegitimate daughter of an ex-con was now working at a church-type camp. Bizarre.

"And, of course, your guard dog is welcome," he added. "I think we'll all feel safer with her around."

Mikayla laughed. "Good. I'm not sure what I'd do with her otherwise."

"We have two on staff. Bruno you met. The other is a German shepherd, Pal. He's out with a True Adventure crew. We always have one of them up at camp with each group."

She stroked Lula's silky head. "She's obviously a bit protective of me so I'll keep an eye on her as they get used to each other. Wouldn't want her to scare them."

He winked. "I'll be sure to prep them. You can move your stuff in before supper tonight if you want."

It seemed she had a new job. What had she gotten herself into?

- 20 -

Mikayla sat beside the cold fire ring, typing furiously. As *Hik-er Girl on a Mission* took shape, she'd realized there was so much to say about her adventure. The trick was keeping her identity hidden as she shared her thoughts, and questions, and photographs. The simple blog tempered her loneliness. It was a relief to talk to someone, even the anonymous cyber-world.

Under their new assumed names, Lindy and Maggie had shared comments that made her laugh, and a few that knotted her throat. Surprisingly, a few strangers had chimed in as well, praising the photos and sharing their hiking and camping experiences.

Since returning to her campsite, she'd wrestled with the realization that she'd accepted the job without thinking through possible consequences. What if the search for Kenny led her away from Winter Park? Was that fair to Dawson? Once she'd talked to Old Joe, she should go home. Lindy would be thrilled. From his emails, it seemed like Dad would be okay with it. Mom...

Nope. She closed the laptop resolutely. She needed a little more time away. She'd be home for the wedding just like she'd promised Lindy, but not before. She set to work tearing down the campsite and packing the jeep. Working would keep her occupied as she waited a few weeks to talk to Old Joe. The added benefits were working outside with kids, learning from Dawson, and gaining experience to use for her own camp.

She slid sunglasses on and headed toward Outlook, hair flying in the wind. What could be better than new experiences to add to her own outdoor adventures blog? She grinned. Okay, maybe having those new experiences while working with a cute guy.

Once her belongings were stowed in the room next to Brenda's on the upper level of the bunkhouse, she joined Dawson outside the main lodge. Since there was just the rest of this week before her first True Adventure Camp started, he told her they'd use every free minute to get her acclimated—learn the curriculum, policies, and procedures, practice the skills she'd teach, and hike the most used trails to get oriented to the area.

Within the first two hours, Mikayla realized she'd have to do some training of her own. Whether it was because she was new or because she was a girl, Dawson dumbed things down to an almost insulting level. Yes, she could tie each of those knots, hiding a grin when she did so faster than him. No, she wasn't afraid to put slugs, worms, or anything else on a hook, or take them off. She'd show him her filet skills once she hauled in a big one.

By the time the dinner bell rang, she was exhausted and

out of patience. There was no way for him to know her level of skills and knowledge, of course, but simply asking her to demonstrate would have been better than giving her step-by-step instructions. She'd suggest that tomorrow.

Joining the team in the bunkhouse kitchen, she learned that each staff member was responsible for one dinner each week. Tonight Kyle served burgers, brats, and chips, which, from the razzing the others gave him, was his usual choice. Mikayla enjoyed her meal quietly, watching the staff's interactions. Four of the crew were out with adventure groups, and Bucky was home in Denver recuperating. While Brenda, Dawson, Rob and Kyle teased each other throughout the meal, Mikayla was surprised at the level of respect that remained.

She answered their questions and laughed at the joking while fighting to keep her eyes open. The stress of the past month had finally caught up with her. Lula seemed to feel the same; she snored quietly on Mikayla's lap.

"Looks like our new recruit is ready to turn in," Rob commented during a lull.

Mikayla offered a tired smile. "Sorry. I'm usually more fun than this. What's the cleanup routine?"

"New recruits do cleanup for a week," Kyle said, then flinched when Brenda punched his arm. "Ow!"

She looked across the table at Mikayla. "Whoever is up next for cooking picks someone to help them clean up. Since Kyle cooked today, if you can call it that, he picked Rob. And since I'm cooking tomorrow, I pick Kyle."

"What?" he protested. Under her steely gaze, he sighed dramatically. "Okay, fine. Sheesh."

Mikayla stood, stifling a yawn. "Anybody mind if I turn in? I promise I'll be more fun once I've gotten a good night's sleep."

They waved her away, welcoming her again to the team before she trudged up the stairs. Dawson caught her before she shut her door.

"Hey. We didn't talk about tomorrow. Want to do some fishing? I've got a meeting from 8:00-9:00, then we could head out after that. It'll give us a chance to hike one of the trails and talk more about camp."

"That would be great." She missed being out on the lake with Dad, missed the banter and the comfortable silence. "Are we on our own for breakfast?"

"We have Rosie, a local woman who comes in for breakfast and lunch when we have campers, so if you want anything in the morning, make sure you get over to the lodge by 8:15."

"Will do. And then I'll see you at 9:00."

"Great." He stuffed his hands in his pockets. "I'm glad you're on the team, Mikayla."

She smiled. "Me too."

"Get some sleep. I'll see you in the morning."

After a brief walk for Lula to do her business, Mikayla managed to change into sleep shorts and a T-shirt and brush her teeth at the small sink in the corner of her room before falling into the bed someone had kindly made for her. As she sank onto the pillow, she marveled at the comfort of sleeping on a mattress rather than the ground. Her eyes closed, and she smiled at the mosaic of images that lulled her to sleep. Lindy, Violet, Dad, Brenda, Lula, Dawson...

A boisterous greeting welcomed Mikayla into the main lodge as soon as she opened the door.

"Hey, sleepyhead!"

"Somebody better tell the new recruit we're all out of bed by five a.m."

"I wonder if Daws knew he was hiring a late sleeper."

Mikayla laughed at the comments and glanced at the clock, relieved it was only 7:15. For a second, she'd believed them. "Very funny. I've already been out for a walk, which is more than I can say for Kyle." She slid into a chair at the table and raised an eyebrow at him. "Unless that's the hairstyle you actually chose for today."

"Whoa! Good one!" Rob laughed.

"Told you she'd fit right in," Brenda said.

Kyle threw a wadded napkin across the table at Mikayla. "Watch your back, Gordon."

"Better be sure you know who you're tangling with before you issue threats," she shot back. "I'm the master of payback."

Brenda gave her a high-five as Rob laughed and jostled Kyle. Mikayla shared a wink with Kyle, then the kitchen door swung open. A petite woman with a waist-length black braid emerged, balancing a tray of food that set them groaning.

"Man, that smells amazing, Rosie." Rob inhaled deeply. "Didn't get enough to eat for dinner last night."

"What is this, pick-on-Kyle week?" he grumbled. "I figured two burgers per person was all anyone needed."

Rosie set a plate of pancakes and bacon before Mikayla

and laid a hand on her shoulder. "Welcome to the crew, Mikayla. I'm Maria-Rosalita, but everyone calls me Rosie."

"Maria-Rosalita is a beautiful name. Breakfast smells delicious. Thank you."

They exchanged warm smiles, then Rosie handed out the rest of the steaming plates.

"Please let me know if you need anything," she said to Mikayla before returning to the kitchen.

After Rob said a blessing, conversation flowed, and Mikayla smiled to herself. She wasn't going to question how she'd come to this point; she'd simply enjoy it while it lasted. It would be over all too soon.

After helping Rosie in the kitchen, Mikayla wandered the grounds. Lula and Bruno had become friends, the pixie clearly in charge of the brute as he loped along behind her. They'd trotted off together when Mikayla had headed to the lodge for breakfast and now they were nowhere to be seen.

A pile of logs, a few already split, sat behind the shower house. Flexing her arms, she glanced around. She hadn't chopped wood since last fall, but it was worth a try. If she couldn't do it, no one would know.

She tossed her baseball cap aside, then got the feel of the splitter handle, Dad's instructions ringing in her ears. She set a log on the stump, planted her feet and swung the splitter over her head. The blade bit nicely into the wood but didn't split it completely. She wiggled it a few times, and the pieces separated with a sharp crack. *Thanks, Dad!* She added them to the stack and set up the next log.

Once in a rhythm, it was satisfying to hear the crack and

split. She doubted her former coworker Leif could do this. She grinned, setting more pieces aside. It might mess his hair before a hot date.

"I've never seen anyone smile while splitting logs." Dawson's voice came from the side. "You like doing it that much?"

"Had a funny thought. Not about splitting wood." She set the axe aside and brushed off her hands. "Good morning. How did your meeting go?"

"Long. Sorry to make you wait." He looked at the pile she'd created. "Or maybe I'm not. Nice work."

"Thanks. Who usually does this?"

"Me. Or Bucky. Anyone who has some extra time."

"I'll do some. I enjoy it." She rolled one shoulder, then the other. "Although I might not be able to lift my arms tomorrow."

He laughed. "Then it's good we're goin' fishin' today. I grabbed a couple of walkies on my way out of the lodge." He held one out. "If you're not on the clock, you don't need one, but working staff never leave the grounds without one."

"Does it matter which one we take?" She hooked it to a belt loop and then scooped up her baseball cap and pulled it back on, tugging her ponytail through the opening in the back.

"There's a sign-out sheet, and each walkie is numbered. That way we know who's out and where they've gone. I'll show you where the gear is." He looked around. "Where's your guard dog?"

"She and Bruno are off exploring together. Rob said he'd keep an eye on her. Apparently I've been replaced."

"By Rob or Bruno?"

"Both!"

With a laugh, he turned toward the pole barn. Mikayla kept pace with his long-legged stride as they gathered fishing gear, signed out the equipment, and then followed a winding path to the Fraser River. Dawson explained the procedures used with the kids. She nodded, itching to get her line in.

"Need help with your lure?"

"Done. You?"

His gaze snapped to hers, and she swallowed, holding her breath. It was one thing to tease Dad, but she barely knew this man.

The corner of his mouth twitched, and he turned away. "Touché," he said.

"Sorry. I've always fished with my dad so I forget other people might not have the same sense of humor."

"We'll see who's laughing in an hour."

She grinned. "You're on."

They cast in silence, Mikayla's shoulders lowering as she drank in the stillness. She watched a hawk circle overhead and sighed.

Dawson followed her gaze. "Red-tail. He's a beauty. Look at the strength in those wings."

"It looks effortless."

His line jerked. "Like my fishing," he said as he played the fish.

Mikayla reeled in her empty line, then grabbed the net to scoop the trout from the clear water. When he held it up, she nodded. "Good one. Eight pounds, maybe?"

"'Bout that. Since it's a rainbow, the rules are catch and release." He unhooked it and set it back in the water. "Two-fish limit on the others."

She sent her lure zinging toward the middle of the river. "Sorta hate to catch the rainbows and then put them back with a hole in them. Hopefully I'll catch something else."

"So you're a fisher with a heart for fish."

She felt his glance and shrugged. "I have a few issues like that." Fishing just for fun had never really made sense to her. "When I was little, I'd cry if Dad had trouble removing a hook from a fish I caught. Fishing for a meal is different."

They stood in silence under the sparkling morning sun, watching a deer cautiously approach the opposite shore. Mikayla drew a slow breath. "I can't get over how beautiful it is here, how clean the air is." She kept her voice low. "We're proud of our clean air in Minnesota, but it's different here. Fresher, I guess. Sounds weird, but I can't get enough of it."

"I'm a native of Colorado and I feel the same way."

At the tug at her line, she pulled sharply to set the hook, satisfied by the response at the other end. "Watch how it's done," she said, playing the fish in to shore.

Dawson had the net ready and whistled in appreciation. "Look at you! That's gotta be ten, eleven pounds." He scooped the brown trout. "And you got your wish. It's a keeper."

She held it aloft and mugged as he took a picture, then un-hooked it and slid it on the line. "Any questions?" she teased.

His laughter rang across the water, startling the deer back into the woods. "Pretty cocky for the team rookie."

Their chuckles slowed as they turned back to fishing.

"Have you fished your whole life?" he asked.

"Since I could hold a plastic fishing pole."

"You mentioned a twin sister. Does she fish too?"

Mikayla shook her head with a snort. "Oh my gosh, no. Fishing might ruin her nails. And she'd be bored silly out here. She's a fashion director." *And she's not my twin anymore.*

"Ahh."

"Our older sister always had her nose in a medical book, so she never had time. She's a pediatric surgeon now." Mags, a surgeon. It still filled her with pride.

"Wow. How about your mom?"

"Hardly. It's been just me and my dad. He taught me about fishing, hiking—"

"Chopping wood."

She shot him a grin. "And everything else I know." A sigh escaped. "He's amazing. The most patient, encouraging, funny man I know. I miss him," she added softly.

A breeze ruffled nearby cattails and danced across the water. "He's in Minnesota?"

"He and my mom and my twin. My older sister practices in Boston. Dad can tie the tiniest knots, create the most detailed wood carvings, and clean a fish perfectly in minutes, but I swear he's all thumbs when it comes to typing. Must be a mental block."

Dawson chuckled. "Well, I may be some competition for him then. Seems like I always have a million things to do, so I shoot off half-done messages with bad grammar and no punctuation. And that includes emails. I thank God every day for Brenda's attention to my lack of detail."

"She seems awesome."

"She is. Definitely an answer to prayer." His lure flew over the water and disappeared with a tiny splash. "When Walt got sick, I was handling all the details myself *and* guiding *and* recruiting. I knew I needed help but didn't realize how much until she showed up. Good thing God did."

Mikayla gazed across the river. What would it be like to be needed like that? To be an important part of a team? She hadn't been at the magazine. She hadn't even fit in with her own family. Maybe now...

"Here comes a winner," Dawson exclaimed, reeling in his second catch.

"If it's not," she commented, retrieving the net, "you'll be stuck fixing *my* catches for dinner."

He laughed as he pulled the fish in, then held up a brown trout nearly the same size as hers. "Voila."

Once each had their limit, Mikayla prepared to showcase some of the filet tricks Dad had taught her. Dawson's hovering, however, set her on edge. When he grabbed the knife she'd set spinning, Dad's signature finish, she faced him. "What is your problem? I'm not a child playing with knives, for heaven's sake!"

"Looks like it," he said, arms folded as their gazes locked. "We're teaching responsibility, safety, and focus. This will absolutely not happen when the kids are around."

She jammed her hands on her hips. "Of course it won't! But I don't see any kids around here. It was something fun my dad taught me."

"Hopefully not when you were a kid."

Nobody bad-mouthed Dad. She stepped closer, chin angled as she glared. "For your information, my dad is the most responsible, knowledgeable, safety-conscious guy on the planet. But he also likes to have *fun*. Maybe you should try it." She spun back to their makeshift filet station and scooped scraps into a bag, her jerky movements sending some to the ground.

In the distance birds sang, leaves fluttered overhead, the river lazed past. She paused and closed her eyes. So much for impressing her new boss. Obviously he thought her incapable of good judgment with the kids. Or he'd be impossible to impress and she should get out now.

There was a long breath behind her. "I'm sorry," he said. "I overreacted. That was stupid."

"I'm not a dumb blonde," she ground out without looking up. "Do I seem that irresponsible to you?"

"Not at all. It's just... A few years back I hired a girl right out of college who told me she had lots of experience. Turned out she had pretty much none. She cut herself really bad when she was trying to filet, somehow cut her wrist. There *were* kids there that time."

Mikayla looked sideways at where he stood quietly, eyes closed under a pained frown. He shook himself from the memory and handed her the knife.

Her shoulders lowered. "Sounds awful."

"It was." He squatted and picked up fish pieces from the ground. "Afterwards, we changed a lot of our policies. I don't take people's word for it when it comes to what they know, or don't know."

Thus the overload of teaching. "You took mine."

"My introduction to you was on a trail where you professionally wrapped a stranger's ankle." He glanced sideways and gave a half-smile. "And I called your boss at the magazine."

"You called Ted? When?"

"After you and I talked on the phone. You'd mentioned the magazine, so I called. We had a great chat. He said I'd be stupid not to hire you. And I hate being stupid. Like I just was."

She hid a smile and returned to cleaning. They worked quietly side-by-side until the area was clean and the filets neatly wrapped and stored in his backpack.

As they started back, Dawson paused. "Mikayla, I have no questions about your abilities. And I haven't for a second thought you're a dumb blonde."

"I know there's a lot for me to learn about how the camp runs, but I will never intentionally put the kids or staff in danger."

He held her gaze then nodded. "I know you won't. And I'll try not to overreact."

She put out her hand. "Deal?"

His grip was strong. "Deal. Now let's get these fish back before every bear in the county is onto us."

"Onto *you*, you mean," she said, starting up the trail ahead of him. "I just have to run faster than you."

His chuckle followed.

- 21 -

Cresting the hill that afternoon, Mikayla released a delighted laugh. Layers of jagged mountain peaks surrounded them, from green and detailed in front to a hazy blue in the distance. Thick forests spread like carpeting, a river winding through the valley. This was where they'd camp with the kids? Her heart danced and spun in her chest. "This is amazing!"

"Part of why we picked it." Dawson pulled out his water bottle, then slid his backpack to the ground. "That and it's a tough enough climb that the kids have to work."

"I'd say so." She drank deeply from her hydration pack. "Especially if they're carrying supplies."

"Work is necessary for anything worthwhile. That's a good lesson to learn early."

She settled beside her backpack on the clover-covered slope and leaned back on her elbows. "Beautiful as it is back home, there's nothing like this."

"I've never been to Minnie-*soh*ta." He dropped down beside her. "Tell me what it's like."

His exaggeration of her accent made her smile. From the

montage of images that flashed before her, she focused on her favorites. "You know we're called the Land of 10,000 Lakes, right? For starters, we have way more than that. There are reservoirs, marshland, manmade lakes—pretty much water everywhere you look.

"It's so green," she added. "Such a variety of nature across the state. Lots of parks, campgrounds. Miles of walking, biking, and inline skating paths. The Boundary Waters area in the northern part of the state has wonderful camping, and pristine lakes great for canoeing and kayaking. It's a beautiful wilderness."

"So a lot like here, just no mountains."

She pursed her lips as she looked across the panoramic view. "I guess so. Maybe that's why this place speaks to my heart. Minnesota with mountains." And she'd get to spend the next week looking at this with a group of campers. How lucky was that?

Dawson chuckled. "We don't have as many lakes, but there are plenty of waterfalls, streams, creeks and rivers."

"We have lots of good fishing as well."

"Trout?"

"And walleye, bass, northern, muskies, crappies, sunnies, perch."

"Mmm, nothing like a great meal of perch."

She giggled. "Those are appetizers. Oh, and we have lovely bullheads and carp."

He wrinkled his nose. "No thanks."

"My dad can make even a bullhead taste good over an open fire."

"I'll take your word for it." He studied her. "You know your Minnie-sohtah fish."

"I had a great teacher. We also have brown and black bear, wolves, deer, cougars, elk, fox, moose, porcupines, otters—"

"Sounds crowded. What pulled you away from such an amazing place?"

She turned back to the view. "I needed to find someone, a relative I didn't know. Problem was nobody knew much about him, so I've had to do a lot of digging. Started in Michigan, then Jackson Hole, and eventually here."

"Did you find him?"

"Not so far."

Dawson sat quietly.

"I have a good lead, so I'm not giving up yet. But," she added, sitting up to brush off her elbows, "the silver lining is I discovered Colorado."

"And I'm glad you did. Let's eat before I get into details about what we do up here with the kids for five days."

"I'm starved. Something yummy from Rosie again?"

"As always. Would you get a fire going for coffee while I get the food out? I brought some fire starters, if you need them."

She was up to the challenge. Hopefully the more he saw what she could do, the less explaining he'd need to do. Within minutes she had a fire blazing in the fire ring, the fire starters still in the package. His appreciative smile gave her a shot of satisfaction.

Over roast beef sandwiches and fresh fruit, Mikayla asked about the camp. "You said Walter started it but now you run it. How did that come about?"

Dawson chewed thoughtfully, staring at the fire. "My childhood was... It had some rough spots." His gaze touched hers, then returned to the flames. "When you talk about how great your dad is, I'm pretty jealous. Mine was mean. I hated being in the house. My folks fought all the time. I started getting into trouble. Going-to-jail trouble. That's when my mom sent me to Outlook."

He gave a snort. "To say I didn't want to come was an understatement, but the judge agreed we'd give it a try before sending me to juvie. That's when I met Walt and life started to turn around."

"Was it him or being outdoors or being away from your dad?"

"Yes," he said, a half-smile flickering. "Walt himself was great—laid-back but no-nonsense. We were welcome as we were, but we had to follow the rules. He sent kids home when they didn't. And being outdoors is good for everyone, even angry teens. Especially them."

"It started as a camp for kids in trouble?"

"Not really, but there were quite a few of us who came. He had a way of accepting people for who they were. Because he'd gotten in trouble at times in his life, he was somebody we could relate to, which made us want to do better. Be better."

He pointed at a bald eagle soaring overhead. "I always wanted that kind of freedom, that strength. Walt taught me that with strength comes responsibility. Freedom has a cost. I could have both if I understood that and put it into practice."

It seemed he'd forgotten she was there as he watched the

bird continue its path. Mikayla followed the majestic bird, hoping Dawson would continue.

"It was confusing at first, trying to figure out how to make better decisions, how to not be so angry. But the more time I spent with him, the more I understood. And it all stemmed from his faith in God, and how he modeled his life after Jesus. Once I got that, life just...fell into place."

He looked across the flames at her. "I know you said you don't really believe. I get that. I was there. I hope working here gives you a better understanding of what I learned from Walt."

She wanted peace far more than freedom or strength. Dawson's calm, cheerful demeanor relieved some of the ache in her heart; his smile always pulled one from her. In these few days together, she'd found her shoulders relaxing and her circling thoughts slowing. Maybe there was peace to be found here, answers to the questions that still made her heart ache in the quiet of the night.

She nodded, the corners of her mouth lifting. "I hope so too."

After dinner that evening, playing cards with the staff at the picnic table, Mikayla jumped when her back pocket buzzed. Having grown accustomed to the limited reception, it was a surprise to receive a call. She glanced at it and nearly returned it to her pocket, then answered. "Shouldn't you be picking out his-and-her pillows or something?"

From Lindy's end there was only sobbing.

"Lin? What's wrong?" Plugging her ear, she hurried toward

the lodge, where reception was the strongest. "Come on. Deep breath. If they spelled your name wrong on the napkins, I'll call them and get it fixed."

"N-no n-napkins."

"They didn't come? I'll call them about that too. I'm your bulldog, Lindy. I'll get it done."

Lindy sighed so deeply Mikayla's chest shuddered. "Take your time. A few more deep breaths. It's nothing we can't fix." She passed Dawson as he emerged from his office. "My sister," she mouthed at his raised eyebrow. He nodded and went outside.

"I n-needed to hear your v-voice," Lindy managed.

"Here I am. Need me to keep talking for a bit?"

"No. I'm okay. I just..." A shaky sigh. "I got an email from Dad."

Mikayla settled onto the leather couch and propped her feet on the log table. "Wow. He's really improving on his tech skills."

"It was meant for you."

Her heart slammed against her ribs. "And?"

"I know why you left."

Silence stretched over the mountains and across a thousand miles. "Oh, Lin. I'm sorry you learned it that way."

"Our family is a mess." Lindy gave an unladylike snort. "If it's even a family."

"I'm still working on that," Mikayla admitted. "What did the email say?"

"Just enough that it made me think something big was going on. So I asked him and Mom at dinner last night."

183

"Uh boy."

"The restaurant got an earful of our family drama. Mickie, why didn't you tell me?" The accusation pulsed with hurt.

"I wanted to so bad, but I felt the way you do now. I was either crying or yelling or throwing up the days before I left. And I didn't want to ruin the wedding. I figured we'd talk about it afterwards."

Sniffling silence then, "We aren't getting married."

"What?" Mikayla was on her feet. "You have to! This doesn't affect you and Beau, Lindy."

"Of course it does. He can't marry someone who has no clue who she is!"

"Yes, he can." She paced before the window. "And we know exactly who you are—someone perfect for him. And my best friend, and an amazing fashion director."

"You know what I mean."

She did. But she wasn't about to marry a great guy. "Have you talked to him about it?"

"Not really. I was pretty incoherent last night."

"Lin, don't over-react to this."

"Over-react?" she screeched.

Mikayla flinched. "Bad choice of words. I meant don't throw your future away because of Mom and Dad. Talk to Beau. Let him be part of this. That's what people who love each other do—they face the hard stuff together." She sounded all wise and sisterly while she still floundered on her own journey. "Does Maggie know?"

"I don't think so. I don't know. What a mess."

"Yeah." Maybe they would have been better off not

knowing the truth. She pinched the bridge of her nose. It would have come out eventually. "Lin, what we're learning through this is the importance of being truthful, no matter how hard it is. You need to start your marriage with Beau that way. Don't make any rash decisions. Let this sink in for a bit. Talk to him. I really think you can wait until after the wedding to decide what to do about it."

"I don't know."

The defeat in her words sent a surge of heat through Mikayla. She continued pacing to keep from screaming in frustration. If their mother hadn't gone to Aunt Cindy's, this wouldn't be happening. What was wrong with people? Couldn't they see how their actions affected others?

Lindy sniffed. "You *are* coming home, right?"

"Of course, sillyhead. I promised, didn't I?"

"Yes, but..."

"I know. Right now we're not feeling too trusting toward other people. But, Lin, I promise I'll always be honest with you."

"Always?"

"Yup."

"Even about my wedding dress?"

That was progress if she was talking about her dress. "It's absolutely perfect for you. And it would look ridiculous on me."

Lindy giggled. "What about the shoes I picked out for the bridesmaids? Do you like them?"

Mikayla rolled her eyes. "No. They're too girlie for me. Will I wear them? Happily, because it will make *you* happy.

But I can't promise I'll keep them on through the reception."

"Don't you dare wear your boots!"

"Fine." She gave a noisy, dramatic sigh. "Not the boots but something more comfortable. I *can* promise I'll do my best not to embarrass you."

Their giggles faded into silence.

"Are you finding the answers you're looking for out there?"

"Not many. More digging to do."

The sniffling resumed. "We'll still be sisters?"

"Forever and a day." Mikayla closed her stinging eyes. "Up to now we've been stuck with each other. Now it's our choice."

"I like that." She sighed. "But I'll know it's your choice for sure when I get a picture of you in our ugly sweater."

"Argh!" Mikayla released a disgusted groan. "I hoped you forgot about it. Fine. I'll send one tonight. If it shows up on social media, however, you'll be fired as my sister. Now, you promise you'll talk to Beau?"

"I promise."

When they hung up, Mikayla stared blindly out the window. Such a mess her mother had created. Now that Lindy knew and was equally devastated, the anger ramped up. How could she ever forgive their mother? Did she even deserve forgiveness? She hadn't seemed sorry in the least.

"Everything okay?" Dawson's voice came from behind, and she turned.

"No," she admitted, "but it will be. Someday."

He studied her a moment. "I've been told I'm a good listener."

She slid the phone into her pocket. "I would believe that."

"How about a walk into town for one of Vi's world-famous cookies?"

His hopeful smile lifted the cloud that formed during the call. Time outside would allow her to breathe again. "Sounds great. I'll put on different shoes and meet you outside."

He was a boss who cared about his staff. A lot like Ted. But she'd never considered Ted a friend. Dawson was already that. And way cuter.

- 22 -

"Welcome to Outlook True Adventure Camp!" Dawson stood on the picnic table before a mostly silent group of ten teenagers Sunday afternoon. "We're glad you opted to spend a week with us when there are a million other things you could be doing."

"Wasn't a choice for some of us," a boy behind Mikayla muttered. He stood alone, slouched in baggy jeans and a faded striped T-shirt, unruly blond hair over one eye.

Dawson continued his welcome, either unaware of or ignoring the comment. Mikayla moved to the side to study the kids with whom she'd be spending the next seven days. Six boys and four girls, all shapes, sizes, and attitudes.

Two of the girls stood close together, apparently already friends as they whispered back and forth. In fashionable boots, ratty jeans and crop tops, they were hardly ready to head up the mountain. The other two focused on Dawson, one biting her short nails while the other twirled a lock of curly brown hair. At least they were dressed more appropriately in jeans, tennies, and hooded sweatshirts.

She turned her attention back to Dawson, swallowing against the nauseating sense of being out of her element. *What am I doing?* If they'd only come for the camping experience, she'd be fine. But if they wanted answers to their faith questions, the week would fall flat for them and her. She didn't want to disappoint Dawson or the kids, and she was bound to do both. She should ask Brenda to switch camps—

"The other half of the team is Mikayla Gordon."

Dawson grinned down at her from his perch, hand extended. His wink set her feet in motion and she climbed up beside him.

"Mikayla is new to Outlook but not to the wilderness experience." He turned toward her. "Give everybody a quick rundown on what you did before joining us here."

Try to piece my life back together. Figure out who I am and what I'm supposed to be doing. "I've been camping since I could walk," she said, "and fishing since I could hold one of those teeny plastic rod and reels."

The girls smiled back at her.

"I'm from Minnesota where there are a gazillion trails and even more lakes. Great hunting, hiking, and tons of outdoor stuff to do."

"What do you do in the winter in Minnie-*soh*ta?" Dawson asked.

She punched his shoulder and the kids laughed. "Well, there really isn't all that much to do except maybe camp, ice fish, hike, skate, ride snowmobiles, ski and snowboard, have snowball fights, build snowmen, play hockey or broomball—"

"Okay, okay," he interrupted. "I've never been there, but

obviously there's plenty to do. You've done all of it?"

She tapped her chin with a forefinger, then nodded. "Yup." She cocked her head. "Have you ever been ice fishing?"

"Can't say that I have."

"You haven't truly fished until you've sat on an upside-down bucket on a frozen lake with a line dropped through a hole in the ice."

He looked at the kids. "Not sure why anyone would think that's fun, but I'd say that was a challenge, wouldn't you?"

The boys cheered.

With a hand over his heart, he turned back to Mikayla. "I promise I'll make time this winter to become a true fisherman and try ice fishing." He gave an exaggerated shiver.

She folded her arms and nodded, enjoying their banter. "And I'll hold you to it."

"Do you do anything outside of all those activities?"

"For the past few years I've written a column for *Outdoor Experience* magazine, focusing on women in the outdoors. I was the only female on the writing staff." Was. Still hard to comprehend that she'd walked away from the job. "And I've done lots of camping and trail guiding, like we'll be doing this week."

Dawson raised his eyebrows at the teens. "I think we're all going to learn something from her. Okay, in a few minutes the camp bell is going to ring. That's your signal to get washed up and head back to these tables. You've got ten minutes from the time the bell rings to when we eat. If you're late, you eat after everyone else. No exceptions.

"For now, leave your gear on the flatbed. We'll sort it out

after lunch. Shower house, where you can wash up, is right over there." He pointed, then glanced at his watch. "We have about twenty minutes before the bell. Explore the camp but stay on the property. Nobody goes off alone, or even in groups, without a staff person with you. Got it?" At the half-hearted response, he repeated loudly, "Got it?"

"Got it," they called back.

"Good. See you back here after the bell."

Mikayla jumped down and headed toward the girls. "Ladies, let's get introduced since we'll be rooming together this week."

The two friends shared a look. "All of us?"

"Yup. Sharing a 6-person tent. So I'm Mikayla from Minnesota." She looked at the taller of the two. "And you are?"

"Joy. And this is Heather."

Mikayla smiled at the other girl. "I'll bet Heather can speak for herself."

She blushed and nodded. "I'm Heather."

"You two came from...?"

"Denver," they said in unison, then giggled.

The other girls, Britt and Tiffany, had come from Aurora and Colorado Springs. Mikayla continued the conversation as she led them on a tour of the camp. "I'm curious as to how you found Outlook."

"Our youth pastor told us about it," Joy said. "He knows that leader guy from somewhere. High school, maybe. I'm not really into camping, but it sounded cool. And the guys are cute. So is the leader."

She and Heather giggled. Mikayla caught an eye roll from

Britt and steered the conversation toward the tour. They'd covered the camp when the bell rang, and Mikayla pointed out the shower house before heading toward the lodge. She found Dawson standing at his desk, sorting through papers. His welcoming smile warmed her heart.

"How did it go with the girls?"

"Good, I think. Two are from Denver. Their youth pastor knows you. They're more into boys than camping, so that'll be interesting. The other girls found us online, looking for something like this. How about the guys?"

"Good group. Three have solid outdoor experience. We'll have to keep an eye on the newbies. After lunch we'll hit the first session about camp basics, get the tents set up, and then do the river hike."

She nodded, anxious to get started. A rhythm would settle her nerves, as would getting back on the trail. "Let's do this!"

On Day Three, Dawson and Pal led the kids up the mountain path, Mikayla following at the end of the line. The first two days of camp had been interesting. And exhausting. Since only about half of the teens had some semblance of camping experience, it hadn't taken long for frustration to set in as they struggled to erect the tents. Once the girls' tent was up, they'd crawled inside and collapsed while Mikayla sat outside and pondered the greater challenges awaiting them, and her ability to follow camp procedures.

Now heading toward the campsite, her spirits soared with

the hawk overhead. Dawson's program was impressive, every detail considered as the kids learned basic camping skills, and rules and procedures while getting to know each other. The initial awkwardness had been replaced by chatter, teasing and laughter that occasionally startled birds out of trees as the group climbed upward.

Lula had seemed fine being left at camp with Bruno and Rosie, probably due to the scraps she got from the kitchen. Strange how the absence of the itty-bitty dog felt more like a gaping hole. Pal trotted beside Dawson, eyes ahead, tongue lolling. His black coat shimmered in the sunlight, his piercing eyes intimidating. He was friendly with her and the kids, and devoted to Dawson.

Mikayla watched Dawson's backpack at the front of the line swivel back and forth as he turned to chat with the kids directly behind him, then turned back to the path. He was comfortable in front of the group and focused when talking with just one or two. She had a lot to learn over the coming days if she wanted to create a similar program.

She shifted her backpack, aligning it with her shoulders. She'd never used a pack like this. It's height and framework required concentration as she adjusted to the feel of it on her back. A smile touched her mouth as Dawson's laugh floated from the front of the line. He'd laughed hard when she nearly tipped over the first time she tried the pack on. She'd repaid him during last night's water fight.

At the halfway point, with the kids' shoulders drooping and conversation muted, they settled in for lunch. As they ate, Dawson led a conversation about effort, focus, and determination that morphed into a discussion about faith. While most of the kids openly wrestled with understanding and raised more questions, Justin's stubborn silence was a clear reminder he was there under protest.

Dawson pulled out his guitar and started a song that most of them seemed to know. Maybe something they sang with their youth groups? His warm voice was filled with an awe that brought tears to her eyes. The quiet melody stayed with her as they packed up the remains of their lunch. *Light of the world, have mercy on us.*

"Remember, LNT," Dawson called, shrugging into his backpack.

Heather looked at Mikayla and whispered, "LNT?"

"Leave no trace," she whispered back.

The girl rolled her eyes. "Duh. How could I forget that?"

Mikayla gave her a quick hug, then slid her backpack on. "Glad *I* remembered." Dawson had drilled that message into them the past few days, along with plenty of other instructions. While most of it wasn't new to her, Mikayla's mind still swirled with information. No wonder the kids got confused.

Once they reached camp, setup went more smoothly than it had two days ago. Most of the kids were confident in their assignments and worked together with little disagreement. After the tents were up and secure, high fives were exchanged with laughter and compliments.

Mikayla watched Dawson joking with a few of the boys. She knew logistically how to lead groups, but she didn't have the touch he had with the kids. Was it even something she could learn? He seemed to have an endless reservoir of patience and good humor, a quick wit that diffused frustration, and cheerful encouragement the kids soaked in.

He looked across the campsite and raised an eyebrow at her. Cheeks flaming, she shrugged and turned away. Nothing like getting caught gawking at the leader, *by* the leader. She had her own assignments to complete before the sun went down; there'd be time later to wonder how he did it.

Around the campfire that evening, Dawson taught several new songs, then shared his story, his expressive face accented by firelight.

"First time I came to Outlook, I thought it was a stupid idea." He glanced at Justin. "But my mother and the juvenile court judge thought otherwise. I had no idea it would change my life.

"My dad was a mean, abusive man until the day he died. No one cried at his funeral." He looked around the circle. "That's a sad testimony to a life poorly lived. I'd cried plenty through the years, but by then I was just mad. At him. At the world. At my mom for not leaving him. And definitely at God. Mostly at God."

He fingered the worn leather bracelet on his left wrist. "I was headed down a path that would have eventually made me just like my dad. Then God stepped in and physically put me on the right path."

Mikayla blinked. God? He thought the court judge was God?

"My mom could see where my life was going, so when I ended up in front of the judge for the third time, she asked if I could be sent here for one last chance to turn my life around."

He gave a short chuckle. "Can't tell you how mad I was at her."

"I can," Justin said. Resting back on his elbows, shaggy hair still covering one eye, he glared at the fire.

Dawson nodded. "It's pretty frustrating being forced into something when you just wanna live life your way. Back then the camp was run by its founder, a guy named Walt. He had an interesting history. He'd had great success in his life, but also made lots of mistakes. Prison-time mistakes. He could relate to what some of us were going through, and he had a good idea what the future held for us. But he also knew how healing it was to be out here, away from the stuff that was part of our poor decisions."

"In the middle of nowhere." Disdain dripped from Justin's words.

"In the middle of nowhere—" Dawson agreed, looking at the angry boy then up at the blanket of stars against the black sky—"and in the middle of everything. There's nothing out here to distract us from who we are and who God is. Nothing for us to hide behind. It's scary out here, but not because of wild animals."

Joy slid closer to Heather and linked arms. Mikayla hid a smile.

"Because facing ourselves, discovering who we've been and who we're meant to be, can be a lot scarier than anything with teeth. Many of us have been told lies our whole lives. We're stupid, ugly, fat, skinny. Too tall or short, too this or that depending on what the voices decided. We won't amount to anything, we're too much trouble, we can't learn, we're stupid, we'll never fit in."

Images of a childhood on the outside looking in wove through the flames, stabbing her with familiar pain. Never the pretty one. Never the one guys wanted to date. Never welcomed into a circle of friends. But Dad's encouragement and pride in her attempts had balanced the loneliness, and, she was realizing now, developed a strength and resilience she relied on.

"Over the coming days," Dawson said, "we're going to discover a whole lot of things about ourselves. Some of it will be exciting, some a little painful. But my prayer for each of us is that God shows up big time here on the mountain to speak truth into our lives."

His gaze met hers, then touched on each teen. "So I'm asking you to be fully present in every moment. Ask questions. Challenge ideas. Share your thoughts. And always be respectful of each other. This is a safe place to discover the real you, to find out who God created you to be."

He stood. "And I promise you, if you're open to learning and growing, you will go home different than when you came. In a good way. Let's sing that first song again then hit the hay. The sun comes up early on the mountaintop."

- 23 -

Up early, Mikayla rekindled the fire and made a fresh pot of coffee. With her first cup in hand, she strolled to the edge of the campsite to enjoy the view, savoring her favorite morning aroma—fresh coffee. But this crisp mountain air might take over that top spot. She'd already come to love this sense of renewal, of being part of something so big, so...awe-inspiring.

"Quarter for your thoughts," came Dawson's voice nearby.

She glanced sideways. "Wow. Didn't it used to be just a penny?"

"Some thoughts are worth more." He sipped from his travel mug. "Sleep well?"

"Surprisingly yes. It's been a while since I've shared a tent with four teenage girls, so I wasn't sure any of us would sleep. They went out the second they climbed into their bags, and I think I was two minutes behind. You?"

"Always do when I'm up here."

Her gaze roamed across the panorama, from distant white peaks to nearby pine-covered slopes. "I was marveling at how amazing it is here, even when it's forty-eight degrees and my nose is running."

"That's what I paid a quarter for? I thought it might be a bit deeper than that."

"Hey, that was pretty deep!" They shared a laugh as Heather and Joy emerged from the tent, disheveled and shivering. Heather pointed toward the wooded area that had been designated as the girls' latrine, and Mikayla nodded. Plastered together, they disappeared.

Mikayla turned back to the vista. She could never tire of such a sight. She needed to take a boatload of pictures, to remember this when she got back to Minnesota. The thought pulled a sigh out of her.

"Another quarter?"

A half-smile lifted her mouth. "I don't ever want to forget this place."

He stood quietly sipping his coffee. "Aside from the wedding, is there anything keeping you in Minnesota?"

She shrugged. "Not really. I'll have to get my stuff moved into a smaller place that I can afford, which means I'll need to find a job. So there are things needing attention."

"Will you look for another writing job?"

"I don't know. What I really want to do—"

Joy and Heather emerged from the woods and scurried to the fire where the coffee-pot sat atop a grate.

"Heather!" Mikayla called sharply. "Watch your scarf near the flames."

The girl snatched the dangling accessory and stuffed it inside her jacket.

"Good catch," Dawson said.

"I'd rather not have one of my kids burst into flames on my first trip." She shot him a twinkling look. "Not a good way to impress the boss."

As she stepped away, his chuckle made her grin. Now to keep the kids alive and well for the next four days.

The shriek sent a chill through Mikayla, and she leaped to her feet from where she'd relaxed beside the fire ring that afternoon with Britt and Tiffany after a short hike.

"Bear! There's a bear!"

Sprinting toward the frightened voices, Mikayla checked her belt for the bear spray. The girls burst out of the woods, blowing the whistles they were required to wear. Mikayla skidded to a stop, ordering the girls toward the camp as she scanned the wooded area. Heart banging against her ribs, she yanked the canister from her belt and held it in front of her, arms locked and feet planted as she waited.

She strained to hear something that would warn of a charge. Birds twittered overhead, a breeze rustled through the leaves, but no sounds of an animal in the woods. Feet pounded from behind, and she glanced over her shoulder.

Dawson stopped beside her, breathing hard. "Anything?" he asked.

"Not that I've heard or seen, but we'd better check."

"Wait." His hand on her arm stopped her. "If it was an actual bear, I'm thinking that scream scared it into the next county. I'll look. You go back and check on the girls."

When she opened her mouth to argue, he held up the rifle she hadn't noticed. "I won't go looking for it. I just want to do a perimeter check. This is mainly to scare him off." He whistled and something crashed in the underbrush. Mikayla tensed, then sighed when Pal bounded into the clearing. "And since Pal's not alarmed, neither am I."

The dog loped toward them, and Dawson squatted to greet him. "Good boy. Did you scare the bear away? Or"—he glanced up at Mikayla—"maybe *you* were the bear."

"You think the girls didn't recognize him through the trees?" She hadn't considered that.

He stood and shrugged. "Probably. But we'll make sure. Back in a few." He motioned to Pal, and they went into the woods.

Mikayla turned and approached the group standing near the fire. "Dawson and Pal are doing a perimeter check," she assured them as she neared, "but whatever it was is long gone. Where are Heather and Joy?"

Justin motioned toward the tent with a smirk. "In there. Or back at the lodge."

The other boys' chuckles stopped when Mikayla frowned at them. "It's easy to laugh at someone else's fear, especially if it seems unfounded. The bigger person offers encouragement."

Huddled together in the center of the tent, the girls jumped when Mikayla swung the flap open. "Just me," she said, joining them. Tiffany and Britt followed her in and completed the circle. "You guys okay?"

"No one believes us, but we *did* see a bear." Joy lifted her chin, eyebrows tented above the fear in her eyes. "We're not just stupid girls."

"No one is saying you didn't, and no one thinks you're stupid," Mikayla assured them. "You did the right thing by making a lot of noise."

"That scream probably scared every bear on the mountain," Britt said. After a silence, Heather giggled, then the rest joined in, laughing until tears ran.

When they finally quieted, Mikayla held out a hand to the girls on either side of her. Once they'd all connected, she smiled at each one. "It took courage for all of you to register for camp, and greater courage to show up. You aren't 'just' girls. You're brave, and strong, and truly amazing. I'm proud of every one of you for being here learning, growing, trying new things. As Daws said earlier, you won't go home the same person you were when you came."

They exchanged smiles with each other, then Heather looked to Mikayla. "Would you pray for us to stay strong while we're here? I'm not feeling it right now."

The fear of facing a bear paled at the abrupt pounding of her heart. Pray? Out loud? "Of course."

She lowered her head and squeezed her eyes shut, picturing Dawson. How would he do this? "God," she started slowly, "sometimes we feel small and helpless, especially before a bear. But we have strength and courage inside we're not even aware of. We want to dig deep and bring it to light. Help us do that. And thank you for keeping us safe here. Amen."

The simple prayer seemed to be what the girls needed as they broke into happy chatter and squeezed together for selfies. Mikayla smiled for a few photos, then climbed out of the tent. Dawson, relaxed beside the fire ring with the boys, raised an eyebrow at her. She gave a thumbs up, then pointed toward the latrine area.

If God planned to strike her dead for daring to pray when she'd never acknowledged His existence, she didn't want it to happen in front of the kids. She bypassed the latrine area and headed toward an outcropping of rocks she'd seen earlier. The wobble in her legs was either waning adrenaline after the bear-scare, or a growing fear of God.

Settled on the flattest rock, she lifted her face to the warmth of the sun and focused on slow, deep breaths. The girls were okay. *She* was okay. God wasn't going to strike her dead for a simple prayer. And she was in the most beautiful place ever. The soul connection she felt to the mountains, to Dawson and the staff, to being here with the kids filled her with such strange joy she trembled deep inside. She was supposed to be here, in this place at this moment.

As a tear slipped down her cheek, she caught it with a finger and studied it in the dappled sunlight. Had the threat of a bear scared her to tears? Or was it the thought of leaving all this? She'd been terrified and yet not, filled with a courage that had allowed her to stand her ground. Maybe that was how mothers felt when their kids were in danger—they'd do whatever was necessary to protect them.

With a sigh, she propped her arms across her knees. Since learning it would be weeks before she could talk to Old Joe, she'd felt even more lost than when she first left Minnesota. A week later here she sat, bewildered yet content.

"You okay?" Dawson dropped down beside her.

He seemed to always have her back. "Yup. Just needed a minute. We'd better get back since they're unattended."

"Mikayla." He held up his hand before she stood. "Pal is standing guard. We can take two minutes."

"Oh." She crossed her arms over her knees again. "Okay."

"Your response to the girls was amazing," he said. "Instinctual."

She shrugged. "They're my responsibility while we're out here, and I just...reacted." She glanced at him. "Stupid of me to consider charging toward the supposed bear on my own, though."

"You did exactly what you should have—had the spray in hand while standing between the danger and the kids. Going alone into the woods would have been stupid," he added, then chuckled. "And against procedure."

"Thank goodness I wasn't *that* brave."

"Mikayla, I know it seemed weird that I asked you to come work with me when we'd just met, but it was what I call a 'God prod'."

She raised an eyebrow. Sounded painful, like something to use on cattle.

"A prompting from God," he explained. "I didn't want to cancel any camps, so I'd been praying about getting someone hired fast to replace Bucky. And then there you were up at Lone Pine. You were a natural with the kids and didn't hesitate to help Hannah. That night, when I was trying to get to sleep, it was clear I was supposed to hire you. But finding you was the problem."

She looked sideways at him, warmed by his smile.

"Leave it to God to solve that problem too. I laughed when

I saw you at the coffee shop since I'm not usually in town during the week. Sometimes God makes it perfectly, abundantly clear what to do next."

The silence between them was comfortable. "I'd been feeling a bit lost," she admitted. "The best lead I had to find my person was gone for a few weeks, and I wasn't sure what to do in the meantime. That's when I realized it made sense to talk to you about the job."

"I'm glad you're part of the team. You're a natural at this. How are the girls?"

"A little shaken. I think it drew them all closer together which was neat to see. But..."

When she hesitated, he prompted, "But?"

"They asked me to pray for them. I didn't know how to say no so I prayed."

"Cool."

"Cool? God won't strike me dead for doing that?"

He swiveled on the rock to face her and crossed his legs. "Why would He do that?"

"Well, because...I don't believe in Him."

"Good thing He believes in you." A smile danced at the corners of his mouth. "If you don't believe He exists, then praying won't matter because He's not really there, right?"

"I think...wait, what?"

"If you don't think He exists, but you prayed anyway to help the girls, then that was a kind thing to do. If He *does* exist—" he added, eyes sparkling—"then He'll have heard you. The Bible tells us He hears every prayer, spoken out loud or in our hearts."

She gnawed her bottom lip, wanting the peace exuding from him. "But how do you know He exists? Really know in here." She tapped her heart.

He swung his arm toward the view. "If for no other reason than this. The beauty, the harmony and coexistence of the eco-systems of the earth. The instinct of His creatures. The rhythm of life. He inhabits His creation and enjoys it like we do. It's all here for us. There's no way I can believe this is an accident."

She followed his gaze. Was that why this place soothed her, called to her? God was here? She blinked. Pretty simple answer to such a big question. There had to be more to it.

"Let's head back," he said. "Pal's good, but he's a dog, after all. We can talk about this more tonight if you want."

Walking behind him, hands stuffed deep into her pockets, she tried to corral the stampede of questions. Was believing in God as easy as looking at the beauty around her? But what about the ugliness that also existed? Where was God when she was conceived, and when Lindy and Maggie were given away?

It would be easy to believe in God when enjoying the beautiful solitude of the mountains, but stepping back into the real world would blow that simple belief away as easily as the wind tossed leaves and twigs. No. That kind of belief could come only with solid answers based on proof, not fresh breezes, birdsong, and wildflowers.

She seemed to be on as much of a journey as the teens who now stood proudly beside the lunch they'd made on their own. Scary as this path might be, she'd have to keep her heart and mind open, just like them. She had so much to learn.

- 24 -

"I can't believe we go home tomorrow," Joy said with a deep sigh.

The others nodded where they'd gathered around the fire. Mikayla studied each face, already missing them. In a mere six days, she'd come to appreciate their uniqueness and admire their new-found confidence, including Justin. After days of hiking, fishing, games, and discussion he smiled easily now, the edge of anger gone from his young face. No longer hiding behind his hair, he even wore one of Dawson's bandanas.

She moved her gaze casually to Dawson and pushed down the surge of affection. They'd worked well together, developing an easy rhythm that kept the schedule flowing. The shared laughter and unexpected opportunities for learning from each other put her slightly off-balance. He treated her as an experienced partner, not the newbie she was. He hadn't made one off-color comment, was respectful of her and the girls without condescension, and talked easily about his faith in a way that set a yearning in her heart.

"He's cute," Joy whispered, settled beside her on the log.

Mikayla turned. "Who?" she whispered back.

"Daws."

Grateful for the darkness that hid the sudden flush in her cheeks, Mikayla rolled her eyes. "Are boys all you think about?"

"Only when the cute ones are right in front of me. And he thinks you're cute too."

What? "Joy, you're a stinker. He's my boss. I think he's just glad I didn't lose any of you off a cliff."

"Whatever," came the knowing whisper before she leaned closer for a selfie.

Mikayla grinned for the photo, then hugged the girl she'd been sure wouldn't last one day on the mountain. Every assumption she'd started the week with had been obliterated, every guess she'd made about the kids' reactions wrong. Even things she knew about herself had changed. She shook her head. Once they climbed back down fifteen hundred feet, she'd probably go back to normal—whatever that was now.

"Okay, listen up." Dawson had pulled his guitar onto his lap. "There's one last thing I'd like us to talk about before we head back tomorrow. It's something that comes up a lot, so I want to be sure we get a chance to share our ideas.

"The other night I talked about how I came to Outlook, and I mentioned that my dad was a mean, angry man. When I first started hearing about God here at camp, Walt called Him 'Abba'. Maybe you've heard someone use that word for God— Abba. It basically means 'Daddy'."

He strummed a few times, shaking his head. "I couldn't relate to that at all. The last thing I wanted was another so-called daddy waiting for me to mess up so he could slap me around. And that's what I told Walt. I'd rather have *no* dad than someone like that."

Mikayla rested her folded arms on her knees. How lucky she'd been to be raised by such a wonderful man. Would Kenny have been like Dawson's dad or hers? She shivered.

"Walt didn't lecture me or try to convince me that God wasn't like that. He just lived his faith in a way that helped me see who God was. When I compared God to my dad, God came up short in my expectations because the bar was so low." He strummed again. "But when I compared my dad to who the real Father is, it was my dad who came up short. Way short. All of us do. We can't expect perfection because no one except Jesus is perfect. However, that doesn't mean we accept abuse, neglect, anger, or any of that stuff as normal or okay. It's not. It's sin and it's wrong."

The chords and notes came together in a gentle melody. "God isn't like us. He's not mean, vindictive, neglectful. The Bible says He's the same yesterday, today, and forever. He won't change His mind—decide He doesn't like you and just leave one day." He shook his head, smiling. "He never goes back on His word. And God doesn't lie. Ever."

Unbidden tears filled Mikayla's eyes, and she looked up at the star-covered black sky, blinking rapidly. She'd never thought her mother would either.

"How do we know He doesn't?" Justin asked from his usual spot next to Dawson. "I mean, people who aren't 'sposed to lie to us do anyway."

So true.

"We know because He says so." Dawson reached for his tattered Bible on the log beside him. "In here. And He proved it over and over. He's made good on every promise throughout history. Because of that, we know we can approach Him without fear."

"How do we do that?" Joy asked.

"Through prayer. We can talk directly to Him like we're talking now."

Mikayla gnawed her bottom lip. She'd prayed with the girls after the bear-scare and hadn't been struck down. She hadn't heard a big voice booming a response, but they'd certainly all felt better afterwards. It'd be nice if God sounded a bit like Dad—comfortable, encouraging, with some laughter thrown in.

"My dad left when I was ten." Justin tossed bits of bark into the flames. "Got himself a girlfriend and started a new family. Guess we weren't good enough."

"That's rough," Dawson said. "The good thing with God is that you are good enough for Him. That doesn't mean we don't sin every day and make a mess of our lives, but because He made each of us, He will never leave us. Never give up on us. Never stop forgiving us and helping us be the best we can be. And He'll never stop wanting the best for us, and that 'best' is Him in our hearts."

"I don't even know who my dad is," Joy said, eyes down. "Just some...guy my mom slept with. She doesn't know who it is because there were so many."

Mikayla's eyes went wide. What if she'd found out about her mom at Joy's age? How would she have handled it? Her heart squeezed. Maybe she wouldn't be sitting here living her dream.

"I had a great dad," she said, surprised she'd spoken aloud. "Then I found out recently, accidentally, that he's not actually my dad." She met Joy's gaze. "I came out here to track down my bio dad."

"Did you find him?"

"Still looking." She'd give it a few more weeks and then head back to Old Joe's.

Joy sighed and leaned her head against Mikayla's shoulder. Mikayla looked toward Dawson, who looked back at her with a sympathetic lift to his brow.

"But you already have a dad," Heather said. "What about him? Isn't he your real dad?"

"He is," Mikayla said, forcing a normal tone over the lump in her throat. "But he didn't know I wasn't his either, so...it's a mess. We'll have to figure out a new normal when I go back."

The gentle sounds of the guitar continued behind their conversation, draping peace over the pain being shared.

"God knows how hard it is on us when our earthly dads don't do the right thing, when we're left hurting and angry," Dawson said. "That's why His promise to never leave us means so much."

"But God's in heaven. What good does that do us here? I need a dad with skin on," Joy said.

"That's where people like Walt come in. I knew he wasn't my dad, of course, but he became a good friend, someone who taught me stuff, listened to me." His eyes sparkled in the firelight. "He saw my potential to be a better person and helped me see it too. But most importantly, he taught me to rely on God more than any person."

He looked around the circle. "He puts people in our lives to fill some of the hole left by our earthly dads—people we can lean into, learn from, share life with. Who do you already have in your life like that? Might be a teacher, youth director, coach, boss."

The hissing and snapping of the fire grew louder as they pondered his question.

"My soccer coach is pretty cool," Justin said. "We've met for lunch and dinner a few times. He's easy to talk to."

"Great! Who else has someone like that in their life?"

One by one, each spoke up. Several had intact families and dads they enjoyed. Others mentioned a choir teacher, youth director, coworker. The shadow that the earlier conversation had brought now swirled upward with the smoke as their young faces lit with understanding.

"I guess I never thought about those people like that," Justin said, his spine straightening. "My mom's pretty cool too, so my dad's missing out."

"That's a great way to look at it," Dawson said.

"But...why doesn't God stop people from doing stuff like that in the first place?" Joy asked, chin quivering. "He could stop dads from leaving, or moms from, you know..."

Mikayla held her breath.

"He could," Dawson nodded, "but then we wouldn't have free will, would we? We'd all be like puppets He controlled, and He doesn't want that. He wants a real relationship with us, so He allows us to make our own choices even when He knows it will hurt us or someone else. Sometimes we learn from those mistakes and change our behavior. Sometimes we don't. Making choices gives us ownership over our lives, but it also makes us responsible."

He looked at Justin. "For whatever reason, your dad made the choice to walk away from his responsibility and promise to his family. That really hurt you guys, and it hurt him, whether he'd admit it or not. Your choice now is how to respond. Stay angry and keep acting out, or decide you want something better. Live a life of anger and resentment or find a way to move past it. They're choices we never asked for but ended up with anyway."

Mikayla stared at the flames, family images dancing among the colors. She had a choice. Forgive or not. Work at patching severed relationships...or not.

Dawson strummed louder and said, "Listen to the words of this song in the context of what we've talked about tonight. Take it in; make it your song. *This* is what's true about you right this minute, and every day for the rest of your life. You are loved unconditionally by God. The word used in the Bible is 'beloved'. Each of us is the beloved of God."

Mikayla closed her eyes as he sang, questions mixing with the lyrics. *Beloved?* The illegitimate daughter of an ex-con? The words proclaimed she wasn't an accident. Wait—she *wasn't?* But that would mean God planned things to go the way they did. Or He'd allowed it anyway.

Now she had a choice—figure out how to live with the new truth about herself and move forward or continue to be angry. The lyrics described the heaviness in her heart but assured her again she was beloved. Her fingers curled as if to grasp the words and hold them close. Dad loved her. Lindy and Maggie did too. Even Mom. The song encouraged her to rise above the hurt. Could she? The deception, the cover-up, and even the truth had split her life in two—life before and after.

The final notes faded into the stillness she'd grown accustomed to on the mountain. No one moved; gazes fastened on the flames dancing quietly.

"It's been really great sharing this week with you," Dawson said. His gaze moved across the fire and locked on Mikayla. A corner of his mouth quirked before he looked around the circle. "Thanks, all of you, for being here."

Her toes curled in her hiking boots.

"The schedule for the morning," he continued, "will be early breakfast followed by breaking camp. Joy and Britt are on for breakfast, Justin and Brent for clean-up. Your assignments for set-up are the same for tear-down, in reverse obviously. We'll start the descent at 10:00 sharp. If you don't have your stuff in your backpack when we head out, you'll have to carry it, which makes hiking difficult. Got it?"

"Got it," came the muted response as they got to their feet.

Hugs were exchanged, comments and quiet laughter mingling before the girls filed into the tent and the boys headed toward their latrine area. Dawson propped his guitar against the log and moved around the fire ring to settle beside Mikayla, where they watched the kids disperse.

"What a week," she sighed. "They look wiped out and yet... content, I guess. At peace."

He nodded. "Means God's been working in them, changing

their hearts, opening their eyes to see Him in daily life."

She wrapped her arms around her knees and glanced at him. "How do you know that?"

"I've seen it happen over and over. Most of them send emails when they get home, sharing some of what they learned, how they changed, and what it all meant to them. Really cool testimony of what God was up to during camp."

"I wonder what this group will have to say," she mused.

"That they had the best staff ever."

She giggled.

"Seriously, 'Kayla. You did great work with the girls, and the boys commented on how they wouldn't want to be in a skills contest with you."

The highest form of compliment. And the nickname warmed her heart. "Good to know."

"Did you enjoy it? Enough to do it again?"

"Definitely!"

"Phew." He wiped his brow with a flourish. "There'd be no way I could replace you."

"You'll have to come September."

"Don't remind me."

She sighed and rested her chin on her arms. She didn't want the reminder either. She'd already become far too attached to this job. And this guy.

"I'm sorry about what you've been going through," he said eventually. "The whole dad thing."

"Thanks. It's been a rough couple of months. What started it all was finding out I had a hole in my heart."

"Seriously? It sure hasn't slowed you down."

"They repaired it about a week later. I guess it's not that uncommon. But because my twin didn't have it, or anyone else in my family, it got me looking through family medical history. Then a comment from my soon-to-be brother-in-law prompted me to do some DNA work. One thing led to the next and the next, and here I am." Still trying to find answers.

"God's funny like that."

She straightened and met his gaze. "Do you give God credit for everything?"

"Mostly. Not when it's something stupid I've done, but since I don't believe in coincidence, it's easy to see God at work in the world."

"You don't see anything as coincidence?"

"Nope. I see a bigger picture. I don't know why you didn't know the truth earlier, but for some reason it came out now through that particular series of events. And I, for one, am glad because it led you to Winter Park and then to Outlook."

Something to consider. "Aren't you afraid of giving God credit or blame for stuff He didn't do?"

"I give God credit for turning my life around, for putting the right people in my life at the right time who shared their faith with me. Over time I realized that none of that was co-incidence, and that's taught me to look for God in everything that happens no matter how small. Your being on the Lone Pine path wasn't a coincidence. Neither was your being at Vi's coffee shop when I didn't know where to even start looking for you."

Her heart fluttered at his decisive words, at the thought God had been controlling her steps. "Doesn't that take away the idea of free will?"

"Not at all. God knows us, the choices we'll make, what we need when. This will seem weird, but I see it as a big chess game, except that there aren't any opponents. Now, this isn't something I learned at a church; it's just the way I've been able to make sense in my own head of how life unfolds."

Chess wasn't her thing, despite Dad's many attempts to teach her. Lips pursed, she raised an eyebrow.

"As we make moves, decisions, choices each day, God makes counter-moves."

"Such as?"

"Well...what led you to end up on the Lone Pine trail?"

She thought back to her arrival in Winter Park. It seemed so long ago now. "I'd just arrived in town and needed a hike to clear my head before starting my search. I found a map and just...picked it."

"Okay. And we got a later start than I'd planned because we had to wait for Hannah to find her hiking boots. If we'd headed up at the scheduled time, we'd have missed you completely."

"So God hid her boots?"

A grin flashed in the firelight. "Possibly. Would we have seen her boots mysteriously slide under the couch? No. But I've seen things unfold like this over and over in the past ten years. Just a moment here or there and the results would be drastically different. Someone's throw-away comment speaks directly to another's unspoken question. Three different people mention going to hear a speaker, so I go and sit next to someone who becomes a major donor to the camp."

"And you don't see that as God moving you, the chess piece, around."

"I don't, because at any point I could make a different decision, decide not to go to the conference or make the remark that someone needed to hear. And I believe that happens. After the fact, I've learned that had I said whatever it was I felt nudged to say, that person would have changed their plans, been encouraged, or made a different decision.

"So God doesn't *make* us do things, but there are times when we get a feeling or a persistent thought that prods us one way or another, and we realize later it's exactly what we needed to do or say. For our benefit or someone else's. Or we might never know if there was a reason for the nudge."

"A God prod."

"Exactly."

Mikayla sighed. "This is a lot to figure out."

"It's taken me ten years to get to this point, so don't rush it. Just be open to the world around you, and watch God move. You might not realize it 'til later but eventually you will. And if the chess analogy doesn't work, you'll come up with something that makes better sense. Now let's turn in, or we'll be the ones carrying our stuff down."

He stood and held out a hand, pulling her to her feet, then kept a light grasp on her fingers. "I meant what I said earlier, Kayla. This has been a great week leading camp with you. You aren't afraid to jump right in. You're brave and funny. And I've learned a few tricks from you along the way."

A shy smile lifted her mouth. "I loved every minute. Thanks for taking a chance on me."

He squeezed her hand and let go. "God wouldn't have it any other way."

She rolled her eyes and laughed. "Touché and good night."

Snuggled in her sleeping bag later, she smiled into the darkness. She wouldn't have it any other way either.

- 25 -

Bidding farewell to the kids the next afternoon was more painful than Mikayla had expected. Every group she'd led in college had started with strangers and ended with friends, but this was different. In the past it had been about what she could teach them. This time she'd gained far more from the kids and Dawson than what she'd given.

Within hours of their departure she received numerous texts and emails from all four girls with the expected number of exclamation points and emojis, but also heartfelt thanks and musings about what the whole week had meant. Their enthusiasm warmed her heart. They'd learned about camping and trying new things, but it was what they'd learned about God, who He was and what that meant to their lives that changed them most.

Their revelations brought back the fireside conversation with Dawson. The questions that had stirred then continued to poke at her throughout the weekend as she and Kyle prepared to lead day camp. Needing answers, she sought Dawson out Monday afternoon after the day camp kids had departed,

Lula dancing along behind her.

Daws looked up from the papers strewn across his desk and smiled. "Hey, Mikayla. Come on in."

"Am I interrupting?"

"Thankfully yes. Have a seat." He motioned to the chair. His own squeaked a protest when he leaned back. "This is the least enjoyable part of my job, completing grant paperwork. Brenda usually does it, but she's visiting her boyfriend in Montana until Wednesday, and this stuff needs to get sent in."

"I can come back—"

"No way. I desperately need a break. What's up?" Lula jumped into his lap and licked his chin, making him chuckle.

"Nothing worth interrupting your work for." She lifted her shoulders, and added, "I've just been thinking about what we talked about Friday evening around the fire and comments the girls have shared in their emails."

"This sounds like a conversation best had over ice cream. C'mon, let's walk over to Vi's." He stood and crooked an eyebrow at her. "You do like ice cream, right?"

She faced him across the desk. "Would I get fired if I said no?"

"Of course not. But you'd be relegated to trash pickup for the next two weeks." The sparkle in his eyes countered his serious tone.

"Then I love ice cream."

They shared a laugh as he followed her and Lula out of the office. The late afternoon sun warmed her shoulders as they started the mile hike toward town, and she pulled in a deep breath. "If only I could bottle this air." This moment.

"I'm glad you can't," he said, matching her stride on the path. "This way you have to come back for a fix."

"Oh, I will, believe me. I'm definitely a mountain girl now."

"Yes!" He pumped his fist. "I knew we'd get you hooked."

He asked about day camp and working with Kyle. When she admitted he was far more professional and knowledgeable than she'd expected, he chuckled. "He comes off as a sort of clueless ski bum, but he's got degrees in recreational administration and rec therapy. I know the dude's gunnin' for my job."

"Maybe he'll open a rival camp."

"That would only be good news for the community, especially with how our waiting list keeps growing. He just has to find a different mountain."

"That can't be too hard since there seems to be an abundance," she said with a laugh, scooping up Lula who'd been prancing in front of her.

"You'd think so, but there's lots of federal land and parks that don't allow camping. It will take some work to find a spot as good as ours."

When they reached Violet's shop, Mikayla scolded her heart for wanting to keep on walking. Dawson was cute, smart, fun, and extremely knowledgeable, but he was also her boss. Temporarily. It did her no good to get caught up in thoughts unrelated to camp, especially when she had to leave soon. Much too soon.

"Well, two of my favorite people!" Violet met them in the doorway of her shop. "And my favorite four-legged friend," she added, stroking Lula's head. "What brings you kids wandering into town?"

They glanced at each other and answered, "Ice cream!"

"It's a perfect afternoon for a treat, isn't it? Daws, I've got a new flavor I think you'll like."

They followed her and stood at the counter. She gathered two sampling spoons and scooped a bit of ice cream. "See what you think of this."

Dawson tasted it, then nodded quickly, smacking his lips. "You know me well, Vi. It's obviously white chocolate, but what else?"

"White chocolate and brownie cheesecake."

They nodded in unison. "Yes, please!"

"On sugar cones," Dawson added.

Violet laughed as she scooped their choice. "Two peas in a pod."

"Hmm. Pea-pod ice cream," Mikayla said, nose wrinkled. "That wouldn't cut it."

"Vegetables don't belong in ice cream," he agreed.

Settled outside, they enjoyed their treat in silence, Lula daintily chewing a tiny dog bone from Violet. When Mikayla looked up, Dawson was frowning at her. She quickly wiped her face. Apparently she ate ice cream like a two-year-old. "Am I making a mess?"

"What? No! Sorry. You just...you remind me of someone." He went back to his ice cream. "Certain expressions. I thought it a couple times during camp, but nobody's come to mind. Maybe someone I knew in high school. So tell me what you've been pondering."

Between bites, Mikayla talked about the questions that

continued to pester her, and the wonderful emails the girls had sent. "But while they seem stronger in their faith, I'm only more confused."

"About?"

She shrugged. "Who God is. *Why* He is. How people get guidance and answers from Him. Why do terrible things happen to good people?"

"Ahh, the simple stuff," he said, a teasing glint in his eyes.

She laughed. "Exactly. I'd like to hear your story, how you came to believe. I know it has to do with Walt, but there's got to be a lot more."

"There is." He popped the last of his cone into his mouth and leaned back to stare up at the sky, eyes narrowed. "Like I said before, I wasn't too thrilled about being at the camp, and was pretty obnoxious about it. Walt was probably the most chill guy I've ever met. He took me and my attitude the way they were and let the work of the week do the talking. Where now we bring a lot of supplies up ahead of time, back then we had to haul all of it, so when I say work, I mean it. Those first few days we were exhausted, which kept things low-key."

His gaze grew distant, a smile toying at his mouth. "I think Walt was happy I was too tired to mouth off. But once I got my strength back, the challenge was on. I didn't believe God had anything to do with my life, or it wouldn't have been so messed up, so Him being part of it now was a little late, in my opinion."

He leaned the chair back on two legs. "Walt let me talk my macho teenage self into one corner after another, running into dead ends every time. Some kids had similar views, some already had a pretty strong faith, so there were interesting discussions around the fire. Walt shared parts of his story throughout the week, which had a bigger impact on me than I knew at the time. Once camp was done and I went home, there were things I just couldn't shake."

"Like?"

"Things he'd said about God, stuff in the Bible. And needing to consider the consequences of our choices and actions. He'd challenged us at the end to make our lives stand for something, and to be the ones to decide; not a judge or parole office, or anyone else. How we lived our lives was our choice. That had the most impact."

Stand for something. The words reverberated, both an exciting challenge and a frightening prospect. It was up to her where she went from here, how she wanted to live. What relationships she wanted to have. Or not have.

On the return walk, they exchanged stories of previous camping and guiding experiences that kept them laughing. Before they parted outside the lodge, Dawson leveled a serious gaze on her. "It still holds true, Kayla. Whatever you decide about your family, your job—it's up to you. God's happy to provide guidance, but you'll need to ask." A smile lightened his expression and he winked. "I guarantee you won't be sorry if you do."

She nodded. "I have a lot to learn, don't I?"

"We all do." He held up a finger. "Wait here. I'll be right back." He went into the lodge, then reemerged with a book in his hand. "We keep these on hand for anyone who doesn't have one."

He held out a Bible, which she accepted automatically. "Thanks." It felt heavy in her hands, yet it lightened her heart. This would help her decide if faith was an idea worth pursuing.

"Don't start at the beginning," he said, taking it back and opening it to the middle. "Read some of the Psalms, which is a book of conversations, really—people being honest with God when they were angry, scared, questioning, or just plain happy. Then read though John, which will help you understand who Jesus is. We can talk about it whenever you want."

She clutched the book to her chest and smiled. No one had ever given her something of this magnitude before. Not even her parents. "Thanks. This means a lot."

Kyle stuck his head out the front door and told Dawson he had a call. He nodded, then looked back at Mikayla. "Seriously. Whenever you have questions or want to work through something that doesn't make sense, let me know."

As she chopped wood later, the Bible sitting on a nearby stump, Dawson's challenge echoed in her head. She had decisions to make in the coming weeks that would affect the rest of her life. A daunting prospect and yet...if God helped her, maybe not so hard to do.

She split another log. Tonight, when she got in bed, she'd check out this book that meant so much to him and see if it spoke to her. If not, no harm done. She'd just make those decisions on her own as she'd planned. She sighed, setting up the next log. She was tired of being on her own.

- 26 -

After breakfast Wednesday morning, before the day campers arrived, Mikayla plopped onto her bed for a quick email check. The one from Lindy about Dad's tuxedo fitting left her giggling. Then there was one from Dad. Probably about the fitting. She opened his with a smile.

> Hey kid. Ive tried to call a couple times, but the calls aren't going through. Whatd you do—go to Siberia? Ha. Anyway, there's something I need to tell you. I didnt want to share it this way but I want you to have time to think about it before you come home. I hope when Im done you can find it in your heart to forgive me.

Unable to pull in a full breath, she massaged the sudden throbbing in her temples. She couldn't imagine him doing anything that would require forgiveness. Heart beating disjointedly against her ribs, she read on.

> Early in our marriage I did something stupid that almost ended things before they really got

started. We got Maggie not long after we were married. Maybe 6 months. We were barely in our 20s. I worked long hours at one job, then took on a second job so your mom could stay home with Maggie. She was alone a lot. That was hard on her but the good thing is it gave her a chance to learn how to be a great mom. The bad thing is I felt ignored whenever I was home because they didnt seem to need me.

I was young and self-centered. I'd go out with the work crowd and have a few beers. When I got home I wasnt always in the best shape, so we argued a lot. I worked even more hours just to stay out of the house.

Hand at her throat, Mikayla lifted her gaze to the window. *No. This isn't going where it sounds like it's going. He wouldn't do that.*

Things got rough between your mom and me. Life was all about me. I was frustrated that she didnt appreciate all my work so she could have the house she'd wanted. So when a girl at work came on to me and seemed to appreciate me, I figured I deserved some fun.

Tears splattered onto the keyboard. *No, no, no...*

It didn't last very long, and I felt so guilty I told your mom. I've never forgotten the look on her face. I hope I never do. She took Maggie to Cindy and Jim's that summer to decide if she wanted to stay married. It was the longest couple months of my life. I sent letters promising Id never do it again and

I never have. I was the luckiest man in the world when she and Maggie came back. I've spent the last 30 years making it up to her.

Mikayla leaned her head back against the wall, eyes closed. The splintering of her life was complete. Drawing in a jagged breath, she finished reading.

Im sorry, Mikayla. I know you don't want to know any of this, but your mom shouldn't take all the blame. This mess is both our making but I started it. I hope someday you can forgive your old man. I don't deserve it but at least I can ask. And I'm sorry you girls are the ones paying the price. I hope you'll still call me Dad when you come home.

Closing the laptop in slow motion, she sat rigid as the room spun, a hand at her stomach. There were no thoughts, no raging emotions. Just the sensation of the last truth she'd clung to being flushed away.

She dashed down the hall to the women's restroom and released the bile of her old world. It didn't go easily, but finally she slumped against the wall, sweat gliding down her spine where she rested against the cool cement.

What did she have left? Her family wasn't her family. The man she'd trusted and adored was a mirage. She'd lived thirty years in a glass house that now lay shattered at her feet.

The swish of the restroom door, then Brenda's voice. "Mikayla? The day camp bus should be here any minute. You coming?"

"Yeah," she croaked, then cleared her throat. "Be right

there."

"You sound awful."

"A little headache, but I'll take some aspirin and be fine. I'll meet you outside in two minutes.

In the silence, Mikayla could almost hear Brenda's eye roll.

"You're sure?"

"Yup." Once the door shut, Mikayla emerged from the stall and wobbled to the sink. The girl in the mirror gazed back at her. Blue eyes dark with pain, skin a grayish white. She leaned on the cold ceramic sink and dropped her head. No, she wasn't fine. They'd obliterated her past, turned her memories inside out. Would she ever be fine?

The thud of her heartbeat came slowly. If Lindy weren't getting married, she'd never go back. Never face any of them again. With a defeated sigh, she lifted her head. But she'd promised Lin she'd be there, and so she would. How she'd manage it was another issue.

"You'll live through this," she told the pathetic reflection. "One step at a time."

She splashed cold water on her face, rinsed her mouth, and pulled the door open. She wouldn't let Dawson or the team down. With one last wobbling step, she drew a deep breath and left the building, chin up, eyes ahead. Her almost-mended heart now fully broken.

By the end of camp Friday afternoon, she was barely upright. It had taken every ounce of concentration to keep smiling, interacting with the kids. Once the bus rounded the corner, she let her arm drop and trudged to her room where she'd hidden the past few nights. Stretched on the bed, she closed her eyes, but the parade of images popped them open again. The room was stifling, the silence mocking. Lula was off with what the staff laughingly called "her boys," keeping Pal and Bruno in line.

Mikayla rolled off the bed and yanked her hiking boots on, glancing at the Bible on her bedside table. With a brief shake of her head, she grabbed her backpack and headed out. She'd discovered a sweet little spot hidden off the main trail where she could disappear into the vastness of the forest, gaze up at the mountains and lose herself in the moment. After Dad's revelation, she didn't want to be found.

Rob was chopping wood as she rounded the corner of the shower house. He paused, wiping his forehead, and called, "You around for dinner tonight, Mikayla?"

"Not tonight. See you later."

"Got your walkie?"

She patted her hip where it was still clipped from day camp and gave a thumbs up. She knew the rest of the staff were watching her, no doubt wondering if she was sick or mad at one of them. Every speck of energy had been consumed by the kids each day, leaving nothing for mealtime discussion.

She followed the trail. Veering into the woods, she trod softly over the path she'd worn the last few days, mindful of Dawson's mantra. She tried to leave a barely noticeable trail. A short climb and she reached the clearing—the perfect size that let her feel part of the beauty and quiet without intruding. The gentle flow of a stream winding through the ravine welcomed her as she dropped onto the log and set her backpack to the side.

No need to put on a cheerful face here, have an answer, or make decisions. It was just her and the mountain. Her parents had each other. Lin had Beau. Mags had her work. She closed her eyes against the stab in her chest. Which left just her. Even as she'd wrestled with her mother's actions and how to face her again, she'd always thought she and Dad would pick up where they left off. But now...

Elbows on her knees, she rested her forehead against clasped hands. If this were Dawson's problem, he'd be talking to God by now, having a good old chat. Did God ever talk to him? A shiver raised bumps on her arms.

She lifted her gaze to the distant jagged peaks. How did she respond to Dad's email? *Oh, it's okay. No problem. It's easier to be mad at both of you.* She stood and stomped back and forth. "No, really. I didn't mind finding out something like that through email. It kept me from freaking out at you." Sarcasm swirled up into the trees. "Lindy and Mags have tried hard to get through on the phone. Unlike you or Mom." Not that she wanted to talk to either of them, but still.

She might be thirty, but she felt more like ten, wanting to throw herself on the ground for a full-blown tantrum followed by a good cry. But that would change nothing. Shoulders drooping, her pace slowed. Decision-making was her thing. Having no clue what to do next was paralyzing. She slumped onto the log. She was so tired—of raging emotions, unanswered questions. And especially of navigating life on her own.

The rustle of leaves behind her made her turn. Dawson was coming up the hill. The pain in her heart eased. At least for right now she wasn't alone.

He raised a hand as he neared, eyebrows lifted. "Okay if I join you? If not, I'll head back."

If it were anyone else, she'd say no. She nodded, not surprised he'd tracked her down. A moment later he settled on the log. In the silence, tears crept toward the surface. *No crying! Not in front of Dawson.*

A moment later his arm came around her shoulders. She rested her head against him and let the tears fall. A few at first, then the torrent loosed, and she sobbed as he wrapped her in a warm hug.

What seemed like hours later, she mopped her face with the edge of her camp shirt and sat up. He dropped his arm and slid a few inches away. Still he didn't speak.

"How did you know where I was?" she asked.

"Hiker's intuition."

She managed a tiny smile.

"The walkies have GPS."

"Ah. Smart. Unless someone wants to hide."

"Then said someone should have left their walkie behind."

"Which would be against policy and get said someone fired."

Their sideways glances met. "Glad to see you memorized the employee handbook," he said. He rummaged in his backpack, then held out an orange and a banana. "Ladies first."

She took the banana. "Thanks."

As they ate, Dawson named a few of the birds darting over and around them, then pointed at an eagle far overhead. Awe filled his smile, as if it were his first sighting. "Man, that never gets old." He cocked his head. "There. Do you hear it?"

She listened. Nothing beyond the splash of water and birds twittering. "What?"

"The mountain is singing."

"I don't hear anything."

"You do. You just don't know it." He looked sideways at her. "Tell me what you do hear."

She sat quietly a moment. "The creek running below. Wind in the trees. Birds. Something running through the leaves." She looked at him and shrugged. "That's all."

"That's all? That's the mountain singing, Kayla." Excitement filled the words. "About God and His creation, His love of detail, His joy in the silence. The wind in the trees makes me think of a choir humming. The birds add the melody. Listen again."

Frowning, she closed her eyes and focused, hearing only those same sounds. Then the wind took on a deep sighing through the trees, sweeping down into the ravine. Twittering became birdsong. The water added a sweet undertone. The woods had come alive with a harmonious symphony, and her throbbing heart sang in response.

Eyes wide, she turned a smile toward him, touched by the joy in his expression. "That's amazing." How had she never heard it before?

"I knew you'd hear it," he said, then added, "Not everyone can. You need a heart for this place to hear the mountains sing, and when you do, you realize God is singing over *you* as well. That you're part of something so beyond comprehension, you have to join the song."

They sat still, absorbing the sounds around them, then he turned toward her. "I followed you out here because I'm wondering if you're not happy working at Outlook."

"I love it."

"You'd tell me if you didn't?"

"Yes, I would." She set the banana peel aside and folded her arms over her knees. "I guess you've noticed I've been... preoccupied."

"Yeah."

She stared at the ground, debating. "I got an email from my dad."

"Today?"

"Wednesday morning. I'm still trying to..." Anger flared that he'd dumped that on her through email. "Apparently he tried calling but couldn't get through." A sigh doused the fire. "I suppose there's no easy way to tell your child, who has idolized you her entire life, that you aren't the hero she thought. That it was actually *your* actions that started the chain of events that brought her to this place."

He shook his head. "No good way to admit that."

She pinched the bridge of her nose. "It changes everything and nothing. I'm still out here on my own with no clue what to do with my life, but now I don't even have that ally to lean on. The person I depended on most to be there for me isn't who I thought he was."

"That's rough," he said. "Do you think you should head back now to get everything straightened out?"

"No!" It was the last place she wanted to be. "I actually thought I was working through things, getting ready to face my mom, coming to grips with my new normal which includes Kenny in my family tree."

"Kenny?"

"Kenny Johnson. My bio dad. My mother's summertime fling." She stared across the ravine. "I'm the illegitimate daughter of a cheater and an ex-con womanizer, raised by someone I'd never have believed had the same moral issues. I'm a mistake, an oops that no one was ever supposed to discover."

The pain in her words echoed between them.

"I'm sorry you're going through this, Kayla." He shifted on the log and faced her. "But I want you to hear me on this. You aren't a mistake or an oops. None of that defines who *you* are. It might describe other people's actions, but it is not who you are."

"Then what is?" she managed over the knot in her throat. She'd become a whining, sniveling mess. Where was the decisive, fearless person she used to be? "I have no idea who I am anymore. Maybe I never did."

"Because no one told you who you were to begin with. You picked up bits and pieces, but not the truth."

She snorted. "The truth is there is no truth. Everyone decides what truth is to them, and that's as far as it goes. Unless they get found out," she added, sarcasm coloring the words. "Then they come up with a new truth."

His expression remained calm. "You did DNA testing to find out who your biological parents were, right? But your DNA goes a lot deeper and means so much more. Your true father is the Creator of the Universe. God has spoken that truth over you from the moment you were conceived. Before that even."

"The truth of my conception is that my mother had a one-night stand." She stood and stepped away, then folded her arms and faced him, jaw set. "And now there's a new truth. My *dad* had an affair first."

He met her challenge, eyebrows tented with sympathy. "Ouch."

The fight vanished. "Yeah."

He crossed the short distance and took her shoulders in a firm grasp. "Mikayla Gordon, the truth of who you are isn't in the actions of your parents. It's in who *God* says you are. You were never an oops in His eyes. Your title isn't illegitimate, mistake, accident, or unwanted. You were created in His image, and He's none of those things. Your true DNA is found in Him. You're identity is child of God, His beloved."

The conviction in his voice, the earnest light in his brown eyes wrapped warmth around her battered, aching heart. If only that were true. "It sounds good, Dawson, but it doesn't apply to me. I was definitely a mistake, an embarrassment."

She stepped back, out of his grasp. "All my life my mother treated me differently. She says she never knew for sure, but I think she suspected and because of her guilt, she didn't know what to do with me. I never fit in. I wasn't pretty and girlie like Lindy, and definitely not smart like Maggie."

She turned and looked up at the mountains, blinking quickly. "I always thought it was because I was so much like Dad, but now..." She didn't want to be like him. Or any of them.

The tone from Dawson's walkie yanked her back to reality. What was she doing, wasting his time whining when he was running a business? She gestured for him to respond to the call. He answered and told Brenda he'd be back at the lodge in twenty minutes. As he returned it to his belt, Mikayla retrieved her backpack.

"Mikayla—"

"Daws, this has been helpful. Really. Thanks for tracking me down." She didn't meet his gaze as she hooked the pack. "There's work to do before the next Adventure group comes in, so let's head back."

He stepped in front of her. "Hey. Look at me."

She hesitated, but it seemed ridiculous to stare at his chin, so she lifted her gaze. "I'm okay. Or I will be. I promise."

"I know you will," he said, "but it's going to be a process. You're dealing with a lot, and I don't want you to go it alone. I'm available to talk anytime. I mean that."

She nodded, a smile softening the tension in her jaw, lowering her shoulders. "I know. I appreciate it."

They stood quietly for a moment before he shook his head. "You really are stubborn, not to mention frustratingly independent."

"And proud of it," she agreed with a cheeky grin that faded. "But not too stubborn to ask for help. When I need to talk, I'll find you."

He hesitated, then hooked an arm around her and pulled her in for a playful side hug. "I'm holding you to it. Let's head back and start getting ready for the Sunday group. Good thing there's no reception up on the mountain. We don't need more emails like that next week."

She laughed and started toward the trail. "That's for sure." The hike back in comfortable silence allowed Mikayla to mentally leave the pain and anger behind. She'd been living with the DNA results from her mother and Kenny. She'd never considered she had God's DNA. It was an extraordinary idea, freeing and a bit overwhelming.

What she did know was that this solid, caring man had her back and that was enough for now. Once she went home, it might be a different story. In the meantime, she'd listen to the mountains sing every chance she got.

- 27 -

The next week's True Adventure camp, followed by a week of day camp, and then another True Adventure camp passed without major issues. The summer was drawing to a close, and Mikayla was desperate to slow it down. Dawson now deferred the skills teaching to her, and the appreciative glint in his eyes kept her off-balance. All but two in the second True Adventure week's group of ten had wilderness camping experience, and Mikayla was delighted to gather new ideas from them as well as share her own.

While her days were busy teaching, learning, and listening, the nights in the tent were long and silent as she wrestled with Dad's revelation, and her inability to formulate a response. Without knowing if he'd told Lindy and Maggie, she couldn't work through it with them. It was his news to share, just as her mother had had to come clean on her own. She could barely digest this herself; she had no words of wisdom for her sisters.

During the second week of True Adventure camp, they were soaked by a heavy rain, received several visits from a curious fox, and caught a total of three fish during two outings. Several times she encountered Dawson's quizzical gaze through the flames, or a startled glance when she laughed with one of the boys. She'd liked to have been flattered, but his expressions held questions rather than admiration.

On the return hike Saturday morning, corralling the end of the line of kids, she caught glimpses of Dawson at the front of the line. Had she said the wrong thing at some point? He seemed to be questioning something about her. While she'd developed a serious crush on him, he obviously didn't return the sentiment. She rolled her eyes. He was her boss, for Pete's sake. He'd never mentioned a girlfriend, not surprising given his crazy life, but he no doubt had a policy to protect himself from swooning staff members. *Too much time in the sun, kiddo. Once you leave here, you won't see him again.*

She stumbled, knocking the boy in front of her off-balance before landing on her hands and knees. Sucking in a breath through gritted teeth, she sat back and pulled her bloodied knees up for inspection.

"You okay, Mikayla?" The boy crouched at her side. "Sorry if I wasn't going fast enough."

"Totally my fault," she assured him, eyes stinging from the shooting pain in both knees. She shrugged out of her pack and unzipped the first-aid pouch on the side. "I took my eyes off the trail."

Word had spread through the group, and they gathered around her. Dawson squeezed through and knelt beside her. "What happened?"

She waved him off, flinching as she patted the cuts with

the medicated pad. "Not paying attention. Dumb move."

With a gentle touch that sent a tingle down her legs, he inspected the damage, then pulled bandages from the pouch. "Managed to hit those rocks square on," he commented, glancing at the rock-strewn path.

"Always try to do my best," she quipped.

He looked up at the kids crowded around them. "Everybody take a water break. We'll be done here in about five." As they moved away, he turned her stinging palms up. "Not quite as square on here."

The skin was scraped, but not bleeding. "Sorry."

He chuckled and sat back on his heels. "I'll let it go this time. Your knees are gonna be sore for a few days. Keep moving anyway."

"Yes, sir."

He held her gaze, his smile deepening. "Gordon, you sure aren't the typical staff person."

Hardly sounded like a compliment. "I've been called worse." She shifted and got slowly to her feet, brushing off her shorts to hide her disappointment.

"Hey." He waited until she looked up. "I have other words that can't be used while we're working."

"I've probably heard them all," she said, her tone light. Tough, fearless, strong, unfeminine, scrapper, one of the guys. Atypical fit right in. "Wrap up your break," she called to the group. "Let's keep moving."

She ignored Dawson's hesitation and picked up her backpack, sliding into it. "Let's get these knees moving before they get too stiff."

Releasing an irritated breath, he moved to the front of the line. "Everybody here? Missing anyone?"

They counted off to show they were present, and he waved them on. Mikayla limped behind, flinching every time there was a steep decline that jarred her knees. One of the boys found a long stick for her that took some of the pressure off and eased the jolts of pain. *Eyes up, watch where you're going.* Dad's words rang in her head.

She'd yet to respond to his email, unable to formulate anything appropriate. Her heart had continued to ache as if someone had died, and she'd finally realized something had—the relationship that had been the foundation of her world. With her departure date only two weeks away, she had to figure out how she'd get through the wedding without ruining it for Lin.

Once they reached camp, Mikayla kept moving so her knees didn't stiffen up. She greeted a dancing, yipping Lula who would not be ignored, then turned her attention to the campers' families. She hugged each teen and shared a favorite moment of them with their parents, and finally waved the last one off the grounds before limping toward the bunkhouse.

Brenda emerged and stopped, hands on her hips. "What in the world?"

"Took a little tumble on the way down. Just need to re-dress them, and I'll be back out to get the gear cleaned up and inventoried."

"I'll do that," Brenda said firmly. "You helped with that massive mailing for the Founder's Day Celebration. This way you can put your feet up for a bit."

"Really?" She sighed. "A few minutes would be great. But

I won't rest too long, or I won't be able to bend my legs."

"True." Brenda gave her a quick hug. "I'll check on you when I'm done. And I'll let Daws know I ordered you to rest for a bit."

Continuing her hobble toward the building, Mikayla smiled at Brenda's thoughtfulness. She'd become the first girlfriend Mikayla had who loved what she loved and didn't think she was weird for being able to bait a hook or filet a fish. She was awed by their similarities, the hours of shared laughter and talks, even their disagreements that ended peacefully. How amazing to have a friend who appreciated her for who she was.

With Lula ahead of her, Mikayla gripped the handrail to pull herself up the stairs to her room, and turned her thoughts to the team. The guys treated her as a true equal. During free time in the evenings, she'd bested them in hatchet throwing and tying flies. They'd taken the losses with good-natured groaning before beating her soundly, digging a firepit and creating a shelter. She was so fortunate to call them her friends. She'd never felt so comfortable in her own skin.

After thoroughly cleaning her battered knees and tossing down a few aspirin, she shuffled to the bed and lowered onto her back, propping her legs on her duffel bag. With a deep sigh, she closed her eyes and stroked Lula who snuggled against her. Just a few minutes and she'd get back to work. Helping Brenda with a mailing wasn't nearly as time consuming as wrapping up the end of a True Adventure week.

A gently persistent knock at the door brought her eyes back open as Lula leaped from the bed with a shrill bark. So much for a nap. Mikayla moved her feet to the floor and stood, sucking in a sharp breath. Even those few minutes had stiffened the injury.

She snapped a light on, squinting as she limped to the door. Dawson waited, a tray of food in hand. "You missed dinner."

"I what?" She ran a hand through her hair. "What time is it? I just lay down a few minutes ago."

"More like three hours ago."

"Three *hours*? Why didn't someone wake me? I'm so sorry! I was going to go back to finish the inventory."

He chuckled. "It's okay, Kayla. How about coming down to eat while it's still hot. That'll get your knees working again."

She hobbled down the stairs behind him to the bunkhouse kitchen and slid into the chair he pulled out. "Thanks. This is really nice of you, but you didn't have to."

"I know I didn't, but you knocked yourself out the last three weeks so it's the least I could do. I'm just glad you didn't literally knock yourself out when you fell."

"Me too." The aroma of meatloaf and potatoes made her stomach growl. She pulled in an appreciative breath. "Who made dinner?"

"Me." He laughed at her blink of surprise. "Hey, I *can* cook more than burgers over a fire."

Her mother would use that to prove her point.

"I'm impressed." With the first bite, she sighed. "Mmm. You really can cook."

"I'll try not to be offended." He dropped into a nearby chair. "How are the knees?"

"Sore. I can't believe I did that. At least it was on the way down."

"We all do it at some point. I'm just glad you didn't break anything. A few days and you'll be running sprints up the mountain."

She could swing an axe, bait a hook, and hike up a mountain, but she'd never been fast. Faster than her sisters maybe, but that was hardly a contest. "I'll be happy to just walk up. Sorry I left you to do the equipment wrap-up."

He shrugged. "Brenda helped. It gave us a chance to talk over details for the party."

She finished the last bite of her meal with a satisfied sigh. "That was really good, Dawson. Thanks. So I'm assuming the Founder's Day party is about Walt?"

"Yup." He fiddled with the salt and pepper shakers, frowning. "About that. I was thinking about something you said after you got your dad's email. You mentioned that your—"

"Well, there's the lazy bum." Kyle's voice interrupted as he led the staffers into the building. "Falling down the mountain *and* sleeping through dinner. Nice work, Gordon."

They settled around the table, and he dropped several decks of cards in front of her tray. "We're playing Rummy. You've been elected scorekeeper."

She looked at Dawson. "What were you saying about the email?"

He waved a hand and stood. "It's nothing. Good luck keeping score with this group."

"You're not playing?"

"I've got to get a list of supplies going for the celebration," he said, and slapped Kyle on the back. "No cheating."

"What? When have I ever—"

Rob cut him off, reaching for the cards. "Don't even go there or we'll tell you when." He looked at Mikayla as he shuffled. "Ready?"

She set her napkin on her plate, surprised when Dawson reached for the tray. "You don't have to do that. You brought dinner. The least I can do is bus my own dishes."

"I'll do it this time," he said over his shoulder. "You're on kitchen clean up the next two days."

Amidst the razzing of her teammates, she watched him leave the building, then turned her attention to the game. As much as she enjoyed every staffer at the camp, Dawson's presence provided a sense of...something. Safety? Reassurance? Calm.

He was going to say something about the email from Dad. She shook the thought away and studied her cards. Probably just that God would help her deal with it.

- 28 -

Propped in bed after the raucous card game, knees neatly re-
bandaged, Mikayla opened her email and sucked in a breath.
Mom. There'd been one brief email of apology over the past
months but no phone calls or texts just as she'd said to her
mother before leaving town. One of the many ugly things
she'd said in her anger and hurt.

Her heart squeezed as her finger hovered over the email.
Nothing could be worse than Dad's.

> Hi sweetheart. I hope you're doing well and find-
> ing the answers you need. Your dad told me he sent
> you an email about why I was at Aunt Cindy's that
> summer. I know how much he wanted to talk to
> you instead, but it seems reception is pretty poor
> out there. I know you don't want to talk to me, so
> I'm going to tell you what happened that summer,
> and you can call me if you want to talk about it.
> Anytime, night or day.

Mikayla shook her head. *If you all keep dropping bomb-
shells on me through email, I'm changing my address.*

After your father told me about his affair, I took Maggie and went to Cindy and Jim's. I was devastated but also feeling guilty. Your dad knew how much I wanted a house, so he took on a second job. I was so wrapped up in caring for a baby and setting up our home, your father came in a distant 3rd for my attention. That wasn't at all fair to him.

At the resort, I was usually outside with Maggie, so I got to know Kenny because he was so friendly. We talked a lot about life, relationships, jobs. Eventually I told him why I was there. He gave me some good advice, believe it or not, and encouraged me to go back and work on my marriage. He'd never been married because he moved around a lot, but he'd always wanted a family, so he was serious about me going back to your dad.

Kenny talked her into saving her marriage? Kenny who then got her pregnant? Her family was a virtual soap opera.

I don't know what all you've learned about him on your search, but the Kenny I knew was funny, thoughtful, and hard working. I listened to his advice and decided I'd go home and do everything I could to make my marriage work. From the letters your father sent that summer, I knew he would too.

The night before I left, the resort had a big end-of-summer party. Unfortunately, I didn't eat much all day because I was helping with set up, and then I enjoyed too much wine, as did Kenny. To this day I don't remember most of the evening, especially after I got back to my room. Kenny had been very kind, but he was also pretty drunk.

What I do know is that he didn't take advantage of me. We were mortified to wake up together in the morning. I headed straight home. I should have told your father right away, but I was too embarrassed. That was my second mistake.

Mikayla dropped her head against the wall and thumped gently. *Great tactic. Ignore it and it will go away. We've seen how well that works.*

Honey, your father was over the moon when you were born. Then, as we were packing to move to the Cities for his new job, we were offered another child we named Lindy. It was overwhelming to have a toddler and two new babies, but we felt so blessed. You and Lindy instantly took to each other. We decided we'd tell you when you were a little older. I see now what a mess that decision has created.

I'm so very sorry, sweetheart, for turning your life upside-down. Please don't let this ruin your relationships with your sisters. Now is when you need each other most. I'm counting the days until you come home for the wedding. I love you with my whole heart. Mom

Mikayla stared at the email, the letters blurring. The explosion of emotions she'd expected at finally hearing her mother's explanation didn't happen. It was far less offensive than the story she'd created in her head, especially since her version had her father as the wronged party. Now she had two sides, but she'd never get the third if she couldn't locate Kenny. Would he remember it the same way?

She closed the laptop, shut off the light and slid under the covers, Lula snuggled close. "It's time to see if Old Joe is back, Lu," she said. "Time to solve this mystery and put it behind me for good." Old Joe had to know where Kenny was. She was running out of time.

"Maybe when I wake up tomorrow," she added as her eyes closed, "this will all have been a dream." Except for Dawson. He needed to be real.

With the Founder's Day Celebration on Saturday, no camps were scheduled for the week, which freed Mikayla to head to Tabernash Monday afternoon. Lula stood beside her with bright-eyed anticipation. Old Joe had to be home by now.

Pulling to a stop on the dirt driveway, she smiled at the older man relaxed on a bench near the front door, a gray braid hanging over his thin shoulder. He watched her climb out of the jeep and approach, nodding a greeting as she got closer. "Afternoon."

"Hello. I'm Mikayla Gordon. Are you Joe?"

"Yep."

Mouth suddenly dry, she swallowed with difficulty. "I'm looking for Kenny Johnson, and someone at the resort in Winter Park thought you might know him."

He returned his attention to whittling the block of wood in his gnarled hands. "Kenny Johnson."

Mikayla waited, glancing back toward the jeep, where Lula waited in the front seat. If Old Joe didn't like dogs, the animated pixie wouldn't help Mikayla get information out of him. "I stopped by about a month ago and heard from your neighbor Pete that you were recuperating at your daughter's. I'm glad to see you're home now."

His head bobbed as he whittled. "Not my time to go." Rheumy blue eyes glanced at her from beneath a black knit cap. "Haven't heard the name Kenny Johnson in a long time. What would a young lady like you want with him?"

Hope fizzled. Maybe he didn't know where Kenny was. She explained her tie to the magazine. "I'm hoping you can get us connected so I can set up an interview with him. I have to head back to Minnesota soon, and I hope I can talk with him before then."

"Huh." He set the knife and wood aside and pushed slowly to his feet. "Just made some coffee. I'll get us both a cup."

Before she could reply, he swung open the flimsy screen door and went into the tiny cabin. When it slammed shut, she flinched, waiting for it to fall off the house. When it didn't, she breathed slowly to calm the chaos under her ribs. Joe hadn't said he didn't know Kenny, just that he hadn't heard the name in a while. And he was getting them coffee. Those had to be good signs that answers were within reach.

He emerged with two blue tin cups and motioned toward the chairs with his head. "Have a seat, young lady. And by the way, I don' mind if your friend joins us."

Mikayla looked back at Lula and smiled when the feathery ears dropped down as if pleading for her to agree.

"Go on," Old Joe encouraged. "Haven't enjoyed a dog in quite some time."

Mikayla opened the jeep door and swept her up before the imp could make a dash for the older man. "Behave yourself," she whispered as they joined him, "or I'll put you right back."

Settling carefully onto a lawn chair, praying the webbing would hold, she kept Lula on her lap and accepted the cup. "Thanks. This is Lula."

"Lula. My wife's name was Lola. She didn't have those ears, however."

Mikayla laughed at the twinkling look he shot toward the dog. "Thank goodness."

Old Joe set a small plate with chocolate chip cookies on the wobbly wooden table between them. "Can Lula have a bite of cookie?"

"I think she'd like that." An understatement. Lula ate anything. Keeping a grip on the collar, Mikayla set her down. Lula's tail swished against the dirt.

Old Joe broke off a tiny piece of cookie and held it out. Her dainty acceptance drew a chuckle from him. "She's got some good manners."

Mikayla told him how she and Lula had become partners on this winding journey, releasing her grip on Lula's collar when Old Joe reached for her.

He nuzzled his gray, scruffy chin against the soft fur, smiling. "It's a privilege to care for one of God's creatures," he said eventually. "Still miss my old Monty. He was a good friend. Took a snake bite meant for me."

"That's awful."

"Sure was, but it showed how much the old guy loved me."
He cleared his throat and set Lula on the ground. "Haven't
wanted to try replacing him. Ain't no dog that could live up
to that."

Mikayla sipped the surprisingly good coffee, tasting hazelnut and nutmeg. "This is delicious, Joe. Thank you."

He nodded and they sat quietly, surrounded by peaceful
sunlit woods. Finally he looked at her. "So what do you wanna
know about Kenny?"

Everything. "I've heard from different people he's quite
the...character." A nice word. Far less colorful than what she
wanted to say.

"I met Kenny thirty-odd years ago," he mused. "Skied
the circuit together an' worked jobs around the country in
the off-season together too."

Anticipation churned. "Did you work with him at Iron
Mountain in Michigan?"

He frowned, scratching his head through the cap. "Hmm.
Don't think so. How long ago was that?"

"About thirty years." Give or take nine months.

"I met him in Jackson Hole, first race of the season.
Might've been before or after he was in Michigan."

Lula scampered after something moving in the underbrush, then trotted back as if she'd done her job.

"Do you know where I can find him now?"

His eyes narrowed in the silence. "He died a few months
ago. Early February."

"He... In February?" The revelation punched the air from
her lungs, and she dropped her gaze to the cup she clutched in

her lap, blinking rapidly. Of all the scenarios she'd considered, that wasn't one of them. He couldn't have stayed alive a few more months so she could have her say? The selfish thought stung.

"Sorry if that was a bit harsh." Old Joe released a heavy, wheezy sigh. "I still expect him to come roaring up the mountain on his bike."

There were no words, only swelling defeat and anger.

"You didn't know him?" Old Joe asked.

"No." *Nobody gave me the chance.* "I thought I could—" What did it matter now? She loosened the clench in her jaw. All this way for nothing. Relationships ruined. For nothing! Why did she ever have to find out about him? "I won't take any more of your time. Thank you for your help. And for the coffee."

With trembling fingers, she set the cup aside, then managed a weak whistle for Lula and stood. "It was nice meeting you," she said with difficulty. Unable to fully meet his gaze, she turned toward the jeep on wooden legs. Kenny had taken the answers she needed to his grave and robbed her of the opportunity to have her say. Her medical history would remain a question mark, as would that part of her identity.

A mosaic of emotions bounced in her chest as she followed the rutted dirt road. All this way. Why had she bothered? Had he ever known about her? He wouldn't have cared. Fear of commitment, Squinty had said. More like an aversion.

She'd never have the chance to tell him what she thought of him. Never look him in the eye to see his reaction. A tear slid down her cheek. Never know the actual person behind the

name she'd detested as soon as she heard it. Perhaps he would
have cared if he met her. Probably not.

She'd never know.

256

- 29 -

After an endless night of broken dreams and restless sleep, Mikayla took her raging headache to Violet's for a strong cup of coffee, grateful she wasn't running any camps this week. While she'd had trouble focusing after Dad's email, now she couldn't form coherent thoughts.

Vi's smile faded when she approached the table where Mikayla and Lula sat. "I'd say you had a wild night, but you don't strike me as the wild living kind of girl." She settled her large frame in the opposite chair. "What's the matter, sweetie?"

The kind inquiry knotted Mikayla's throat. *I will not cry over that man.* "I found out yesterday that the guy I've been looking for is dead." She managed a strangled laugh. "Put a lot of miles on my poor old jeep for nothing."

"Oh, hon, that's rotten news." Vi reached across and squeezed Mikayla's arm. "Does that mean you'll be heading back to Minnesota soon?"

She dropped her gaze. There was still so much to see and experience here, people to spend time with. "I guess it does," she said. Defeat had a bitter taste.

"Well, I have something that will make you feel better right now, anyway. And I'll have Abe bring you a cup of my strongest coffee."

She bustled off, and Mikayla swiped a finger under her eyes. *There's no use crying over someone you never knew.* In the early morning hours, as she'd watched the sun come up, she'd decided to go back to Old Joe and tell him everything. He was her only source of information about Kenny, so she'd ask questions until she was satisfied.

Abe ambled out with a steaming, hand-painted mug in such vibrant colors she couldn't help but smile.

"Vi's got some of the wildest cups I've ever seen," he said with a sheepish shrug, setting it before her along with a plate of creamers. "You might need a bunch of these to make the coffee drinkable. It's Brazilian. The strongest they've got down there, or so they told Vi. Definitely the strongest in Winter Park."

Mikayla thanked him before he headed back to the shop, then took a tiny, tentative sip. Whew! Abe wasn't kidding. The bitter liquid scalded her tongue and burned her throat. She emptied three creamers into the mug and stirred until the black brew turned a caramel hue. *Mmm. Better.*

Vi brought out a small white box crowded with a scone, an apple turnover, and a chocolate-frosted donut with sprinkles. "Don't let my granddaughters know I stole one of their donuts. There now, see? I knew one of these would make you smile."

"Who doesn't smile at chocolate and sprinkles? But I don't

want to get you in trouble, so I'll take the turnover."

"You'll take all of them. The girls won't miss one donut. What do you think of the coffee?"

"Strong enough to take the curl out of my hair."

Vi slapped her thigh as she laughed. "That's true! Now, you enjoy the sunshine and share some of these"—she placed three small dog treats on the table—"with our sweet Lula. I'll check on you in a bit."

Mikayla watched her return to the shop, her gauzy, multi-colored blouse fluttering behind in the warm breeze. She released a heavy sigh. What a gift to have gotten to know such a dear person. She wouldn't get to meet Kenny, but she'd met many wonderful people along the journey.

She savored the warm turnover and offered bites of the dog treats to Lula, letting the angst of yesterday fade with her headache. When the treats and the turnover were gone, Lula jumped off her chair and stood with her paws on Mikayla's knee. Mikayla smiled and lifted her for a snuggle. "Fine, Lu. We'll get going. But I suspect all you care about is getting another cookie from Joe."

Carrying the empty cup and plate into the shop, she tried to pay Violet, but the woman crossed her arms and gave a firm shake of her head. With a roll of her eyes, Mikayla started to leave, waiting until Vi turned away, then snuck a ten-dollar bill under the edge of the register and hurried out into the sunshine.

As she slowed to a stop at Old Joe's cabin, he glanced up from his whittling and nodded, then focused on the wood. Either he didn't surprise easily, or he'd expected her to return.

She collected the white box and climbed out to follow Lula as she raced toward the old man. The crunch of gravel under her feet echoed in the quiet.

"Mornin'," he said, bending over to pet Lula who danced at his knee.

"Good morning. I came to apologize for the way I left yesterday. That was rude of me."

He lifted a shoulder. "Didn't seem like the news you expected to get, so it made sense. I'll get us some coffee while we talk some more."

"None for me, thanks. I just had a cup of Vi's Brazilian coffee."

He threw back his head with a raspy laugh. "Good on ya if you finished it. That's one strong cup. Should keep you awake for the next three days."

"I finished," she said with a proud smile, "but it took three creamers for my tongue to handle it." She held out the white box. "And she also provided some pastries, so I brought them for you."

"That's mighty nice of you. I sure love Vi's baking." He accepted the box and motioned toward the chair she'd occupied earlier. "Set yourself down while I get a cookie for our waiting friend."

Lula whimpered, her tiny rear wiggling where she sat at his feet.

"Lula," Mikayla scolded. "That's rude. No begging."

Old Joe retrieved another plate of cookies, then settled onto the bench and took up his whittling project again.

Mikayla sat quietly, debating how to start.

"Always good to start at the beginning," he mused.

Perceptive old guy. He'd known she'd come back with more questions. Drawing a slow breath, Mikayla plunged into her story from her collapse at the office. He nodded occasionally, lips pursed as he listened. The pressure in her chest lessened as she told the uncensored version for the first time.

"So that brings me to today. The answers I was looking for are gone." She sighed deeply. "And I'm not sure what to do next."

"Been a tough road for you," he said.

Tears prickled. "It never occurred to me he'd be gone," she admitted. "Stupid not to consider every angle. I'd thought about what I'd do if I couldn't find him, but to find out he's dead wasn't on the list of potential endings." She nibbled at the last of the cookie she'd been tossing to Lula and stared into the woods.

"Kenny was my best friend," Old Joe said. "I knew him better'n anyone, but I still didn't understand him. Pretty complex fella. By the book in some ways, devil-may-care in others. But I can tell you one thing for sure, missy..."

In the silence that followed, she moved her gaze to his.

"He'da been thrilled to know he had a child. 'Specially a daughter. He taught skiing to little ones the last few years and loved it. Had a soft spot for little girls who were brave enough to get on skis."

She rolled her eyes. "I'd have been a disappointment then. I hate downhill skiing."

Old Joe chuckled. "That'd have been a challenge," he acknowledged. "But he'da changed your mind eventually."

"And I'm afraid of heights."

"Huh. The higher and faster, the better he liked it."

She hid a relieved sigh. So she wasn't all that much like him. "If you have time, I'd like to know more about him. Try to put together a picture of who he was, what he was like. And I need to know what he died from so I can add it to my medical file."

"Got all the time in the world for someone related to Walt."

She smiled. "You mean Kenny."

He waved a hand. "Sorry. Can't keep names straight anymore. I'm happy to talk about him. Never thought I'd be lonesome without his big mouth around here."

The morning sun climbed into the cloudless sky as Old Joe shared memories and insights. His stories painted a confusing picture of Kenny—a fierce competitor who sent money every month to his mother in Montana. A ladies' man unable to settle down. Someone who was generous with his friends, but occasionally landed on the wrong side of the law.

He handed her a blue-speckled cup of water and resettled on his bench. Lula jumped into his lap and looked at him with wide-eyed expectation. He offered a bite of his cookie. "He didn't talk much about his family. I always figured there was too much pain. And he weren't one to dwell on the past. Up until the injury, whenever he got knocked down, he'd get right back up."

His gaze became distant and Mikayla waited. She didn't want to know Kenny had been a regular person with dreams and ambitions, friends and some enemies. She wasn't about to forgive him for the mess he'd made of her life. Old Joe's snort startled her.

"He shouldn'ta been on the slope that day," he grumbled. "Bad weather was settin' in. But that was Kenny. Cocky to a fault. He couldn't let the challenge go."

"Challenge?"

"Some idiot new to the circuit had been braggin' about being the fastest skier, making remarks about some of Kenny's record runs." He shook his head, brow dark with memories. "I tried to tell Kenny it was jus' talk. And I reminded him he'd had a couple of beers already. Maybe that's what clouded his judgment."

Mikayla watched pain shadow his sun-wrinkled face and held her breath, silently urging him to continue.

"With the other guys eggin' him on, he just couldn't walk away. So he told the kid they'd do one race before the snow closed the mountain that day. I knew it was gonna end badly. I could feel it."

She shivered.

"They went up with a couple of the guys an' the rest of us waited at the bottom." He sat quietly staring at the memory. "Seemed like we waited forever. Snow started comin' down heavier. Wind was blowin'. The kid finally showed up yellin' something about Kenny going off-course. Guess visibility was worse than we'd thought an' Kenny missed a turn. Took the medics two hours to find him and get him down." He sighed. "Longest hours of my life."

"How bad was it?"

He blinked and focused on her. "Worst I'd ever seen on

the circuit. He'd gone right off the hill, fell about forty feet. Broke both legs, pelvis, a couple ribs. Got a concussion. He was out for days. They didn't do surgery on his legs right away 'cause of the swelling in his head, so when they finally did, they couldn't set things right. Never skied another race."

Mikayla pushed back against an unexpected pang of sympathy. Kenny wasn't a man who made good choices, in any area of life. It was his own fault. But still...

"He weren't the same after that," Old Joe mused. "The fire went out. Lost most of the attitude that made him a great competitor. Still shot off his mouth though. That got him in some big trouble so he hadta live under the radar."

"What kind of trouble?"

Joe thought a moment, shaking his head. "Won a bunch of money at some card games. They said he cheated, but I know that wasn't true. He was a lot of things, but not a cheat. But then he got involved with the guy's girlfriend. That weren't too smart, I'll give you that. The guy told people he was gonna fix Kenny good. I heard he was real mean so I think he meant it.

"Wrong guy to mess with." He sighed. "Anyway, Kenny pretty much lived off the grid after that. When I moved here, he came too. Built a good life. He was happiest outdoors."

That's a bit too close to home.

"What did he die from?"

"Liver cancer. Hated doctors and wouldn't go in. Stubborn as the day is long. By the time he made an appointment, there was nuthin' they could do for him."

"So it wasn't a heart issue?"

"Not that I know of. He wanted his organs donated, and I

remember them sayin' he had the heart of a man twenty years younger."

Mikayla leaned back in her chair, a weight lifting from her heart. If Joe was right, her issue was a fluke. *Thank you, God.*

He refilled their cups, then they sat in companionable silence.

Old Joe stroked Lula where she'd sprawled across his lap. "He had a reputation with the ladies, for sure. Some of it was real but most of it was made up. He liked the image, but he weren't the ladies' man everyone said. He had too much respect for women."

"Not my mother."

"Don't know the story behind that," he admitted, "but I'm sure there's something. He was the life of the party, but not too many knew the loneliness behind that."

The strength in his words tangled her thoughts. She'd come here to demand an answer, even an apology. But her mother's email, and now Old Joe's declaration, softened the edges of that mission. His memories painted a different picture of the man whose lifestyle and choices she'd disdained. He wasn't who she'd have chosen as her biological father, but she could live with it. She'd just make sure her lifestyle and choices never reflected his.

"This is a lot for you to figure out," Old Joe said. "I ain't goin' anywhere, so you can come by anytime with more questions. I'm happy to keep his memory alive." He waited for her to look at him. "The Kenny I knew was complicated, but he was a good guy who paid the price for some bad decisions."

The compassion in his eyes warmed the chill in her heart.

Maybe Old Joe didn't know everything about Kenny, but it was clear how much he'd cared for his friend. And mourned his loss.

"An' you might not want to hear it, but you've got his eyes and his spirit. I thought it when you showed up yesterday asking about him, and now I see it plain as day. It makes this ol' heart happy to meet his blood. To know part of his spirit will live on."

She bit her lip and looked away. She didn't want to be Kenny's legacy. Nor her mother's. She'd have been happy to be Dad's until the email.

"But I'll bet you got more of your mom than Kenny," he added kindly. "Can't imagine you in jail for shootin' off your mouth or doin' stupid stunts on a challenge."

She didn't always censor what came out of her mouth, so that might be from Kenny, but she preferred to think the rest was from Dad. "I've had the most wonderful father my whole life. Everything I know I learned from him."

"Glad to hear it." Old Joe nodded. "Walt prob'ly wouldn't have been half the dad for you. Not 'cause he wouldn't have cared, but he just wouldn'ta known how."

Kenny, or Walt as Joe kept calling him, would never have measured up to Dad. "Well, thank you for your time, and your openness." She got to her feet. "You're right. This is a lot to take in."

"Say, have you stopped by the camp? You'll find out lots more about him there."

She frowned. "What camp?"

"The one not too far from the resort. The, uh..." He shook

his head. "Something about adventure…"

"Outlook Adventure Camp?" The name squeaked out.

Old Joe snapped his fingers. "That's it."

"What does Kenny have to do with the camp?"

"He started it. 'Bout fifteen years ago. Needed somethin' to do when he moved here, and he loved bein' outdoors, so it made sense to try that."

Mikayla watched his mouth move, the words coming down a long tunnel. "But the guy who started it was…" Walt.

"That's the name he used once he moved here," Old Joe said with a nod. "His real name was Walter. Walter Kenneth Johnson."

A memory flashed before her—Sara reading the personnel record. "His real name is Walter."

Joe was still talking. "When he came here, he wanted a fresh start so he went back to Walter and used Smith so those thugs couldn't find him. Don't know if too many people 'round these parts knew him as Kenny Johnson. It took me a while to get used to callin' him Walt. He'd get after me good if I slipped up."

So that's what he'd meant when he said he hadn't heard the name Kenny Johnson in a long time. She sank back into the chair, which Old Joe seemed to take as an invitation to say more.

"I helped him build that first lodge. Took us nearly six months." A fond smile filled his whiskered face. "We had a good time workin' on it. And it brought him back to life, gave him a purpose. He needed that bad. That's when he really became Walter Smith."

He'd been right under her nose this whole time. If she'd taken the time to look at the camp photos more closely, she'd have seen it. And the one behind Dawson's desk—the one she'd thought was him and his dad—that was Kenny too. *Her* bio dad.

Her breath hitched. Had Dawson known and not said anything? She raced back through their conversations. Did she ever mention Kenny's name? Not that—wait. After getting Dad's email, she'd ranted about her bio father. Was that why he'd looked at her strangely the last few weeks? He knew and didn't tell her?

No, he wouldn't do that. Not after everything she'd shared with him. But she'd never have believed her parents could hold out on her, and she'd known them far longer than three months.

Dawson had only lived here for ten years—when everyone knew Kenny as Walt. If she hadn't been so fixated on finding who her mother called "Kenny," all she'd had to do was ask about Walter when she first arrived in Winter Park, and she'd probably be back in Minnesota by now. But the name "Kenny" had burned into her brain from the moment she heard it. Even the newspaper clippings had referred to him as Kenny.

"You're lookin' a little green all of a sudden. You need more water?"

She blinked and focused on the concerned lift to Joe's brow. The chaos in her head made her nauseous. "No. Thank you. I'm fine." *I don't even remember what fine feels like.* "I've taken up far too much of your time, Joe. Thank you so much for all the information."

Pushing to her feet, she paused to stop her spinning thoughts and forced a smile. "It's been a pleasure getting to know you."

He stood and handed Lula to her, then walked beside her to the jeep. "Pleasure's all mine. It gets a bit lonely out here sometimes, so I'm always happy for visitors. You bring that little girl back for a visit sometime."

"I will." She climbed in and rolled down her window. Much as she wanted to race back to camp, she couldn't be rude to the sweet old man again. "I hope you'll think about getting yourself a new friend. I'll bet there's the perfect one just waiting for a new home. It's good to have a sounding board that doesn't give advice." It was astonishing she could form coherent sentences with her brain in chaos.

"A true friend," he agreed with a chuckle, then held up a hand. "Hold up a second. I got somethin' to give you."

He returned to the cabin and emerged with a faded camo duffel bag. "You should have this."

A faint musky aroma lifted from where she set it on her lap. "What is it?"

"All that's left of Kenny's belongings."

A tremor shot through her, and she lifted her hands from where they'd rested on the canvas. This was way too personal. "No, Joe. I can't take this. You were his family. You should keep it."

He stepped back. "They gave it to me after the funeral, right after Dawson went away for a while. I forgot I had it. You might find more answers in there. Go on now." He shooed her away with a smile. "Share it with the team at the camp."

She set it on the floor behind her. She'd give it to Dawson. Or maybe throw it at him if it turned out he'd known all along. "If there's anything you decide you want back, let me know." She reached into the glove compartment for a business card. "Here's my cell number."

They exchanged a smile as he nodded. "Will do. Now you get out there and live your best life, Mikayla. Do your father proud. Both of 'em."

With a wave, she pulled away from the tiny cabin. He stood alone in the road, a hand raised, until she went around the bend. With everything he'd told her about Kenny, or Walt, nothing shocked her more than learning Dawson's friend and mentor was her bio dad.

Now she had a new mountain of questions, but this time only Dawson had the answers. As close as the men had been these past years, he had to have known Walt had also gone by Kenny. Right? How dare he not tell her? He knew how she valued honesty, knew how messed up she'd been by so many lies.

She'd trusted him, worked beside him all this time. And she'd fallen for him. Maybe that's what hurt most. It hadn't occurred to her he'd withhold something so important. She lightened her foot on the gas pedal. She couldn't go back to camp and demand answers until she had her emotions under control. Questions and thoughts ricocheted through her head while her head ached and her heart burned. She needed to process everything Joe had told her. Once she could think clearly, she'd have a calm, rational conversation with Dawson.

And then she'd be free to go home.

- 30 -

The last few days before the Founder's Day celebration, the camp was a hive of excitement and activity. Mikayla helped decorate the lodge and grounds, unloaded vanloads of food and equipment, and ran errands into town. Anything to keep from dwelling on her conversation with Old Joe, and the duffel bag still in the jeep. And from wondering if Dawson had chosen not to tell her the truth.

With anger still simmering below the surface, she'd yet to figure out how to broach the subject without blasting him with the pain of another betrayal. When they crossed paths, she was polite and professional, keeping their interactions brief. Several times she caught him watching her with a quizzical frown, and quickly put her attention elsewhere.

In the quiet of her room each night, snuggled in bed with Lula, she looked through hundreds of photos on her computer, trying not to dwell long on those that captured Dawson's smile. Then she continued reading the parts of the Bible he'd suggested. She could easily identify with the angst, anger, and grief in many of the verses. Discovering people from long ago who had experienced similar issues and emotions created an unexpected connection to the readings.

Her blog entries had become more personal as she mused about honesty, living in truth, owning up to mistakes so others didn't have to deal with the fallout. Hiker Girl found solace in the stately silence of the mountains, the calm of the forest, and the simple beauty of wildflowers. Nature didn't lie or shade the truth. After the sudden downpour of a rumbling mountain storm, the sunshine that followed made everything fresh and clear, from the air to the sparkling drops that fell from overhead branches.

Each time she finished a post and turned out the lights, she lay in the dark, wondering what God would say about her tangled thoughts. She should pray about it, like Dawson said he always did, but what would she say? Maybe she'd just try talking to Him like the psalm writers—putting it all out there. And each time she fell asleep pondering how to approach God with her messy thoughts and questions, and hoping it would be okay when she found the courage.

Friday afternoon as she helped hang twinkle lights in the lodge, her phone buzzed. She pulled it out of her back pocket, then stared. Why would Ted be calling? From her post atop the ladder, she drew a deep breath and answered. "Hey, Ted."

"Mikayla! Am I catching you at a bad time?"

His familiar voice made her smile. "Not at all. What can I do for you?"

"Well, I'm not sure how you'll take this, so I'll just jump in. The board has been reconsidering your proposal, and they've decided they'd like to continue the discussion. With you this time."

"They what?" The ladder wobbled as she clambered down and then dropped onto the arm of the couch. "You're sure it was *my* proposal they were looking at?"

He chuckled. "Very sure. It might have to do with my directing them to a certain Hiker Girl blog."

"You've seen my blog?"

"Stumbled across it when I was researching women in outdoor recreation. I'd recognize your writing anywhere— clean, concise, personal but factual."

She sat in stunned silence. Her blog brought the proposal back to life? Ted had seen it? The *board* had seen it?

"Once most of them read it and saw the comments and the interest, they got a better sense of the potential market. They've asked for clarification on some parts and shown great interest overall. So that brings us to the main question—are you still interested?"

"Well, I..." Was she? Why wasn't she dancing through the lodge? "Of course I am, but there's so much going on right now, I don't know how we'd pull it off."

"You had mentioned your sister's wedding in September. Are you planning to come home for that? Unless you're already back?"

"I'll be leaving here on September fifth. The wedding is on the twentieth."

"How about we meet after the big event and get caught up. We can talk about next steps at that point. Long overdue changes have begun at the magazine, some of which were triggered by your proposal and the Hiker Girl blog. I think it's great timing. What do you think?"

Activity humming around her, she tried to focus on what he was saying.

She'd spent many nights in the tent on the mountain thinking about starting her own camp, even using the proposal idea as marketing. But it would take time to get it up and running—create a business plan, find a location, raise the funding, hire staff. In the meantime, this could be the answer to get in position. She'd make new contacts, rebuild her savings, and develop a plan.

"Mikayla? Did I lose you?"

"Sorry, no. I'm still here. This is just...wow."

"I know the initial rejection was hard on you, and you've been traveling all summer, but I'm hoping this is still on your radar. I think there's a lot in our favor since they're coming back to us. You hold the power at this point."

She smiled sadly. He had no clue how much she'd changed since she left the magazine. "I'm still interested," she said, "but I really just want to make sure it's done right."

"And that's where holding the reins will make all the difference. Let's plan on meeting after the wedding. Give me a call when you're ready, and we'll get lunch on the calendar."

"Sounds good. I'm sorry if I'm sounding confused, but this was not at all what I was expecting."

"I figured that. Mikayla, I'd love to work with you again. You're a terrific writer, and one of the best photojournalists I know. You've got a bright future, and I'd like it to be at *Outdoor Experience*."

His praise warmed her. "Thanks, Ted. I've always valued

our relationship. Thanks for the call. I'll be in touch when I get back."

With the phone back in her pocket, she sat quietly. Did he really offer her another stab at the women's mag? Did she want it? With sudden, unexpected clarity, she knew who she needed to talk to.

"Brenda," she called across the room. "I'll be back in a few minutes."

When Brenda gave a thumbs up, Mikayla signed out a walkie and went to her room for her backpack and hiking boots. Back outside, she whistled for Lula, who dashed around the shower house. "Let's go for a walk, Lu. I've got some thinking to do."

Minutes later they reached the clearing. Lula explored while Mikayla settled on the log, backpack beside her. This had become her place to think, wonder, question. To listen to the mountains sing over and around her. And now to pray. Heart hammering against her ribs, she swallowed hard and lifted her face.

"God?" Pathetic start. She cleared her throat. "It's me, Mikayla. I know you know that but...I don't know how to do this. So I'll just talk for a while, and then if you have anything to say you can, you know, say it."

Rolling her eyes, she plunged on. "As you know, I came out west ready to blast Kenny to pieces, and we know how that played out. But when I look back, I realize it wouldn't have solved anything, would it?"

The hammering slowed. "I'm mad I didn't get to meet him, but since that can't be changed, maybe you can help me let go and move on? I'm so tired of thinking about him."

Lula hopped onto the log beside her and licked her hand. A half-smile touched her mouth. "Thanks for the perfect little companion for this journey." She picked her up and cuddled her close. "She was just what I needed. It's going to be hard to give her back."

In the peaceful silence, the last of her fear slid away. She couldn't be sure God was listening, but there was a sensation deep inside that she wasn't alone. A warmth had grown as she shared her thoughts and struggles, and now it gently cradled her heart.

"Thank you for introducing me to Dawson. He's amazing, as you know," she added with a short laugh, "and I'm so grateful to have spent this summer with him. He's doing such great work here. Keep him safe and make the camp really profitable so it can keep impacting kids.

"I know I have to talk to him about Kenny being Walt. Give me the right words and attitude. Don't let me lose my temper." She swallowed against long fingers of loneliness that tightened around her throat. "I'm so going to miss him," she added softly.

"Ted called, but I guess you know that too. What do I do about the proposal? Now there are other things I want to focus on, like the girls' camp. But I don't have a clue how to do that. Could you maybe show me somehow if I should go back to work with Ted? I don't want to lose a great opportunity if the girls' camp is just a pipe dream. I don't know how you talk to people, but Dawson says you do, so if you could let me know what to do, I'd appreciate it. And...things are a mess with my family. Could you show me what to do about that too?"

She ducked her head slightly. "Sorry if I'm asking too much or not doing it right. Mostly, I'm just thankful you brought me out here. I really want to come back someday." A tear spilled over, and she pressed a hand against her heart. "When I leave, I hope I can feel you with me at home as much as I do now. Sorry I've been so slow in knowing that you're, you know. God."

With Lula sprawled across her lap, she sat quietly enjoying the simplicity of just being with God in His creation. Life would straighten out. She knew that without words. Dawson was right. Talking to God wasn't all that scary.

- 31 -

Saturday morning sunshine bathed the camp in sparkling splendor as final touches were put in place. Mikayla glimpsed Dawson at his desk, feet propped, intently reading something.

"His speech for the dedication," Brenda explained over coffee. "He's been working on it for the past month, at least. It means a lot to him that people know who Walt really was."

Mikayla nodded. Old Joe would have plenty to say on that subject. She could add a few things as well. She swirled the dark liquid in her cup. But what would be the point? It would end up hurting people who didn't deserve it, who'd had a good relationship with him. Like Dawson, Brenda, and the rest of the team.

"Dawson has told me a little about him." He'd no doubt tell more when he finally admitted he'd known Walt was Kenny.

Brenda sipped her coffee. "They were good for each other. Walt was the dad Dawson needed, and Daws was the kid Walt never got to have."

Guess it never occurred to Walt he might actually have a child somewhere after his exploits.

"It was fun watching them together." Brenda smiled absently. "Sometimes they bickered like an old married couple, but most of the time they thought the other hung the moon. It was actually pretty sweet."

"It must have been awful for Dawson when he died."

"He was absolutely devastated. We all knew Walt was really sick, but he suddenly went downhill. Nobody was prepared for him to die then, especially Daws. After the funeral, he took off for a few weeks, just traveling around. I was relieved when he came back," she added. "I wasn't sure he would. I think Daws thought the camp would be owned by a trust or something, so he was stunned to find out he was the new owner. It meant the world to him—that Walt believed in him so much, he entrusted the camp to him."

Mikayla blinked away moisture. As she'd learned from Old Joe, Kenny was a complicated, multi-dimensional guy.

"It's been a process for Dawson to come back to life, but this summer has been good for him." An eyebrow lifted as she looked at Mikayla. "He thought you were the greatest find ever. Not sure what that says about the rest of us."

They shared a laugh. "It says he was super desperate when I came along."

"Well, there's that," Brenda acknowledged, "but not just to fill a slot. Anyway, let's get the rest of the flowers on the tables. Then I think we're ready to party."

Within the hour, guests began filling the festive grounds. Mikayla stayed in the lodge to help Rosie and the caterers. Dawson stepped into the kitchen looking adorably nervous in clean jeans, a cotton shirt and a sporty vest.

STACY MONSON

"I can't thank both of you enough for doing this."

Mikayla nodded before turning her attention back to the cookie trays she was filling.

Rosie hugged him, her smile broad. "We're happy to do it, aren't we, Mikayla?"

"Definitely."

As the tiny woman bustled out of the kitchen, Dawson stood quietly, hands stuffed in his pockets. "Kayla, when the party's over, there are some things we need to talk about."

"Yes, there are."

His eyebrows leaped up, and she forced a weak smile. "Like how you'll never find someone so amazing to replace me."

"That," he agreed, "but some other things I've been meaning to talk to you about. Tonight let's go for a walk, okay?"

"Sure, if you're not wiped out." She kept her tone light. "We can play it by ear."

"I won't be—"

"Hey, boss." Rob stuck his head into the kitchen. "Need you out front. Lots of people are arriving."

Dawson lifted a hand in acknowledgement, still holding her gaze. "Tonight."

As the doors swung behind him, Mikayla released the breath she'd held and closed her eyes. She'd have to get her thoughts in order before the party ended. It would undoubtedly be their last walk once she'd had her say. The anger had faded since her visit with Old Joe, leaving behind a pool of sadness and regret.

The Founder's Day Celebration was a huge success if attendance was any indication. Mikayla swiped her forehead as she stirred the umpteenth batch of lemonade, then poured it into a bright orange thermal beverage container. One of the hired catering staff swept into the kitchen, set an empty container on the counter and collected the filled one, then disappeared through the swinging doors.

"Thirsty group," Rosie commented from her spot slicing vegetables.

"That's for sure." Mikayla turned to look across the kitchen, rolling her head to ease the knots in her shoulders. "How many RSVP'd?"

"About two-fifty. Seems we have lots of walk-ins. But that's fine," she added with a warm smile. "It's good for Dawson to see the impact our camp has had on people. He works so hard. Always trying to live up to what he thinks were Walter's standards."

Walter had standards? Interesting concept. Mikayla wiped down her area. "Dawson works harder than anyone I know," she said. She'd never met anyone more dedicated to improving the lives of others on a daily basis. He was the standard she'd use to create her own camp. Definitely not Kenny's. "And he's developed an amazing staff too."

"You were a God-send for him."

Mikayla moved to the sink and rinsed out her rag, glancing sideways at her. "I'd hardly say that, but it worked out for all of us. I've so enjoyed my time here."

"You have to leave?"

"My sister's wedding is September 20th, and there's a possibility of going back to my former job." Back at her counter, she started a new batch of lemonade. "Plus there's unfinished business that needs attention."

"I see. We will miss you."

Mikayla tossed a smile over her shoulder, then started slicing lemons. Her family was unfinished business. Relationships that needed to be repaired, or perhaps started fresh. None of them could go back to the way life was before her collapse.

"Mikayla!" Brenda's voice slid between the swinging doors before she did. "Rosie, come out here. They're going to unveil the statue."

There was nothing Mikayla wanted to do less than see Kenny presented as a permanent paragon of virtue. "Rosie, you knew him, so you go. I'll keep working in here."

"Both of you," Brenda insisted. "It'll just take a couple minutes, and we have plenty of food out right now." She flung an arm around Mikayla and propelled her toward the door. "Come on, slow poke."

"Okay, okay." Mikayla stopped. "Can I at least take my apron off?" She flung it on the counter and looked back to make sure Rosie was following.

As they stepped out onto the deck, the fresh, cool air was a pleasant shock after the warmth of the bustling kitchen. Mikayla paused to pull in a deep breath, then stumbled down the steps when Brenda pulled her arm.

"Brenda, what—"

"Dawson wants the whole team up front."

"No!" She yanked away and planted her feet. There was no way she would be on that stage. People nearby looked toward them, so she lowered her voice. "I didn't know him, and I don't need to be up front," she hissed.

Brenda turned back, wide-eyed. "What? It's not a request, girlfriend. The boss wants us up there with him."

Panic-laced anger clenched her jaw as she shook her head. "You tell your boss I'm busy in the kitchen. I am *not* going up there."

"What is wrong with you?"

"So if we could get all of the Outlook staff up here." Dawson's voice rang out over the crowd. On a small stage, he stood with a microphone in hand beside the canvas-covered statue. "Rob, Kyle." He called their names, including Rosie's. And hers.

"Go up there." She pushed Brenda forward, then retreated to the porch and stood as close to the pillar as she could without blatantly hiding. She wouldn't go up front, but she was curious to see the statue.

Brenda reached Dawson's side on the simple stage and whispered to him as the rest of the staff filled in behind them. Frowning, he searched the throng until his gaze found her where she stood on the porch, arms folded in defiance. For a long moment, they stared at each other, then his shoulders dropped and he looked away. After a moment, he turned his attention to the crowd.

"So, this is a big moment for us at Outlook, to take time to honor the guy who had the vision and determination to make this place happen." He glanced toward her. "Walt was insistent he didn't want the camp named after him. He even said if we changed the name after he died, he'd come back and haunt us until we changed it back. His photo is in the dictionary next to the word stubborn."

Laughter rolled through the crowd.

"After he died, we discussed how best to honor him, and finally decided on a larger-than-life statue to welcome everyone here because Walter Smith was larger-than-life to many of us."

But not everyone.

"This statue was created by a local wood carver who knew Walt well. Steve, come over here and say a few words. Everyone, Steve Roberts."

As the audience applauded, a lanky man approached Dawson, wispy gray hair flowing over bony shoulders. His slight frame was a contrast to the statue looming over him.

"Walt and I were friends from the first day he got to Winter Park," he said. "He was a good man, I'll tell you that. An' he was a storyteller. Man, he'd talk until you were asleep in your chair."

Dawson chuckled and nodded as did many gathering around the makeshift stage.

"He loved the Lord and he loved this camp. I'll tell ya, this was what he was meant to do. He lived quite a life and hoped it helped steer kids right." He paused, looking down at the ground as he sniffed.

From the size of the crowd, it seemed Kenny had touched many lives. Mikayla tightened her arms. He'd touched hers too, just not the same way.

"So anyways, when Daws here asked if I'd do something to honor Walt at camp, I jumped at it. I hope this statue does his big personality a bit of justice." He handed the mic to Dawson who took it and then pulled him into a hug.

Steve moved to one side of the figure as Dawson stood on the other, grasping the end of a long cord attached to the top of the canvas.

"When we're done here," Dawson said, "please stay as long as you'd like. We've got plenty to eat and drink, and we love hearing your stories about Walt. Ready? Ten, nine, eight..."

He scanned the crowd, obviously milking the moment, then went silent when his gaze met hers. Brenda looked from him to Mikayla as the countdown continued. She said something that made him blink and nod. He looked at Steve as the count finished. Together, they yanked the canvas, stepping out of the way as it crumpled to the ground. A roar of approval filled the air.

Mikayla caught her breath. How did anyone do such detailed work in a tree trunk? From the unlaced hiking boots to the wrinkled pants, plaid shirt and unzipped vest, the larger-than-life-sized figure seemed alive. At his belt was a hatchet, a walkie, and a knife.

One hand grasped a fishing pole, a stringer of fish at his feet, while the other pointed upward where his gaze was directed. A joyful smile creased the carved face, sunglasses propped on his head, a bandana around his neck. The smile, his curly hair—just like the photo Sara had given her.

The image blurred as pain creased her heart. An

overwhelming sadness swept over her, and she wheeled around, darting into the lodge, through the kitchen doors, and then out the back door. Standing amidst a cheering crowd lauding Kenny was the last place she could be.

- 32 -

Curled on her bed, arms wrapped around her pillow, she ignored the phone ringing in her back pocket. When it stopped, she relaxed, then stiffened when it rang again. At the third call, she yanked it from her pocket, intent on turning it off, then paused. Lindy.

She sat up and cleared her throat before answering. "Hey, Lin."

"Mikayla, you need to come home."

"I am. I'll leave here next Sat—"

"Now. You need to come now."

She rolled her eyes. More wedding drama.

"It's Mom. They think she had a heart attack."

"What? When? Is she okay?" *I should have answered her emails, at least to let her know I got them.*

"A few hours ago. Dad called from the ER and said they were admitting her. Mickie, please come home. *Now.*"

Mikayla paced the small room. If she flew home, she'd have to fly back for her car, but she couldn't afford that. She could drive straight through and be there tomorrow at this time. But what if Mom died before she got there? She'd been furious with her, but she didn't want her to die! What would that do to Dad? "Do you know for sure it's a heart attack?"

"They're running a bunch of tests. Dad said he'd keep me posted."

"Did you call Maggie?"

"Dad did. He said he tried to call you, but the calls wouldn't go through. I can't do this wedding without you and Mom." Lindy's voice wobbled. "I told Beau we'd have to postpone it until she's better and you're home."

"Don't postpone anything, Lin. Let's see how this plays out first. And I've told you a million times I'll be there. I'd never miss my bestie's wedding. Okay?"

"Okay. Just hurry home."

When Lindy hung up, Mikayla's finger hovered between Dad's number and Maggie's before hitting her sister's. As she'd suspected, Maggie had been in touch with the doctors.

"They're running tests," Maggie said, "that will give a clearer picture of what's happening. I'm glad Dad brought her in despite her saying no. Heart attack symptoms for women are often different from men, so at least now she's where they can monitor her."

"But she's young and healthy. She eats well, she exercises."

"Unfortunately, there are a lot of other factors to consider. Mental or emotional stress, issues like diabetes or a family history of heart problems, high blood pressure."

Mikayla's own heart skipped a beat. Emotional stress. Like the awful words she'd spewed at her mother in anger. "So it's probably—"

"Mikayla, we don't know for sure it's her heart. This is not your fault."

"Is she conscious? In pain?"

"She's been conscious the whole time. Dad said she's had some discomfort, but no pain."

"Could she..."

"Until we know what's going on, there's no way to know what's going to happen. There are no guarantees in life, Mikayla."

She'd come to believe that.

"That said," Maggie continued, "if you can head home now, that would be good for everyone. I have several surgeries scheduled over the next few days that I won't cancel unless I have to. The doc said he'll keep me updated."

Standing at the window, Mikayla looked down at the crowd milling about. Dawson stood near the lodge porch talking with several people. They laughed together, and the older woman hugged him.

"Mickie?"

Maggie's voice startled her. "Sorry. I'll leave first thing in the morning."

"Drive safe, hon. Let me know when you get in."

Hours later the camp was quiet, the celebration finally over. Several staffers stopped at her door and asked if she was okay. She gave brief updates to each, then thanked them for their friendship and hugged them goodbye. Brenda arrived and plopped into the desk chair, watching Mikayla pack as the story unfolded.

"I'm sorry about your mom, but selfishly I thought we'd

have you for another week."

Mikayla sighed. "I guess we can't schedule health issues." She pulled her hiking boots from the closet and stuck them in the duffel on her bed.

"Dawson is taking this hard," Brenda mused.

Mikayla flinched but kept packing. "I haven't told him yet."

Questions swirled in the silence.

"Then why does he look so miserable?"

She shrugged.

"Because I made a really bad decision." Dawson's voice came from the doorway.

Mikayla remained focused on folding jeans despite the sudden tremor in her fingers.

Brenda stood and joined her beside the bed. "I'm not going to say goodbye," she said, as Mikayla turned toward her. "I refuse to think you won't come back. We need you here." She hugged Mikayla tightly, and whispered, "Especially Daws."

Leaning back, she forced a wobbling smile, tears in her eyes. "You have a safe trip and keep us posted on your mom. And don't be a stranger, girlfriend."

Girlfriend. The endearment knotted Mikayla's throat. "Okay," she managed.

Brenda lightly punched Dawson's shoulder as she left the room, pulling the door closed behind her.

Mikayla faced Dawson reluctantly. His dark eyes looked back at her, brows drawn down, hair disheveled.

"We need to talk," he said, then added, "Or *I* need to talk."

The earlier emotions had dissipated with Lindy's call. It

would take the two-day drive home to untangle everything swirling inside. She nodded.

Lula circled him, looking up expectantly as he took in the suitcase and duffel. "Rob told me about your mom. I'm sorry to hear that. Will she be okay?"

"It might be a heart attack, so I need to get back there. I'll head out first thing in the morning. I'm sorry to leave you short staffed."

He took Brenda's spot on the chair, and Lula jumped onto his lap and licked his chin. "We'll work it out. You need to be with your family. I'll be praying for her, and for a safe trip for you."

"Thanks." She slowly folded another pair of jeans.

"Kayla, you have every right to be angry with me."

How big of him.

"It wasn't until a few weeks ago that I made the connection between the person you were looking for and Walt. He's been Walter Smith as long as I've known him. Apparently he started using his given name when he moved to Winter Park, so everyone around here only knows him as Walt."

"Except Joe."

"Except Joe," he echoed. "Since I met you, I've tried to figure out who you remind me of. Didn't occur to me it might be a guy. Then I started noticing that some of your mannerisms were familiar, and the way you laugh. When you said something about Kenny, that sparked a memory from my first year working here. We'd gotten mail for Kenny Johnson, and when I asked who that was, he laughed and said he'd been called that as a kid. I didn't think of it again until you said it. That's when the pieces started coming together."

She glanced sideways. "And that's when you should have said something."

"I should have," he agreed. "But I needed to talk to Joe first, to find out if he knew anything about Walt having a kid. Joe was sure Walt never knew. He wouldn't have kept that a secret."

"So *then* you could have said something."

"I know. I just...I couldn't figure out how. You'd talked about how hurt you were by all this, and I thought it might make things worse if you knew he had a good life here."

She quirked an eyebrow, and he lifted his shoulders.

"It doesn't make sense now, but I didn't know how you'd react. I was chicken, and I'm sorry." He studied her, a corner of his mouth lifting. "Kenny would have been proud of you."

Strangely, she didn't recoil at the thought. It didn't make her happy, but she didn't cringe as she would have three months ago. "He'd never have accepted my fear of heights."

He chuckled. "He'd have made you get over it."

"My dad never did. He's always accepted me as I am—irrational fears and all."

"Now that's a strong man."

She'd always thought he was the strongest, bravest, most perfect man in the world. He might be some of that, but he also had feet of clay. "He's a good guy."

"I'd like to meet him. He raised a pretty amazing outdoor professional."

Quite a compliment. At least he considered her a professional. She set a stack of folded T-shirts in the suitcase, then settled on the edge of her bed.

"Thanks for being here this summer," he said. "You've made an impact on the camp and on the kids. Both the staff and the kids have loved you."

"And I loved every minute." She ached for their easy banter on the mountain.

In silence, they stared at the floor between them. Sadness filled her chest, tinged with anger and regret. She lifted her head and looked at him. "All I've ever wanted is for people to be honest with me. The people I care about most are the ones who've lied to me. Why didn't you just tell me?"

He held her gaze for a long, silent moment, then stood abruptly, making her jump. He set Lula aside, strode forward and tugged Mikayla gently to her feet, then grasped her shoulders. "The main reason I didn't is completely selfish. A rule I've led camps by is to never let things get personal with a guest or a staff member, and I never have. But then you came along and even though I tried not to, I fell for you. Big time. I was afraid that once you knew the truth about Kenny you'd leave. And...I don't want you to go."

Mouth open, she stared at him.

"I figured if you didn't know Walt was Kenny, or Kenny was Walt, or whatever, then your search wouldn't be complete and you'd stay." He released her and stepped backward. "I had no right."

The pounding of her heart made her light-headed, and she sank back to the bed. He'd fallen for her?

He paced several steps one way then the other. Finally he faced her. 'I knew you had to go back for the wedding, but I've been afraid that once you leave, you won't come back. And I want you to." He stuffed his hands in his pockets and held her gaze. "It was totally selfish, and I'm really, really sorry."

No words formed as she looked back at him, tears in her eyes. If he'd just been honest, how different this moment might be. Now she needed space—to sort out everything that had happened these past months, how much she'd changed. And to figure out if she could learn to trust him again.

He swallowed hard. "We'll miss you around here. I'll be praying that everything works out for your family."

Lips pressed together, she nodded. She'd miss him. So much. The curls. Those impossible eyelashes. The dimple in his smile. How he made her laugh and think. And feel.

"Okay, well, I'll get out of here." He moved to the door, sweeping Lula up to nuzzle her. "You take good care of her, Lu. You hear me? We're counting on you."

Mikayla quickly brushed a tear from her cheek as he set the dog down and looked back at her.

"I'll be praying God blesses whatever you do. You have a gift, Kayla," he told her, appreciation warming his words. "And a great opportunity to share it through your work and your writing. Whatever you choose to do is going to impact a lot of people."

The knot in her throat made it impossible to speak. She stood and nodded again, tears still burning.

They looked at each other in pained silence, then he strode back and took her face in gentle, calloused hands. The corners of his mouth trembled, his dark eyes misty. "I already miss you," he said, then pressed a kiss to her forehead.

When the door closed with a gentle click, she remained still. A tear slipped from between her closed lids and slid down her cheek.

- 33 -

Just before midnight, Mikayla quietly took her suitcase and duffel to the jeep. There on the floor of the backseat lay the bag Old Joe had given her. She hadn't found the courage to open it, but now she was out of time. She wasn't going to take it back to Minnesota.

She pulled it out, packed her belongings, and took his bag back to her room. Sitting cross-legged on the bed, she stared at the battered old duffel. There couldn't be anything of monetary value in it, and certainly nothing of sentimental value, to her anyway. She yanked the zipper open, then pulled back from the musky aroma. Kenny's cologne must have been plenty pungent if it had stayed this strong for so long. She reached behind her and slid the window open, breathing deeply.

Lula climbed around and over the bag, sniffing with great interest. Maybe Kenny had owned a dog at some point. Hard to imagine someone with a phobia of commitment taking on a pet. Unless... Her eyes narrowed. Maybe Bruno and Pal had been his. That would make sense.

She squared her shoulders and opened the bag wide. A

worn leather-covered Bible sat on top. Setting it aside, she sorted through the rest. A hatchet, a dorky fishing hat like Dad's, a small tackle box, some books. *Moby Dick? Dante's Inferno?* She couldn't picture him reading anything, let alone classics. A few tattered maps. And a photo album.

She pulled the album onto her lap and flipped slowly through the pages. Parents, maybe. High school buddies. Medals, of course. Lots of guy friends mostly shirtless and holding beers. He was always easy to identify with that curly blond hair and engaging smile. She touched her ponytail where it hung over her shoulder.

There were a few of him with different young women. None of her mother. Why was that disappointing? The last few photos made her pause. Arms folded and wearing a proud smile, he stood on the front steps of a primitive version of the lodge. Probably what he'd built with Old Joe. A hand-carved sign overhead stated *Outlook Camp*. The start of a surprisingly ambitious venture for someone who'd never wanted to settle down.

The next were an older Kenny and a young Dawson fishing, arm wrestling, even praying together. There he and Dawson stood mugging for the camera in front of the new bunkhouse. And the two of them crouched beside a fire in dripping rain gear.

Dawson should have these. He should have all of it. None of it meant anything to her, but he might appreciate the mementos. She'd left Minnesota thinking the worst of Kenny Johnson, intent on uncovering information that would prove her right. Now, with all that was left of his belongings strewn across her bed, she saw the layers of a man she'd never meet. And still wasn't sure she'd want to. If he were alive and she met him tomorrow, her approach would be so different from what she'd planned at the start of her journey. Mainly thanks to Dawson.

She closed her eyes, chin quivering. *God? I'm tired of being angry at Kenny, and Mom and Dad. But I don't know where to go from here, how to fix things. I need honesty from people now. Everyone's cards on the table. And I need some distance between me and Dawson so I can think, but... Why is it so hard to leave him? Even knowing he kept such a big secret from me, I still don't want to go.*

In the answering silence, she released a long breath and waited for something. A lighted sign pointing toward Minnesota. A phone call. Silence. Yet deep inside a gentle nudge started, an ache to see Lin and Mags. A growing desire to see Dad again, even Mom.

Eyes brimming, she nodded. God might have to pry her fingers from the edge of the mountain range, but it was time. She repacked the bag and set it by the door, wrote brief notes to the team, and then wrote one last post on the Hiker Girl blog, musing on the pain of saying farewell, and on what the future might hold.

After snapping off the light, she breathed a prayer into the dark. *Please let me come back someday. Please.*

Mikayla slid a note under each staffer's door, then went out into the brisk pre-dawn air to set Kenny's duffel bag on the lodge porch, propping her note to Dawson on top. She stood a moment, hand pressed against the solid wood door, then set her shoulders and went down the steps to the jeep, Lula at her heels.

Her heart skipped when she saw a white envelope tucked under the wiper blade. She retrieved it and climbed into the jeep. Her trembling fingers struggled to open the flap that was soggy from morning dew. Inside was the bracelet Dawson wore every day, *Remember* imprinted into the leather. The word blurred as she ran a finger across the letters, wrestling against the aching need to stay.

With a sharp, steadying breath, she blinked the tears away, slipped the bracelet on, and started the jeep. Leaving the grounds, she glanced at Kenny's likeness where it stood guard at the entrance and managed a single nod.

Though there was little movement in town, she wasn't surprised to see lights on in the Wildflower Café. Much as she'd hoped to slip away after leaving a note for her special friend, Violet's voice stopped her as she tiptoed away after propping the envelope on the window box.

"Now what in the world has you out at this hour?" she demanded from the doorway, hands on her hips.

Shoulders hunched like a child caught red-handed, Mikayla turned back. "Just leaving you a note."

"Don't you dare think of leaving town without talking to me." She waved an arm. "You and Lula come right in here and talk to me while I get the cinnamon rolls in the oven. Come on."

When Mikayla opened the jeep door, Lula shot out with an excited yip and bounded into the shop. Mikayla followed more slowly. Talking with Vi would only make leaving harder. Settled at the counter with a steaming mug before her, she watched through a window that separated the shop from the kitchen as her friend filled a rectangular baking pan with shaped rolls and slid it into the commercial oven, then set a timer.

She emerged through the swinging doors, poured herself a cup of coffee, and leaned on the counter. "Okay, spill. What has you sneaking away before dawn?"

As the full story unfolded, Violet nodded, frowned, and nodded again. "So you're Walt's daughter. I should have seen that."

"Did you ever know him as Kenny?" Why hadn't she simply asked if she knew Walter at the beginning? If she had, she wouldn't have gotten to know Dawson. She glimpsed a heavenly chess game, and her breath caught.

"Everyone only knew him as Walt," Vi said. "But now I remember a couple of thugs coming in here not long after Walt got to town, looking for someone named Kenny. They were pretty rough and threatening, so I'm glad I told them there'd never been a Kenny Johnson in town. Which was true."

Mikayla smiled. "You didn't even know you were protecting Walt."

"I would have done the same if I'd known," she declared.

"Dear Vi, you are such a gift to this town."

"Go on. You, on the other hand, have been a gift for our Dawson." She sipped her coffee. "Never seen him so happy.

The last time he was in here, he was full of ideas, and all of them included you."

Tears burned again and Mikayla looked away. Vi's hand on her arm was warm, comforting. "Darlin', you need to go home, and take care of your mama, and get things right with your family. But nothing says you can't come back."

Mikayla fingered the bracelet and sighed. Except for the possibility of her proposal getting picked up which would keep her busy for years. "It will be too late by then."

The timer beeped in the kitchen, and Vi patted her arm before going back through the swinging doors. Mikayla had finished her coffee and slid a five-dollar bill under the register when Vi returned carrying a square bakery box.

"Oh, no, you don't." Violet retrieved the money and slid it under the red ribbon tied around the box. "The ten you left me last time pays for today's coffee." She wrapped Mikayla in a hug that spoke calm and encouragement into her heart. "We won't say goodbye because I have a feeling I'll see you again."

Violet leaned back and wiped the tears from Mikayla's cheeks. "Go do what needs to be done, and then be open to what God is calling you to next. Whatever it is, it will be good. Now, get on your way before the Denver traffic gets too crazy." She handed the box to Mikayla, then bent down to stroke Lula's head. "I hope I'll see you again too, Lula."

Mikayla pulled away from the shop with a wave, determined to believe she'd see Vi and Abe, and Brenda and the Outlook staff again. Following the winding road out of town, she squinted against the rising sun at a sign propped in a tree, then laughed. *Minnie-sohtah!* was painted in bright blue letters. No doubt Brenda's handiwork. Another sign was propped against a boulder. *U rock!*

Farther down the road, a sign rested against a tree. *Remember.* Her smile wobbled. These weren't from Brenda. They were Dawson's. She glanced at the leather bracelet. Of course she'd remember. This place had changed her.

Around another bend, a sign up on the hill—*Sing.* Maybe she'd hear music in the woods of Minnesota. She sighed. It wouldn't be the same, but it would remind her of Dawson. The next sign was a cross, and her heart sighed. Perhaps he hadn't been totally truthful about Walt, but he'd shared the greatest truth of all, and for that she'd always be grateful.

One more curve and there, at the end of the straight-away, a sign moved high above the road. As she neared, a strangled sob broke out. Dawson stood on an outcropping, waving a big red heart. Lula jumped up, paws on the dashboard, barking excitedly.

Mikayla slowed to imprint the image in her mind, then gave farewell honks as she passed. She watched him in the rearview mirror until she went around the next bend and cried until Denver came into sight.

- 34 -

"Anybody home?" Mikayla stood in the doorway of the familiar townhome and listened. "Guess I should have let her know when I was getting in." Red roses filled a clear vase on the coffee table, and she leaned close to breathe in the fragrance. "Well, Lu, this is our home until the wedding. Then you'll go back to your mama, and I'll find a new place."

Lindy's text last night said Mom had been released and was resting comfortably at home. No sign of a heart attack or damage. Reading the news, Mikayla had to fight the overwhelming urge to head back to Colorado. No, her journey to find Kenny Johnson was over. Her focus now had to be on building her future.

She set her luggage in her bedroom, then went to the kitchen to make coffee. What a disaster! She now had proof that Lindy was the messy one. Boxes lining one wall of the dining area looked like wedding gifts. Lots of expensive wedding gifts. An assortment of wedding favors littered the table, along with candles, holders, and various-shaped vases clustered together.

Lula darted from room to room, sniffing, exploring, then checking on Mikayla before bounding off on another adventure. Mikayla sighed, watching her happy companion. She'd have to consider getting a dog of her own once she landed somewhere. Life would be way too quiet, not to mention lonely, without a furry buddy to share it with.

The front door opened. "Mickie?"

She popped out of the kitchen, gratified by Lindy's squeal. Bags and a large purse scattered as her sister dashed forward and caught Mikayla in a heart-stopping squeeze. "You're home!"

"As promised." They exchanged tear-stained grins.

Beau joined them, smothering Mikayla in a hug when Lindy finally released her. "Welcome home, Mikayla. You've been missed, especially by me."

She laughed as Lindy elbowed him. "Getting cold feet now that you've had a taste of what life alone with Lin will be like?"

He cut his nod short when Lindy pouted up at him. Wrapping her in an over-zealous hug, he said, "Of course not! What's not to love about life with a crazed bride-to-be who missed her sister more than I think she'd ever miss me?"

Lindy wiggled out of his grasp and hugged Mikayla again. "I didn't know when you were coming, or I'd have been here. Oh, and that must be Lula. She's adorable." She scooped the wriggling, wagging furball into her arms and held Lula's face close to hers. "Wouldn't I be a cute dog owner?" She batted her lashes at Beau.

"No dogs. No. Dogs." His firm response was met with a huff. "We'll have enough of an adjustment learning to live together after the wedding."

"You don't need a dog when you're starting married life," Mikayla added.

Beau mouthed "Thank you" and retrieved the bags they'd brought in. "I'll put these on your bed, hon, and then get out of here so the nonstop talking can commence."

Once he'd left, Mikayla filled coffee mugs and settled beside Lindy on the couch. "Your last text said they let Mom go home."

"Yup. More tests to be done, but they're pretty sure it wasn't a heart attack."

"So what was it? It couldn't have been heartburn if they kept her overnight."

Lindy lifted her shoulders. "The doc said it could be a reaction to stress. And seriously, what could be more stressful than my wedding? I'm surprised *I* haven't had a heart attack. We can head over to see her later if you want, but for now I want to hear everything. Especially about Dawson Dunne. Even his name is cute. You must have tons of photos. I love, love, love the blog. How was the camp? I can't believe you slept on a mountain with bears and such wandering around. I'd never have closed my eyes. What did you find out—"

Mikayla lifted a hand, giggling. "Okay, okay. Give me a chance, and I'll tell you everything, I promise. I just..." She sighed, studying her sister's familiar face. "I need to appreciate being home again. I missed you."

Lindy's eyes filled with tears. "Thank you for coming back. It's been awful without you."

They clasped hands and leaned their foreheads together.

"I can't believe we're not actually related," Mikayla said.

"Legally we are," came the correction. Lindy leaned back and forced a smile. "And in every other way that matters. Just not by blood." She waved long manicured fingers. "That's a technicality."

"We could do that thing where we cut our fingers and share blood." Mikayla watched her sister's face contort. "You know, that blood sister thing kids do."

"Like I said, a technicality. And you know I hate anything to do with blood."

"Good luck with childbirth."

"I'm already planning on lots of drugs."

They shared a giggle, then Lindy waved her on. "Okay, let's hear it. From the beginning."

Mikayla wandered back through months of memories. "It seems like I've been gone a lot longer than three months."

"It felt like three years to me. So you went to Aunt Cindy's and then what?"

Walking through the journey again, this time from an outside perspective, Mikayla marveled at how each day, every new event was a building block. The chess board image flashed again, and she smiled.

"So that's how you met Dawson Dunne? Playing Florence Nightingale on a mountain?"

Mikayla laughed. "I guess that's one way to put it."

"And he was so impressed by your skills and captivated by your beauty that he hired you on the spot." Lindy did love a good romance.

"Not exactly. But we ran into each other at a coffee shop

the next day, and that's when he offered the job."

"Which you accepted immediately, of course."

"Nope."

Lindy rolled her eyes. "You don't know the first thing about romance stories, do you?"

She did now. "I'm not going to change things to fit your romanticized version. Anyway, I called him later and got a tour of the camp, and *then* I said yes."

"Finally! Then what? Wait, let me get us a refill."

With their mugs full, Mikayla shared some of the camping experiences, playing up the bear-scare event.

Lindy sighed at the part where Dawson charged off with his rifle. "A real-life hero. I need to see some pictures before you say any more."

Mikayla retrieved her laptop and clicked through a handful before stopping on one of her and Dawson side-by-side, backpacks on, ready to head up to her first True Adventure Camp.

Lindy's brown eyes went wide. "Wow! Mickie, he's gorgeous!"

She smiled fondly at the photograph, lightly touching his bracelet on her wrist that had been so comforting on the long drive home. "He is. I'm sure most of the female guides he's worked with have had a crush on him at some point." The smile faded, and she clicked on the next photo—Lula with Bruno and Pal.

Lindy burst into a fit of giggles. "Look how tiny she is compared to them!"

The next photo made her laugh harder—Lula standing on

Bruno's back, her expression victorious, Bruno's head drooping. "That is so cute! You need to post that on Hiker Girl."

"Both of those big boys were afraid of her for a while. Even once they got used to each other, she was definitely the alpha dog. It was funny. To the humans, anyway. The boys were always on edge because she wasn't afraid to put them in line."

As they looked through more photos, Lindy's phone buzzed. She checked it and looked at Mikayla. "It's Dad."

Her heart did a two-step as she shrugged.

"Hey, Dad. Yup, she's home. Yes, she's fine." She rolled her eyes at Mikayla. "I don't know. I'll ask." She covered the phone. "Do you want to meet them for dinner? We could go to their house, or out somewhere. Or wait until tomorrow."

"Mom's up to it?"

"Dad? Are we sure it's okay for Mom?" She listened, then nodded at Mikayla.

Both parents her first night back? Mikayla wiped her palms against her jeans. No point putting it off. "Not at the house," she whispered.

"Okay, Dad? Let's meet at that new pasta place. Wellington's, right. And you're sure Mom feels up to it? Okay. Yes, 6:30 would be great. See you there."

The silliness gone, they sat in silence before Lindy tossed the phone aside. "Will things ever be normal again?"

"Not the way they were. This is our new normal."

"I don't like it. Sometimes I'm so mad at them, then other times I just want life to go back the way it was. And then I wonder who my other parents are."

"Yup."

Lindy shifted to face her. "How are you? Really."

Missing Dawson and the camp like crazy. Homesick for the mountains. Longing for a noisy game of cards with Brenda and the guys. "I'm okay. I've done lots of thinking about what really matters, what I want in life, who I want to share my life with."

"And you've come up with..."

"Spending the summer in Colorado made me realize I want to keep doing what I've been doing. Writing about my outdoor experiences, creating ways for girls and women to enjoy what God created. I love being outdoors more than anything, Lin. It's where I feel the most me. And I learned that being me is okay. I don't love fashion like you, but I think I could learn how to be feminine and sporty at the same time." She grinned. "Maybe even wear lip gloss while I'm camping."

"Yes!" Lindy's fist pump made them giggle, then her face lit up. "Hey! Maybe we can create a whole new line of active-wear for women."

"I think that's been done."

Lindy winked. "Not designed by fashionista Lindy Gordon, it hasn't."

Mikayla rolled her eyes. "I also learned I don't need much to live on."

Lindy made a buzzer noise that set them giggling again.

"And most importantly I learned that truth matters. No matter how difficult it might be, honesty is always best."

"Agreed."

"I've also figured out that family matters." She squeezed

Lindy's hand. "But family comes in different forms. I have my family here, where we share a lifetime of memories, and I don't ever want to give that up. But I also have a family at Outlook, where family means working together toward a common goal, depending on each other, sharing daily life."

Lindy studied her. "You're different."

"Tell me something I don't know."

"I mean different from when you left. From who you were before. There's a calmness you didn't have. But sadness too."

"I learned things I didn't really want to know. That's been painful. But I found my way to God, thanks to Dawson. Being out there where nature is breathtaking and there's endless silence, I heard the mountains sing. It changed the way I see life."

Lindy nodded slowly. "I can see that. I want to know more. But now..." She glanced at her watch. "We'd better get ready to meet Mom and Dad."

As Mikayla unpacked and changed, Lindy's words swirled around her. *You're different.* She paused, studying her reflection in the mirror over her dresser. That girl didn't look different on the outside, but there was something in her eyes. She leaned closer. The anger was gone, but there was a new wariness. She'd learned to believe in herself, but lost trust in others. Most importantly, she'd learned to trust God.

She finished dressing and glanced at the girl before leaving the room. There was work to be done starting tonight. *God, lead me and give me strength.*

Following Lindy into the restaurant, Mikayla pushed back against the nerves that made her nauseous. *They're your parents, not the mafia. And they've had a lot to deal with these past months too.*

"They're back there." Lindy pointed toward the corner, then reached for Mikayla's hand. "Ready?"

"No, but here goes." As they neared the table, she bit back tears. Dad had flecks of gray at his temples that hadn't been there when she left. And Mom, always strong and in charge, looked tiny beside him. She slid into the chair next to Dad and managed a nervous smile. "Hey, Dad."

"Hey, kid."

She moved her gaze across the table.

Tears shimmered in Mom's eyes. "Welcome home, sweetheart."

"Thanks, Mom." She'd last seen her mother through the red haze of fury and hurt. "How are you feeling?"

"Better, now that you're home. Really, I feel good. The discomfort is long gone, and they've ruled out a heart attack. I think I wasn't taking care of myself, and it caught up with me." She smiled. "I'm taking it as a warning to get focused. Right after the wedding."

Dad put his hand over hers. "Right now," he said, and they exchanged smiles.

"I'm glad it wasn't a heart attack." Mikayla would never have forgiven herself if her mother had died before they could reconnect. *Thank you for a chance to start over, God. Show me how.*

"Okay," Lindy said. "Let's order, and then we can talk about the last of the wedding plans."

They studied their menus in silence until the waiter arrived with a platter of water glasses. After he took their order, Lindy pulled a tattered notebook out of her oversized, expensive bag. "Okay. So the girls have their dresses except for Mickie. You need to have your fitting tomorrow. And the guys have had their final tux fittings. Dad, is yours scheduled?"

She chattered on about flowers and favors, napkins, and the live band they'd added. Mikayla watched in amusement—Lindy in her element. How different it looked from her own element of climbing a mountain path in hiking boots, jeans, and a T-shirt. The change of attitude surprised her. Instead of feeling threatened that she didn't measure up, she was simply happy that Lin was happy. She blinked at the realization and took a long sip of water.

Dad leaned toward her. "I've seen that epiphany on your face before," he said as Lindy and Mom continued chatting. "Care to share?"

She smiled. "I've learned a lot about myself this summer. Right now it's realizing I'm not threatened by how different Lindy and I are. It's something to appreciate."

"Glad you finally see that. The three of you have skills and knowledge in very different areas of life, and that's how it should be. God designed each of us to be unique, not carbon copies."

"God?" Neither of her parents had talked about faith or God.

His rugged cheeks pinkened. "Through the upheaval of

this summer, your mom and I started going to church. It's made a world of difference for us personally, and for our marriage. I wish we'd made faith a bigger part of your childhood."

Wow. She'd never have dreamed that would happen, certainly hadn't thought to pray about it. Dawson would have.

"I connected with God over the summer too," she said. "My friend and boss, Dawson, shared his faith story with me while we were leading groups of kids, and I realized it's what I've been missing."

He sat back, grinning like the Dad she remembered. "I knew something was different about you, kid."

"I also learned some new fishing techniques, so be prepared," she added. The declaration startled her. She'd wondered how they would start rebuilding their relationship.

His dark eyes were shiny, his Adam's apple bobbing as he struggled for words. "I've done some practicing myself," he managed. "Challenge accepted."

Something heavy fell away from her heart as they smiled at each other.

Lindy and Mom looked at them, waiting.

"One thing I haven't told anyone yet," Mikayla said, "is that Ted called last week to say the board is reconsidering my proposal."

"What? That's fabulous! It's about time." They all spoke at once.

"I don't know what it all means and, to be honest, I'm not sure I want to go back to the magazine. There's a lot to think about. I'll meet with Ted after the wedding and get more details. Just thought it was fun news."

"Very fun." Lindy squeezed her hand. "You amaze me. I can't imagine how you write such beautiful words, take fabulous pictures, and stay so humble. I'd be a total diva."

They laughed at the accuracy of her statement.

"Will you still love me if I am?" Lindy asked Mikayla, a twinkle in her smile.

"Of course, but I'll have to knock you down a peg or two when we're together."

"And I'll appreciate it. After the fact, of course."

By the time they'd finished dessert and left the restaurant, Mikayla was able to walk beside Dad with a peaceful heart. There was a long road of healing ahead, but this was a start. Now if she could stop missing Dawson, she'd face the future with more anticipation.

- 35 -

The following week was filled with activity, laughter, melt-downs, and hugs. Mikayla ran errands, fixed broken heels, and assured Lindy everything would be fine before running more errands. Her heart ached to be outdoors, for peace and solitude instead of endless chatter, to-do lists, and deci-sion-making.

Not yet ready to be alone with Dad, she'd gone fishing on her own several mornings. In the early stillness, she'd listened intently. The lake didn't sing to her, but instead whispered to her heart. It wasn't life in the mountains, but it was good.

Every evening she settled into bed with Lula beside her and the Bible from Dawson on her lap, eager to discover something that would encourage her, challenge her. There was always a nugget or two to ponder, and she longed to share it with him.

By Friday afternoon she'd ignored the persistent niggling long enough. She'd dreaded this conversation to the point of nausea, but it was time, whether she was ready or not. She parked in front of her parents' house and sat for a moment to quiet her pounding heart. "Ready, Lu?"

At the front door she closed her eyes, whispering a prayer for calm and for the right words, then pressed the doorbell with her shoulders back and chin lifted.

The door swung open, and her mother smiled in surprise, then her face crumpled. "Oh, Mikayla." Tears in her eyes, she held out her arms, and Mikayla stepped into the hug, Lula prancing around them on two feet. As her mother released her, she stepped back, eyes burning, and managed a pained smile.

"Come in, please." Mom backed up so Mikayla could enter and bent to pet Lula. "Hello, Lula. I haven't seen you since you were a new puppy."

Mikayla sank down on the couch, grateful for Lula's presence. How would she have managed all these months without her? An image formed of Pal, the hulking black German shepherd, cowering before this bossy pixie. Her guard dog. And her best friend on a bumpy ride.

"I just made a fresh pot of coffee. Can I get you a cup?"

Mikayla started to decline, then nodded. "Sure." When Mom returned, she accepted the mug and pulled in an appreciative breath. "Mmm. Smells great."

"From a new coffee shop we found." Her mother settled in a chair and took a sip. "Just the right blend for us. Not too strong." She offered a shaky smile. "Thank you for coming over."

Mikayla nodded. "A lot has happened this summer."

"Mmhmm. Nothing will be the same, will it? But I think it will be better now."

Better? Mikayla cocked her head. "Perhaps."

"Your father and I have done a lot of work these past months. I've been so thankful he was willing to stay and work on our marriage. It was long overdue. We excel at avoidance, and there were things we needed to face from thirty years ago, as well as current issues."

"He said you've been going to church."

Her pale face lit, a sparkle in her blue eyes. "We found a wonderful church not far from here. It's changed how we see life and each other. And the three of you."

They finally had something in common. "That's great. Faith has become important to me too."

"I'm glad. That's something good that's come from all... this." She set her mug down and folded her hands in her lap. "You didn't respond to my email, but I'm assuming you got it?"

"I did." She'd never figured out what to say. "I appreciated your honesty."

"Everything is out there now, honey. No more secrets." Her eyes filled. "I'm so sorry I created such a mess and didn't own up to it until it was too late."

"It's easier to ignore the hard stuff," Mikayla conceded. "I'm guilty of that too."

Mom blinked the tears away and nodded. "It's hard to be honest, but it's much harder dealing with the fallout."

"And now we know that from experience."

They sat quietly, Lula snuggled on her mother's lap. Mikayla looked around the familiar living room, memories popping out of corners, sweeping down the stairs. Family times. The angst of three teenage girls. Games and holidays and meals.

"Tell me what you've learned this summer," Mom prompted.

Mikayla leaned back, releasing a long breath. "What I've learned. Boy, there's been so much. I guess the first thing is the importance of DNA."

Her mother flinched.

"My primary DNA comes from God." *Thank you, Dawson.* "I'm a child of God first. After that come my human genes. When I left here, I had taken on those human genes as my identity—illegitimate, unplanned, a mistake. While I was on my search, I learned that where those genes came from doesn't define *me*. That was pretty huge." She smiled. "I'm learning to be comfortable in who God made me."

Fingers pressed to her lips, blonde head bobbing, Mom tried several times before words formed. "My mistake never defined who you are. *You've* done that, and it's been wonderful to watch."

"But you never liked who I was." Saying it aloud pinched.

"That's not true." Setting Lula on the floor, Mom sat beside Mikayla on the couch and touched her arm. "Mikayla, you were a miracle to me. The whole pregnancy, labor and delivery, bringing home a child I'd birthed. I never thought I'd have that experience. Every moment was wonderful. But the funny thing was that from the beginning, you gravitated toward your father.

"Nothing I did seemed to work for you. If you were upset, he was the one who could comfort you. When you played with toys, you didn't want anything I chose. While Maggie loved books, and Lindy loved dolls and girl things, you preferred physical activity. And you loved being outside. I was torn between two girls who loved being *in* the house and one who wanted out all the time. I'd have to drag you in kicking and screaming at night. And bath time?" She waved a hand with a laugh. "Only if I bribed you."

"Sorry." Mikayla grinned. "I like baths now."

"You were so comfortable just being you." She smiled at memories Mikayla couldn't see. "You knew exactly who you were and what you wanted. And I felt so..." Her smile faded. "Inadequate."

Mikayla's jaw fell. "You?"

"The stronger you became in who you were, the less adequate I felt. I knew how to communicate with Lindy and Maggie, but it seemed I was an afterthought for you. Off you and Dad would go on your adventures and come back happily dirty, sharing inside jokes. I never knew what I did wrong."

Who was the child she was describing? "But...that's not who I was. I never fit in. I felt so inferior next to gorgeous, perfect Lindy, and Brainiac Maggie. The only things I was good at weren't girl things."

"Oh, honey, *you* were the one who knew what you liked. Lindy always worried about what her friends were wearing, how they did their hair, what makeup they wore. She's grown into a self-assured young woman who has a flair for creating her own trends, but that was never her while you were growing up."

Mikayla stared across the room, seeing her mother trying

to braid her hair while she fumed at the interruption to her outdoor plans. Her mother waving her and Dad off on an adventure, a strangely sad expression in her eyes.

"It was when you hit your teen years that you started to question yourself and your interests," Mom continued. "Those were tough years to be blazing your own trail."

Their eyes met, and they smiled at the choice of words.

"I was off blazing a trail," Mikayla agreed, "but as lonely as a kid can be. I made my first real friend this summer in Colorado—a woman like me who loves being outdoors." She smiled wistfully. "We had so much fun."

Mom returned to her chair and squared her thin shoulders. "Honey, about Kenny. I very rarely thought of him while you were growing up. I hadn't known him very well." Her cheeks blazed pink. "I realize that doesn't make you feel better, but I want you to know I never spent time wondering if you were his. You were so like your father—same sense of humor, love of the outdoors, fearlessness. You idolized him and he adored you."

A shadow darkened her face. "This summer was so hard for him. From finding out you'd gone without saying goodbye, to the reason why, to coming to grips with the mess we'd made of our marriage—he really struggled. We both did. Finding a good counselor and going back to church literally saved our marriage and helped him regain his footing. I'm sure his emails were difficult for you. Especially the last one."

Mikayla glanced away. "You saw it?"

"He showed me every email he sent, and I showed him mine. He cried when he sent that one."

She hadn't responded to that either.

"We've all learned the importance of honesty in a relationship," her mother added. "The truth will always come out, but we can do damage control by owning our mistakes, asking forgiveness, and working through the fallout. It breaks my heart that we all had to learn that the hard way."

They certainly had.

After a lengthy silence, Mom stood. "Let's go bake some cookies before your dad gets home."

Mikayla met her gaze, a smile forming. Making cookies had been the one thing she'd loved doing with Mom. "Sounds good."

As they measured, mixed, shaped, and baked, Mikayla shared snippets of her Outlook experience. The memories made her smile even as her heart ached. Mom asked questions, shuddered at the thought of camping on the mountain, and smiled proudly when Mikayla mentioned beating the guys at some of the staff contests.

While they laughed over Lula's antics at their feet, the door opened from the garage.

"Something smells great in here," came her father's voice. "And it sounds like I'm missing the party."

He stepped into view and stopped when he saw Mikayla. His hesitation broke her heart. Hands sticky with dough, she walked over and wrapped her arms around him. He hugged her tightly, pressing a kiss to her head. "It's about time my fishing buddy came home."

She leaned back and managed a wobbling smile. "Prepare to lose, Pops," she said.

He chuckled. "Remember, I've been practicing." Then he sobered. "Mikayla, you're the light of my life. Nothing will ever change that. God blessed me with three beautiful, amazing daughters, and I will be forever grateful."

His assurance, mirroring what her mother had told her, brought a fresh rush of tears as she nodded. "And I'm blessed with the best dad ever."

"We're good?"

Her smile bloomed. She glanced toward her mother, who watched with tears brimming, and nodded, pressing against him. "We're all good."

Mikayla had sent a brief email to Dawson when she arrived home, then stayed away from her computer to avoid the urge to keep the conversation going. The wedding had forced her to come home, but depending on what Ted had to say, she might not have the chance to return.

Tonight, however, she needed to connect with him. She'd enjoyed baking cookies with her mother, and then having dinner with both parents, something she'd been sure on her journey she'd never do again. Now she sat in the quiet of her bedroom and toyed with the phone as Lula snored quietly on her tiny bed.

He's probably on the mountain, or busy hanging with the team. She set the phone aside, got ready for bed, then slid under the covers and opened her Bible, Lula now nestled beside her. When she'd read the same passage three times without remembering a word, she snatched the phone and called him. Part of her prayed he wouldn't answer—

"Hey! Mikayla!"

The joy-filled greeting knotted her throat, and she struggled to answer.

"Kayla? You okay?"

"Yeah. Sorry." She cleared her throat. "I'm fine. It's just good to hear your voice."

"It's great to hear yours." The smile in his familiar voice warmed her heart. "What's been going on out there in Minnie-sohtah?"

She giggled and relaxed against the pillows. "It's been crazy. I want to hear what's happening out there first. Has the camp fallen apart without me?"

They traded news and laughter, the old banter filling her heart with a joy she'd ached for. When she related the conversation with her mother, he grew quiet.

"Wow," he said finally. "I've been praying for God to create a way for you to reconnect with them. I'm blown away that it's already happened."

She should have known he'd be praying. "I thought maybe we'd somehow start a conversation that would take a while to unfold, but the way it happened, it had to be God directing it. We cleared up a lot of misunderstandings. And I'm going fishing with my dad tomorrow morning, which will give us a chance to do the same."

"Then I'll pray about that conversation too."

"Thanks." She closed her eyes, longing for just a whiff of mountain air. "God changed me this summer, and you were a big part of that. Thanks for being so patient with me."

"That was never an issue, Kayla. Every conversation we had was great. I learned a lot from you too."

She laughed. "Like what?"

"Like a fancier way to filet a fish. And the best way to throw a hatchet."

"And don't you forget where you learned it. Well, I'd better turn in. We're heading into the final week, and there will be a million things to get done. Mainly it's about keeping Lin calm and sane until Saturday. After that it'll be Beau's problem."

His chuckle sent bumps along her arms. "I'm sure you'll excel at that. Thanks for calling, Kayla. It's a relief to know things are going well for all of you."

"Thanks. Say hi to everyone."

She lay still in the dark, pressing the phone over her aching heart. She needed to be here—rebuilding relationships, helping Lin, and planning her future. But she wanted to be there—sitting in awe beneath an impossibly black sky glittering with stars, fishing in a clear mountain stream, listening to the mountains sing. With Dawson.

Turning on her side, she squeezed her eyes shut and listened, straining to hear the music. Almost...

- 36 -

During a lull in the activities of the wedding week, Mikayla called Ted to set a meeting date. After settling on Tuesday after the wedding, he shared his new plan for the magazine.

"We've needed to restructure for a while, but I just haven't had the time to make plans. With this new idea taking shape, however, I made time to look at where we are and where we'd like to go.

"We're establishing a Creative Development department to focus on new ideas and identify new markets. They'll work in tandem with the existing team, so we blend what's working with new ideas and technologies. The goal is to keep our current readership happy while drawing in a new, younger crowd."

"Great plan."

"Good, because I want you to lead it. Initially you'll have an assistant and one full-time staff until we can increase the budget. I know that's not enough for such a big undertaking, but I also know you'll pull it off brilliantly. You've got the visionary skills, plus the creative talent to run with it."

Mikayla stared out the kitchen window, frozen as his words sunk in. He was not just offering her the old job, he was creating a whole department. For her to run.

"The pay would be substantially higher, of course," he continued. "We'll need to discuss whether you want to continue with the column or assign it to someone else. And you'll have the new mag to work on, assuming the board has come to its senses."

"I uh...wow," she managed. "You really have been doing some planning."

"Your proposal and subsequent departure were the kick in the pants I needed to make necessary changes. I think the new plans have energized the board." A muffled voice in the background interrupted. "Mikayla, my next appointment is here. Think about what I said, see what ideas come to mind, and we'll talk next Tuesday. I can't wait to get started. Enjoy the wedding!"

She barely managed a response before the call disconnected. *Wait—what just happened?*

"Hey, Mickie, could you look at... What's wrong?" Lindy stood in the kitchen doorway, a necklace dangling from her fingers. Her brow lowered. "Who was on the phone?"

Mikayla opened and closed her mouth as she tried to absorb the conversation. "Ted. That was Ted."

"Did he offer you your job back?"

"Yes. No. He's creating a new department and wants me to run it."

Lindy squealed and flung her arms around Mikayla. "Yes! It's about time they recognize your talent and importance to the magazine. Are you excited?"

She should be. "I, uh... It hasn't sunk in yet. And nothing's official. We'll talk on Tuesday when I see him."

"Then I'll be excited for both of us. Now, do you think you can unknot this?" She held out the delicate chain. "I tried, but I made it worse."

Mikayla settled at the kitchen table and focused on un-doing the mess Lindy had created. Questions and thoughts became as tangled as the necklace. Start a new department. Implement new ideas. A tingle ran down to her toes. She could create her own outlets focused on women that would bring in new readership. Hold fun events to introduce skills, promote female-focused outings, and raise visibility for the magazine. Maybe some mother-daughter events. Definitely girlfriend outings.

Whoa, there. You'd be back in an office all day. The office where Leif works, remember? When would you have time to be outdoors? Unless you were the one leading those events. Your staff would keep things running in the office while you let the creativity flow, right? But what about going back to Colorado someday?

When the last of the knot loosened, she rubbed her eyes and then her temples. Ted's idea had not only created chaos in her head, now she had an ache in her chest, a longing to grab hold of both worlds. This job was far beyond what she'd hoped she'd get to do someday, and now it was being offered to her with a pay increase.

Dawson had said once that work was necessary for any-thing worthwhile, but he hadn't mentioned she might have to give up part of her heart in the process. Returning the necklace to Lindy's room, she shook the discussion out of her head. She needed to focus on these last few days with Lindy and Mags. Three sisters about to add a brother to the mix. That might be more frightening than running her own department.

"Can I have everyone's attention please? Eyes up here. Thank you." The wedding coordinator stood on the stage in the sanctuary of Beau's church. From the start of rehearsal to now, she'd gone from polished and calm to a bit disheveled, sweat showing on her brow.

Mikayla hid a grin as she turned fully to face the front. Maggie's comment in her ear with the same observation made her snort in response.

"Good. Thank you. Now, bride and groom. Are you ready for a full run-through? Wait, did we lose the groom again?"

The groomsmen traded glances and shrugs. "Probably in the restroom."

She put a hand to her forehead as she searched the sanctuary. "Could someone find him, please? No, just one of you. Thank you. Where's our bride?"

Mikayla and Maggie waved from the back of the sanctuary and pointed at Lindy standing behind them.

"Good. Ladies, you may go out to the foyer and wait for my cue. Dads and moms, you too."

Trailing Lindy and their parents, Mikayla and Maggie shared a grin. "Let's hope tomorrow isn't this big of a circus,"

Mikayla whispered.

"Crossing fingers and toes. If it is, she'll probably look for a new line of work. Lin is holding up surprisingly well, don't you think?"

Lindy stood calmly with the four parents, watching for Beau to appear. When he did, tucking in his shirt, she smiled and turned to Dad, reaching for his arm. Mikayla bit her lip to keep her mouth from falling open. Months of hysteria and *now* she was calm?

Beau stiffly escorted his mother down the aisle, his father beaming behind them as if this were the actual event. He returned for their mother, then took his place beside the pastor, wiping the sheen from his upper lip. The coordinator cued the first bridesmaid and groomsman, smiling as the group performed their duties without the earlier silliness.

Awaiting her turn, Mikayla glanced back at Lindy and mouthed, "Got your back." Lindy nodded and winked. This weekend she'd lose her twin to married life, and next week she'd meet with Ted to design her future. So much change in so few days. No wonder there was chaos in her heart.

Beau's brother offered his arm, which she took with a smile. The groomsmen had barely noticed her. They preferred flirting with the prettier, flashier bridesmaids. Maggie didn't seem to care, and Mikayla tried not to. She wasn't the flirty kind. But it would be nice to be noticed.

Dawson had. Her heart squeezed as they processed down the aisle behind Maggie and her groomsman and took their places at the front. Dawson had admired her skills, encouraged her to try new things. He'd liked her for her. He'd even fallen for her—or said he had. That had no doubt worn off now that she'd been gone a few weeks with no plans to return.

The coordinator cued the music change, then motioned for Lindy and their father to start. Mikayla sighed. Dawson and Colorado seemed so long ago. And now with what Ted was suggesting, that life was becoming just a beautiful dream. She needed to find a new apartment, and that required money. She'd squirreled away most of what she'd earned at Outlook, but it was barely enough for a first month's rent and security deposit.

Lindy and their father reached the front and shared a hug, then Dad proudly put her hand in Beau's before stepping to Mom's side and putting an arm around her waist. Under the watchful eye of the coordinator, Mikayla straightened the pretend train of Lindy's dress, took her paper plate-and-ribbon practice bouquet, and faced the front.

The dream of a camp like Outlook that focused on girls also required money. First, she'd have to get the new department up and running and learn to manage a staff. She had no clue how to do that. She'd never wanted to be in charge. Leading groups on hikes and camping? Yes. Managing people day to day? Not hardly. But watching Dawson lead his crew had been inspiring—

"Psst."

She started and looked toward Maggie who motioned toward the front with her head. Lindy, Beau, and his brother had stepped forward and now waited for her.

"Oops. Sorry." She scooted forward as everyone chuckled and remained focused for the remainder of the rehearsal. After last-minute instructions from the coordinator, she hopped into her jeep with Maggie to drive to the dinner.

"You looked somewhere else entirely for a while there," Maggie commented. "Dreaming about the mountains?"

She sighed. "Always, but mostly thinking about the pros and cons of accepting the new position, assuming Ted offers it."

"Come up with a decision?"

She glanced at her ambitious, focused sister and smiled. "Seems silly to pass it up. The pay raise would help me get back on track after my summer wanderings. And it would put me in a good position to start my own adventure camp someday. I'd make great contacts and have a ready-made audience when I was ready to launch. Which," she added with a forced laugh, "will probably be about ten years from now."

"And by then you could be married with 2.5 kids, living in a house in the 'burbs complete with a white picket fence."

Maggie's teasing pulled a real laugh from her. "Right. And, of course, be pregnant and barefoot in the kitchen."

"Now *that* I could see, without the picket fence." But only if she found a man like Dawson.

"Or the house in the suburbs." Maggie pointed ahead to the right. "Looks like the turn is there." They turned into the parking lot of the country club and stared. "Wow."

"I suddenly feel way underdressed." Though Mikayla wore a dress and sandals, and even had her nails painted, it didn't seem nearly enough. "I hope I don't embarrass Lin. I promised her I wouldn't. On purpose, anyway."

"You look fine. We're not the high-society people she

hangs with, but we're also not her hillbilly folk just in from the backcountry."

Mikayla giggled. "If you put it that way, we look great."

During the cocktail hour, Mikayla shared some of her story with Uncle Jim, Sara, James and Aunt Cindy who had graduated to using just a cane. They laughed over stories of tiny Lula and her "boys," and how the dog had been the saving grace of Hannah's injury on the mountain path.

"Honey, I've been thinking." Aunt Cindy leaned forward and set a hand on Mikayla's arm. "Now that I'm finally back on my feet, I'm feeling surprisingly nervous about falling." She rolled her eyes. "I know it sounds like something an old person would worry about, but it's my reality until I'm fully healed."

Mikayla nodded. "Totally understandable. Once you're back to full strength, I'm sure you'll feel differently."

"That's my plan. But in the meantime, much as it hurts my heart, I'm thinking Lula should stay with you. Permanently. She moves so fast, I'm afraid she'll trip me up at some point."

Keep Lula? She tried not to let her excitement show. "She's fast and tiny to boot, so I'd probably worry about that for you too. But you're sure you'd want it to be permanent? I could keep her through the winter and then see how you feel."

Aunt Cindy leaned back with a sigh. "I've talked it over with Jim and the kids, and given it a lot of thought. Everyone is in agreement that if you're open to it, the best option would be for her to stay with you. What do you think? Be honest."

She bit her lip to keep from blurting out a resounding yes. "Honestly, I wasn't sure how I'd be able to let her go. We went through a lot together this summer, and I absolutely adore her."

A warm smile filled Aunt Cindy's face. "That's what I'd hoped. Sara said Lula took to you instantly when you first met her." She nodded firmly. "Then it's settled. It makes me happy to know she'll have a wonderful new mama and a forever home, and I won't have to worry about falling over her."

After a few more minutes of sharing stories about the dog, Aunt Cindy excused herself to use the restroom, and Mikayla took the opportunity to slip outside. On the spacious patio, she pulled in a deep breath and smiled. Whatever the future held, at least she'd have her sweet little buddy along for the ride.

The setting sun spread golden light across the lush green of the fairway. Not quite the mountains, or even her favorite lake, but at least out here she could breathe. Leaning on the railing, she lifted her face to the waning sunlight. What was that verse she'd read the other day? She'd been trying to memorize it. The words floated by on the gentle breeze. "For in Him we live and move and have our being." It had sounded a beautiful chord deep inside as she visualized living, moving, and being in the openness of God's creation.

The words scattered like the fuzz of a dandelion, and she sighed. Later. She'd be able to do that when she'd gotten the camp going. Maybe she'd have those words put on the main wall in her lodge.

"A penny for your thoughts." Maggie stood beside her.

"Dawson offered me a quarter once."

"Whoa! He must have thought you had some major revelation going."

"He was disappointed," she admitted. "Whatever it was at

that moment wasn't very deep."

"Well, this one looked like it."

Mikayla studied the pretty pale lavender of her nails, lifting a shoulder. "Remembering a Bible verse I read recently that struck me. And I was thinking I'd put it on a wall of my camp someday."

"Then you will. All our growing up years, you were always able to do whatever you set your mind to. I had to work like a dog while you just marched along doing exactly what you wanted and making it look effortless."

Mikayla gaped at her pediatric surgeon sister. "What? That's the most ridiculous thing I've ever heard! You've always been the one with the brains and the determination to reach goals I couldn't even dream of, doing things I can't even pronounce."

"Not without it taking every waking moment of my life. I like science," she said, "but it's never come easy for me. I'd watch you go off with Dad, a fishing pole over your shoulder, stomping along in your boots, looking so happy, and wonder what that would be like."

"To go fishing or wear boots?"

Maggie laughed. "To be happy. I've always had to be so focused on my studies, I never had a free moment to breathe, let alone be happy."

Mikayla studied her sister's profile, stunned into silence. The revelations she'd heard since coming home had turned what she thought about her childhood upside down. None of what she'd learned came close to her own perception.

"Hey, girls." Lindy leaned on the balcony on Mikayla's

other side, a glass of wine in hand. "It's lovely out here, and I'm so tired of visiting, I had to join you. And we all know I don't like being left out. So what are we talking about?"

"I was telling Mags that she's achieved things I couldn't even dream of."

"You're both amazing," Lindy said, "while I walk around like a Barbie doll."

"Looking gorgeous and helping others, like me, figure out how to dress themselves as adults," Mikayla replied. "Without people like you, people like me would always look like schlubs."

"And I for one get sick of scrubs, which is different from schlubs," Maggie clarified with a grin. "Although I feel like a schlub in scrubs sometimes. So I'm thrilled there's someone who can tell me what to wear to look like an actual person."

"You guys think that?" Tears sparkled, and Mikayla reached for her wine glass.

"Yes, we do. And you've had enough to drink until you've eaten."

"There you are." Beau joined them, putting an arm around Lindy's tiny waist. "Dinner is served."

"And none too soon," Mikayla said out of the corner of her mouth to Maggie as they trailed the couple.

"I heard that," Lindy said without looking back. She wobbled on her stilettos.

Mikayla and Maggie shared a silent giggle, then found their places at the linen-covered table with the other bridesmaids. Conversation and the clink of silverware on beautiful china kept the room buzzing through a meal of salad, steak, shrimp, roasted vegetables, and other foods Mikayla couldn't identify.

"Beau's family knows how to party," Maggie observed.

"This is delicious, but way too formal for me."

"Paper plates are too formal for you."

Mikayla covered her snort with the linen napkin. "True. Why use plates when you can just stand around a campfire and eat? Better for the environment. Do you know how long it will take the kitchen staff to wash all this stuff by hand?"

"They can't," Maggie said. "The Health Department would close them down if they didn't use commercials washers."

The ting-ting-ting of a knife against crystal stopped Mikayla's retort. Beau's father stood at the front of the room, behind where Lindy and Beau sat like royalty. "Can I have your attention for a few moments, please? My wife and I welcome you to this dinner to celebrate the marriage of Beau and Lindy. Aren't they beautiful?"

"Nobody will say that about me when it's my rehearsal dinner," Mikayla said during the applause. "I'll be lucky if there aren't leaves stuck to my dress since we'll be outside standing around a bonfire. Maybe I'll put you in charge of checking everyone's hair before we eat."

Stifling a laugh, Maggie pretended to cough and sipped her water.

Beau's father extolled the virtues of his son, welcomed Lindy to their family, and gave a toast that lasted nearly as long as his speech. When he finally handed the microphone to their father, Maggie poked Mikayla without saying a word. Mikayla hid a smirk. The man did seem to love a mic.

"Bob and Jane," Dad said, "thanks so much for this delicious dinner in this beautiful place. Your generosity and your love for our daughter has touched us all."

As Bob and Jane smiled and nodded regally, Mikayla decided she'd never marry into money, not that it was likely.

"Rachel and I have three wonderful daughters of which Lindy is considered the youngest, although she and Mikayla have always shared a birthday."

As the group chuckled, Mikayla met Lindy's gaze. And they would continue sharing it.

"Our girls are all unique, successful, amazing young women. And we're blessed that they are best friends as well as sisters."

Maggie's hand found hers and squeezed.

"We're grateful for Beau and his endless patience, encouragement, and love for our Lindy. He's a welcome addition to our family, especially since I've been outnumbered for thirty-some years." A chuckle ran through the room. "No getting out now, Beau," he added with a wink.

Beau's mock horror followed by Lindy's playful elbowing brought a bigger laugh.

Dad took Mom's hand, then picked up his glass and held it aloft. "As our toast tonight, Rachel and I wrote a blessing for this wonderful couple. Lindy and Beau, may God's light shine brightly upon your marriage. May His love bring you closer to each other as you grow closer to Him. May His Spirit teach you to love, laugh, forgive, accept, and persevere through the coming years. And may His truth be the foundation upon which you start and grow your family. We love you both."

Mikayla forced a swallow of water over the lump in her throat, then laughed with Maggie as they wiped their eyes. These past months had indeed changed every member of her family. She was beginning to see it as a blessing.

- 37 -

Lindy burst into Mikayla's room with a shriek, and Mikayla bolted upright out of a deep sleep. "What? What's wrong?"

"It's pouring outside!"

A roll of thunder punctuated her sobs.

Mikayla pulled herself from the lovely dream with difficulty, wanting to jump back into the stream where she and Dawson had been fishing. "Pouring. Okay."

"You know what humidity does to my hair,'" Lindy wailed. "And the guests will get soaked b-because it's such a long w-walk from the parking lot. And what about the cake?"

"Whoa. Slow down." She rubbed her eyes, then reached for her phone on the bedside table. "Let's check the forecast." And the time: 6:15 a.m.

Lindy flopped back on the bed across Mikayla's legs, like she had as a child, tears running down her temple. "I told you we should have waited. What if this is a bad omen? Maybe my bio parents are actually evil—"

"Huh uh." Mikayla held up a hand. "Not going there. Your *real* parents are Mitch and Rachel. The bio people are just

339

that—biological donors."

"Y-You believe that now?"

Mikayla nodded as the weather app appeared. "It took me all summer, but yes, I do. The people who raised us, sacrificed for us, and nearly got divorced over us are our actual parents. Now see?" She showed Lindy the screen. "Rain until mid-morning, then sunshine by noon. It's going to be a beautiful day for a wedding."

Lindy sniffed. "But my hair will still end up in a bouffant."

An image of a Barbie doll with oversized hair made Mikayla giggle. Lindy glared at her. "It's not funny."

"Yes, it is. What if your hair got so big, you couldn't get through the sanctuary doors? Or you didn't fit in the limousine for the ride to the reception?"

Lindy snorted and sat up. "Stop it! That's not helping!"

Maggie shuffled in, yawning. "What's so funny at this hour?"

"Nothing! It's raining, and my hair is going to be huge from the humidity, and Mikayla is making fun of me."

Mikayla grinned at Maggie where she'd settled on the foot of the bed. "What if her hair gets so big, Beau can't get in for a kiss at the end of the ceremony?"

Maggie tapped her chin, eyes directed toward the ceiling. "Hmm. They aren't actually married without the kiss, are they?"

"I don't think so. That's the binding legal action."

Lindy giggled. "You guys, this is serious!"

They straightened their expressions. "We're totally serious," Maggie said.

Mikayla reached behind her back, then swung her pillow,

hitting Lindy in the face. As Lindy gave a muffled screech, Maggie scooped another pillow from the floor and flung it at Mikayla.

"Oh, you are so dead!" Lindy smacked Mikayla with the pillow she'd thrown.

After ten minutes of squeals and thumps, laughter and finger pointing, they collapsed across the queen-sized bed breathing hard.

"I am totally serious about my hair," Lindy gasped. "You've both made fun of me when the humidity is bad."

"Yeah, we have," Maggie acknowledged with a giggle. "Sorry."

"We also know that you have a fabulous hair stylist that will keep that from happening," Mikayla added.

"Oh." Lindy rolled onto her back. "That's true."

"Having a few wedding-day jitters?" Maggie asked, eyebrows raised innocently.

"You would too if you had three hundred people critiquing your every move."

"Why did you invite so many?"

"*We* didn't. The majority are people his parents simply had to invite. That's why they're paying for the reception venue. What we'd decided on wasn't big enough for all their friends and business acquaintances."

"Ever tried saying 'no'?" Mikayla asked.

"Have you met his mother?" Lindy countered. "We finally decided to just go with it. Then we're moving to the other side of town to get some space."

"I'm sure that will totally thwart her plans for your life."

"Yeah, that'll show 'em," Maggie added.

Lindy laughed, then covered her face. "Oh, you guys. What am I doing?" she wailed. "I'm a mess. I have no idea who my bio parents are or what's in that family history. I can't possibly live up to his mother's standards. And I'm scared to death to do life without you two."

Mikayla and Maggie rolled onto their backs and shifted until their heads touched Lindy's. The only sound was Lindy's sniffling.

"First off," Mikayla said, "we'll always be sisters. Doesn't matter how far apart we might live, that will never change. We won't *let* you do life without us."

"Really?" came the tiny question.

"Really," Maggie confirmed. "And we know exactly who you are, just like we know who Mickie is and who I am. Finding our bio parents will just add a layer to who we already are, not take anything away."

Lindy looked at her. "You're going to look?"

"When I can fit it into my schedule. You?"

A deep sigh filled the silence. "Maybe. I don't know. We haven't told his parents yet."

"Don't. At least not until after the fact," Mikayla said firmly. "Both of you were adopted. That's nothing to be ashamed of. Me, on the other hand..."

"You're the reason their marriage is so solid now," Maggie replied.

"What?"

"That's what Dad told me. They made bad choices early on and never dealt with them when they should have. But when it all came out after your surgery, they had to either work things out or call it quits. Your determination to get answers made them decide it was the least they could do for you. And us."

It was Mikayla's turn to battle tears. "He didn't say that to me."

Lindy bumped her head gently. "He said that to both of us. As hard as this summer was on you, it's because you were brave enough to go after the answers that we're all still together."

Wow. Another chess piece moved.

"I love you two," Lindy said. "Thanks for being the calm in my typhoon. Now, we have hair, makeup, and clothes to attend to. It's my wedding day!"

They scrambled off the bed and into a group hug, then filed into the kitchen. Coffee first.

Through hair styling and makeup application, Mikayla turned Maggie's revelation over in her head. When she'd stormed out of Minnesota at the beginning of the summer, she'd never have believed these changes were possible. But God knew. While she'd been furiously toppling chess pieces, He'd been one step ahead moving another piece. Always one step ahead.

Family photographs kept the tears just below the surface. With her own camera always within reach, she tried to capture those moments when people were unaware—laughter and teasing, quiet moments between her parents, hugs between friends. And she soaked in the happiness she never thought she'd feel again with her family.

The ceremony was beautiful, Lindy stunning in her Vera Bradley gown. The adoration on Beau's face pinged Mikayla's heart. No one had ever looked at her like that. Dawson's admiration had kept her off-balance and tingly, but that moment was gone. By the time she could return to Colorado, he'd no doubt have fallen for a different guide and gotten married on the mountain.

With her hair styled in beautiful curls, makeup on, and wearing a dress she silently admitted made her feel like a princess, she seemed to have caught the groomsmen's attention. She happily danced into the evening, knowing she'd return to her normal, unadorned self in the morning. For tonight, she'd enjoy playing the part.

"You've got every man here going gaga," Lindy whispered when they found a quiet moment together.

"I think it's the unexpected transformation from hiking guide to princess. When they see me in my boots, they'll lose interest."

"Speaking of boots, what are you wearing?" The question was tinged with suspicion.

Mikayla lifted the hem of her full-length lavender gown to reveal dark purple tennies that glittered in the light. Lindy collapsed against her in laughter. "Those are perfect!"

"Told you I wouldn't wear the boots," Mikayla said with a grin. "But tomorrow..."

Beau swept his bride away for another photograph, leaving Mikayla to peruse the crowded dance floor, still smiling. Lindy would do just fine as Beau's wife. Maggie would be a renowned pediatric surgeon someday.

The upbeat song ended and a slower one started. As part of the dance floor emptied and couples came together, she sighed. And she'd find her way. She scanned the room for Maggie then narrowed her gaze. Beyond the swaying couples... Her breath caught.

Dawson stood just off the parquet floor, that adorable grin on his handsome face. Dressed in a dark suit and white shirt, without a tie, he looked like someone from Lindy's world, not hers. Perhaps she'd had too much wine. She blinked several times. No. He was still there.

Heart fluttering like a caged bird, she met him in the middle of the dance floor, under the disco ball that tossed glittering lights over them.

"Hey," he said.

"Hi."

They stood silently looking at each other with silly grins.

"I never pegged you as the wedding-crasher type," she said eventually.

He shrugged. "I heard you needed a dance partner."

"I didn't realize it was such big news." She shook her head. "Are you real?"

He held out his hands, and warm, rough fingers closed around hers. "I am, but I'm not so sure you are. You, Miss Gordon, are more stunning than a mountain sunrise."

The compliment played havoc in her chest. "Thank you. And you clean up very nicely, Mr. Dunne."

"Just couldn't do the tie. Sorry. I'm waiting for security to boot me out."

She laughed, his gentle grasp sending flares up her arms.

"They might have earlier. It's anything goes now. How did you find us?"

"Called your parents yesterday. Once I explained who I was, they gave me the details."

Her eyebrows lifted. Neither had breathed a word to her. Amidst the couples swaying and chatting around them, he tugged her closer and started dancing. It was as easy to follow him now as it had been in the mountains.

"Never pegged you as the dancing type either," she said eventually.

"My mom taught me when I was a kid. Told me it would come in handy someday." He wiggled his dark brows. "She was right."

The song melded into another slow one, and they continued dancing. And smiling. It seemed he couldn't stop either.

"So what are you doing all the way out here in Minnie-sohtah?" she asked.

"I promised I'd try ice fishing, remember?"

She cocked her head. "You're a few months early."

"Am I? Huh. I thought you had snow year 'round in these parts."

"Feels like it sometimes."

He lifted an arm and spun her slowly, then pulled her close again. "Actually, I'm here recruiting for the camp."

She nodded, fighting to keep her smile from fading. Of course. He needed a full staff for next year. "I see."

"I'm working on some new ideas, and I'm hoping you can steer me to the right person."

"I'll try." The delight that had tickled her heart dulled into an ache.

"My first idea is creating a blog that will cover the camps we offer, but also life in the mountains. I especially want to focus on bringing more girls to Outlook. Maybe even expanding to girls-only adventures."

They stopped moving, and she stepped back, frowning. He was going to run with *her* dream?

"The blog would require someone who knows the outdoors," he continued, "and hopefully can take awesome photographs so I don't have to hire someone for that. And of course, they should be able to string decent sentences together to make it interesting. I saw a blog recently about a hiker girl on a journey. Very impressed with the way the author wrote from the heart and shared her perspective on the mountains and life and faith. I'm hoping the person I hire can do something like that."

Her brow lifted as tingling warmth seeped upward from her toes. He'd found her blog?

"The right person will also need to be an experienced outdoorswoman."

"Ah. You're looking for a woman." She could barely speak over the pounding in her chest.

"Not just any woman. I have very specific requirements." He closed the distance she'd created, the light in his eyes brighter than the interest of any of the groomsmen. "A woman with gorgeous blonde hair, eyes as blue as the Colorado sky, and an amazing spirit. She'll have to not be afraid to challenge me, be willing to share the workload, and have the desire to share what she knows with girls and women."

Tears threatened. In the distance she heard the unmistak-able sound of wind in pine trees and the call of an eagle.

His smile faltered. "Mikayla, I told you before you left that I'd fallen big time for you, and I meant it. I thought maybe you felt the same, but you didn't say anything, so I tried to just forget about it. Problem is, that didn't work.

"So here I am, uninvited, apparently a glutton for punish-ment"—his eyebrows tented together—"asking if you'll come back to Outlook. We're not just a summer camp, remember. We have a lot of winter activities too, but while you'd be busy, you'd still have time to write and create your magazine."

The aching heart she'd brought back to Minnesota danced and swirled under her ribs, beating joyfully. She opened her mouth, but no words came out.

"To be completely honest, and we always will be going for-ward," he added with a meaningful nod, "I heard from your sister that you've got a major offer on the table, so maybe mine won't even be in the running."

"You talked to my sister? When? Which one?"

"The bride. And I met the groom too. I introduced myself when I got here so they wouldn't have me thrown out. She introduced me to your other sister, the surgeon? And then I met your parents."

He'd met all of them? "How long have you been here? Apparently long enough to make the rounds with my family."

A corner of his mouth twitched. "I'll play every angle if it means convincing you to come back." The smile vanished. "But Kayla, as much as it kills me to say it, you really need to give the offer serious consideration. It sounds like a great

348

opportunity."

"I've thought about it a lot," she admitted, "from all sides. It *is* a great opportunity. I'd get amazing experience, make really good money, and make contacts for my women's camp idea."

Shoulders set, he nodded. "That makes sense. Much as I'd like to, I can't offer you a lot of money, or a cool townhouse, or even much for benefits."

"Hmm." She pursed her lips, feigning a frown. "What *can* you offer?"

A corner of his mouth lifted. "An office with amazing views. Blue sky and wildflowers. Mountains, valleys, fishing and hiking." He stepped closer, holding her gaze. "A life of adventure and a chance to share that with as many people as we can reach through your writing and our marketing."

We. Our. A life of adventure. *God, you just moved another chess piece, didn't you?* Months ago, she'd have jumped at Ted's offer, but she wasn't that person anymore. She wanted so much more than a desk and a title; she wanted to make a daily difference in people's lives the way Dawson did. And she wanted to do it at his side.

She bit back the smile that lifted from her heart and tilted her head. "Hear that?"

His eyes narrowed.

"I haven't heard it since leaving Colorado. It's the mountain song. I've missed it." Her smile bloomed. "I've missed *you*. There's nothing I want more than to go back to Outlook. With you."

The joy that lit his face was as blinding as sunshine

sparkling above her beloved mountains. He pulled her close, hooking his hands behind her back. "So my recruiting work is done already?"

"Afraid so. You're free to head back to camp."

He smiled and rested his forehead against hers. "Not without my girl," he said softly. "In fact, I think I'll hang around Minnie-sohtah for a bit, get to know the locals. Go on some hikes, do a little fishing. Know any good guides?"

She lifted her head and nodded, barely able to draw a breath. He had to hear her mended heart pounding joyously beneath her Cinderella gown. His danced under her hands resting on his chest. "I do. And I know she'd love to show you her hometown. But then she has a gig to get to."

"Oh? And where's that?"

"It's a place where mountains sing, there's adventure on every trail, and where people meet the Creator of it all."

Dawson slid his hands to her neck, brushing his thumbs against her jaw. "If that's where you're going, I'm going too."

"Let's go together," she whispered before he drew her into a kiss that tasted of joy and wonder and hope.

She was going home.

About the Author

Stacy Monson is the award-winning author of The Chain of Lakes series, including *Shattered Image, Dance of Grace,* and *The Color of Truth,* as well as *Open Circle.* Her stories reveal an extraordinary God at work in ordinary life. She's an active member of American Christian Fiction Writers (ACFW) and the Minnesota Christian Writers Guild (MCWG). Residing in the Twin Cities, she is the wife of a juggling, unicycling recently-retired physical education teacher, mom to two amazing kids and two wonderful in-law kids, and a very proud grandma of four (and counting) grands.

Other Books by Stacy Monson

Open Circle

The Chain of Lakes Series
Award-winning stories of loss, redemption, love, and truth.

Shattered Image
Dance of Grace
The Color of Truth

Dearest Reader,

Thank you for reading *When Mountains Sing*! I hope you enjoyed Mikayla's story, and getting a glimpse of the beauty and majesty of the Rocky Mountains, as much as I enjoyed writing about them.

Identity continues to be at the core of my writing, and Mikayla's struggle to figure out who she is and where she belongs is similar to what most of us wrestle with, although it might not start with shocking DNA news! In a society driven by the worship of youth and beauty, where fitting in is more important than standing for truth, we can often feel like we don't belong. For those who strive to live a life of faith, we wonder where our place is in the upside-down world.

The fact is, we *don't* belong to this world. Our DNA comes from the God who created us, molded us into a one-of-a-kind individual, and gave us specific gifts, talents and interests that the world desperately needs. We are not "of" this world—we were created to be members of God's eternal kingdom—but we are "in" this world to have an impact as only we can.

You don't have to try to fit in; you were made to stand out! So be proud to be who God created you to be. Take your place in the world and make a difference, big or small. The world needs you to be YOU!

Right now you can help others by 1) writing a review, and 2) sharing this book. One of the best ways to spread the news about a book you've enjoyed is to write a few sentences sharing your thoughts in a review. The other way is, of course, to tell your friends and family! I'm sure you know many who are struggling with who they are in this crazy world who could use the encouragement.

My ultimate goal as I write is two-fold: to glorify the mighty God I serve, and to share inspiring, encouraging stories that point people to the Source of all goodness, the One who can and does redeem everyone who seeks Him.

May the Creator of all that is good, bless you and keep you until we meet again!

Stacy

Gratitude Beyond Words

With the experience of each book comes the joy of new friends, learning new things, and discovering new ideas and resources. I am beyond grateful for those who've friended me, taught me, and shared their expertise.

My heartfelt thanks to...

My family who continues to encourage, inspire, and love me through every book.

The **Moms Group**, the **Marriage Group**, the **Tuesday Bible Study** gals, our **PCC Small Group**, the **Hinck Retreat** writers—some of the best cheerleaders in the world!

My Beta readers who were willing to read the rough and the polished versions and provide much-needed feedback: Diana, Brittany, Camry, Brenda, and Tiffany.

Editing geniuses Karen Schurrer and LeAnne Hardy. Nothing like taking out a thousand commas and putting the rest in the correct spot! If you enjoyed *When Mountains Sing*, it's thanks to them!

The Mosaic Collection authors (and sweet friends) Johnnie Alexander, Brenda S. Anderson, Eleanor Bertin, Hannah R. Conway, Sara Davison, Janice L. Dick, Deb Elkink, Regina Rudd Merrick, Angela D. Meyer, and Lorna Seilstad. And the best VA who has kept us in line, shared her creativity, and been our limitless source of encouragement and information – Camry Crist. What a blessing it is to call her my friend as well as my daughter!

And, as always, to...

All of the wonderful, talented writerly people God has put in my life. Critique partners, retreat buddies, chapter-mates (ACFW MN-NICE and MN Christian Writers Guild), brainstormers, chocolate lovers, dedicated servants of Christ. What a joy to create alongside every one of you!

Thank you, Sweet Jesus, for the privilege of serving you through writing.

Coming soon to

THE MOSAIC COLLECTION

Three deaths, three widows, and the ties that bind.

Ruthie Adrian loves ranch life with her handsome husband, Mac and his family. But her fading hope for a child dissolves when Mac is killed in a crash along with his brother and father.

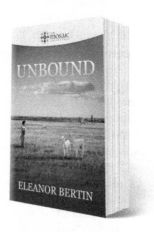

Added to their heartbreak, Ruthie and her mother-in-law, Naomi, now face rejection by her sister-in-law, and impossible barriers as they try to protect their land. Jake, a self-styled prophet steps up with a bizarre offer. A Godsend or a trap?

With raw grief, unexpected humour, and life-giving grace, *Unbound* is a modern twist on a timeless tale of the unique bond between two widows who harbour a few secrets of their own.

ABOUT ELEANOR BERTIN

Surrounded by the rhythms of ranching country in central Alberta, Canada, Eleanor Bertin was inspired by its welcoming people and beautiful, but challenging environment.

Prior to thirty years of raising and home-educating a family of seven children, the author worked in agriculture journalism. She holds a college diploma in Communications and later returned to writing, first with a novel, *Lifelines* followed by a memoir, *Pall of Silence* about her late son Paul. She blogs about contentment at jewelofcontentment.wordpress.com

CPSIA information can be obtained
at www.ICGtesting.com
Printed in the USA
FSHW011254310320
68667FS